NEW YORK, FUN CITY

There were always blasts in Midtown. Responsibility was divvied by the Dreds, or by Mariel; by the Nation of Aztlan, the Black Flag Order, Crimson and Clover, Nouveaux Maroon, Black Wicca Women, the Sons of the Pioneers, or by any of the other lesser, more transitory groups, all toiling daily at their works of disconcertion. Those commanding precautioned. Any vehicle parked in a Control Zone had to have one person near at all times, or it would be blasted. Vehicle searches proved effective; singles entering the pedways were strip-searched, as at museums (for that the Army developed cunning equipment—an Army boy once showed me his inspection glove, like a falconers', with a roof-shingle texture). Some groups levied inside support; some kamikazied. One of the more inventive groups developed an explosive that could be safely swallowed; only later would turn acids grant one last heartburn. X-rays triggered the blast and were of little help. All at play had their ways and reasons.

Army trucks raced down the avenue. "Look at 'em dash," laughed Jimmy, his gold teeth gleaming as if he'd had them buffed. "Won't find 'em now with a sieve."

Tor books by Jack Womack

Ambient
Heathern
Terraplane
*Elvissey**

*forthcoming

AMBIENT

JACK WOMACK

A TOM DOHERTY ASSOCIATES BOOK
NEW YORK

AMBIENT

A Tor Book
Published by Tom Doherty Associates, Inc.
49 West 24th Street
New York, N.Y. 10010

Cover art by Nick Jainschigg

ISBN: 0-812-51605-2
Library of Congress Catalog Card Number: 86-15784

First mass market edition: October 1991

Printed in the United States of America

0 9 8 7 6 5 4 3 2 1

FOR KABI, MY DARLING
12/5/85

AMBIENT

1

"LATER WE SPEAK, O'MALLEY," MISTER DRYDEN CON-
fided to me, climbing into the car that morning; I sat
shotgun next to Jimmy, the driver. ''I've a plan.''

Jimmy loved Fifth Avenue, the safest route downtown. We rode a Castrolite, twenty-three long, eight
across, quite maneuverable when the squeeze drew. We
were secure, to a degree; we were used to it. Dad always said that so long as you had no choice, you could
get used to anything that didn't kill you. He was dead.

"Move," said Mister Dryden.

The car's computer—a number six—awared Jimmy of
internal troubles, gently chiding him if bad tidings
sounded. Armor lined the car frame. A wire skirt ran
beneath; no mollies could be rolled under by any seeking
sport. The electroshield buzzed at button's press, frying
miscreants wishing to lodge grievances. If warranted, less
passive options effected. When all failed, my hands
guarded; there were never safer hands than mine.

"Where?" asked Jimmy.

Mister Dryden, like his father, loved E. "Don't Be Cruel" played on the lasereo as we rolled. He had everything he needed back there: a liquor cabinet, a TVC, a drug compartment topfull with reckers, a Home Army shortwave, two working phones, an IBM XL9000, a Xerox, and a bidet. The bidet was for Avalon; Avalon was for Mister Dryden.

"Bookstore me," he said.

Avalon loved little; she sat beside Mister Dryden. The TVC on her side was tuned, as always, to Vidiac. I couldn't see the screen; could only hear (by listening with care, for Mister Dryden's music played always at top) the sound of tech, chill and remote. Modern music, all tonalities and modulations and flurps and burps and wheeps, never attracted me, and the sharp abandon of Ambient groups—whose music never appeared on Vidiac—overfrenzies my skull. I prefer the music of the dead longaway.

"Rapido," he added.

I loved Avalon; I watched her dress. Her own hair was close-cut, inch-deep topside; she pulled on a curly blond shoulder-length wig. She wore only her wig, that minute; her dishabille was never fully appealing until she slipped in her choppers. Proxies—such as Avalon— were required by law to have their teeth extracted by the Health Service so that they couldn't relieve frustration in an untoward manner. She'd latched Mister Dryden after serving as a lala for the usual period; she was twenty and had been with us for two years. I'd been his chief guard and unofficial business confidant for twelve; she was so happy with her job as I was with mine.

"Ta raas," sighed Jimmy.

Avalon smiled at me, spreading her legs as if to admit the sun. To see her face reshone morning's light, however low dropped the sky's gray wrap. That morning was overcast; most were.

2

"How's by you, O'Malley?" she asked.

"By the by," I replied.

We stopped at the Eighty-sixth Street light. More than I burned; five raw youth had kindled a homebody near the park wall and watched him toast nut-brown. Home Army boys stood on constant guard around the park, and held secure the concrete veldt surrounding the Met; chest-high rolls of razorwire further strengthened those perimeters. Even so, early that morning, innumerable boozhies queued at the Met's entrance, standing snake-lined in tankmuzzle's shadow, waiting to be refused admittance into a major exhibition of Aboriginal art, about which they could later quack as if they'd truly gawked.

Park boys and Army boys—none older than sixteen—stared at our car. Avalon leaned forward, pressing her breasts against the window. She knew that they couldn't see her through the smoked glass, but she didn't mind—nor did Mister Dryden, who ignored her.

"*Jah!*" shouted Jimmy, swerving. A cab—TAILGATE AND DIE scratched into the trunk lid—pulled out, bumping us. The hack screamed at Jimmy and then proceeded up our lane. Using the plow masking our own car's face, Jimmy speeded up, ramming the cab, pushing it onto the curb before we reached Seventy-ninth. The hack's door opened and he fell into the gutter. Jimmy pressed one of the defense buttons, steaming him raw as we passed. He flopped like a fresh-caught fish.

"Quashie won't rax us now," laughed Jimmy, shaking the dreads from his face.

"I shouldn't think so," I said. Urchins hurtled over the park wall and tenderized the cabbie. One smashed the windows of the cab; unfulfilled, he smashed the windows of other passing vehicles. The Army boys laughed; inspired, ever eager for entertainment, they fired into buses inching past. Passengers sprang high, dropping from the sides.

Avalon donned her shopping ensemble: a black leather maillot, cut high over the hips, with open lacing from neck's nape, between her legs, and back to her chin. The ties knotted over her crotch; above the knot was a tattoo of tiny male artillery, with a bloody knife in lieu of the peacemaker. She zipped her thigh-high black boots; tipped the bill of her Death's-Head SS officer's cap below one eye.

"How do I look?" she asked Mister Dryden, who chose Avalon's public wear; his sense of couture had grown rather stylized.

"Yummy," he mumbled, accessing his mail, studying the monitor. He one-handed the keys; with the other hand he scratched away, digging and probing and pulling at his skin, trying to catch the creepies that he perceived to be crawling beneath.

"That's all?" she asked; it was. She looked at me and rolled her eyes. She was a dream printed and punched; the woman you brought home to mother, if mother was home. Mine was dead. To be so evernear while everfar set my feelings on hair trigger; were I a moth I would have freely sizzled in her light.

Two copters buzzed over Midtown, seven hundred feet up, whipping between the buildings. Young pilots in the Home Army did reckers and then took their machines aloft, playing tag among the towers. Dozens were shot down every year, to lessen the damage.

The entrance to the Midtown Control Zone was at Fifty-ninth. There were signs of a recent blast at the pedway: the barricade wall bedizened with red; a greater disarray than might be explained by overuse. On the wall was stencilled the Army's most enforceable antiterror edict:

Speak English Or Dont Speak.

You could wander through any Manhattan zone and not hear English spoken for weeks.

Having 1A plates, we zazzed down our lane while regular-laned trucks, taxis, and buses were stopped, searched, and turned away; it was after rush and traffic was tied for only forty blocks. Flags hung from the facade of Midtown Army Executive HQ, the old Plaza Hotel, long daubed over in dull Army drab. Machine guns and launchers were mounted on the roof, trained on the park. A fountain outside shot scarlet-dyed water into the air, symbolizing the overseas' battlefields' unceasing torrents. Children stood on line outside the Recirculation Center at Fifty-eighth, carted in by the vanload so that they could volunteer their own flow; the Army preferred the blood of the fresh and unspoiled. Army boys kept the detainees amused, shooting pigeons off roofs; those wishing other fare watched Vidiac, broadcast over the street monitors. At Schwartz, across the street, owner's children, guided by tutors and nannies, glutted themselves on their own market's bounty. We passed Bergdorf Tower at Fifty-seventh, Gucci's World at Fifty-third, Cartico at Fifty-second, Saint Paddy's Condoplex at Fiftieth, Saks-Mart at Forty-ninth.

"Any parking places?" I asked. Limos blackwalled the curbs.

"Soon enough, man," said Jimmy. "Soon enough."

A postal van was parked before the bookstore; even the driver appeared covered in graffiti. In Control Zones, mail deliveries were made once a day; in other zones the mail arrived weekly, if at all. As we pulled behind the truck, the driver lurched it away before we might make merry. There were, as ever, few cars in the zone proper; only limos, some taxis, delivery trucks allowed through on their daily runs. Buses were forbidden to enter Control Zones, for they could too handily truck in the ill-mannered. The wind whistled round the

Jack Womack

buildings as if through a graveyard. I opened my door slowly, getting out; I'd injured my shoulder earlier in the week. A blue and white, sirens wailing, sped by.

"Showtime," said Jimmy.

They were slow; further down Fifth a storefront sneezed fire.

"Nipponbank again," said Mister Dryden, looking up, shaking his head. "Stay, Jimmy."

There were always blasts in Midtown. Responsibility was divvied by the Dreds, or by Mariel; by the Nation of Aztlan, the Black Flag Order, Crimson and Clover, Nouveaux Maroon, Black Wicca Women, the Sons of the Pioneers, or by any of the other lesser, more transitory groups, all toiling daily at their works of disconcertion. Those commanding precautioned. Any vehicle parked in a Control Zone had to have one person near at all times, or it would be blasted. Vehicle searched proved effective; singles entering the pedways were strip-searched, as at museums (for that the Army developed cunning equipment—an Army boy once showed me his inspection glove, like a falconers', with a roof-shingle texture). Some groups levied inside support; some kamikazied. One of the more inventive groups developed an explosive that could be safely swallowed; only later would turn acids grant one last heartburn. X-rays triggered the blast and were of little help. All at play had their ways and reasons.

Army trucks raced down the avenue. "Look at 'em dash," laughed Jimmy, his gold teeth gleaming as if he'd had them buffed. "Won't find 'em now with a sieve."

Jimmy claimed his full name to be Man Jimmy Too Bad; he was a Dred until Mister Dryden retained him as his chauffeur, using traditional tactics to gain his access, luring new sharks with warmer blood. Jimmy still professed belief in Ras Tafari, keeping a picture of

6

AMBIENT

Selassie over the dash and the Holy Piby in his pocket. A drawer beneath the steering column held his chillum-pipe and his wisdomweed. He was an excellent driver; we'd never had an accident he hadn't planned.

"Ready?"

Mister Dryden seemed especially underweathered that morning, and mayhap my concern showed over-much; he looked sharply at me, as if I'd disturbed his slumber, and I quickly drained my face of care. His hand shook as he fumbled to close the car door. I met Mister Dryden the first time I left New York; after I was graduated from the Bronx High School of Man-agement, a friend of my father's got me a job as a guard at Yale. Mister Dryden hired me while he was a soph-omore, and I'd worked for him since, big with joy and gratitude. By working so directly for an owner—more particularly, for Dryco—I was excused from Army ser-vice. It seemed for so long that my life was made for what I did, and it was certainly preserved. Half my grad class became business midmen and half joined the Army. As of that morning, I was probably the only survivor.

There was no one for whom I'd have rather worked than Mister Dryden; then the change came clear, dim-ming his eyes, drawing the mindshades down.

"We'll shortterm," he said. He strode toward the store as he always had—briskfooted, as if toward some-thing only he cared to see. But now he moved—when he moved—by snap of nerve's impulse and the rush of vituperation. The bookstore's building was one hundred years old. The store had a vaulted interior, a glass front, wrought-iron balconies, and spiral staircases; a grand marble stairway in the rear and polished brass lamps. To enter the store led even the average owner to imag-ine that he, too, could read. Avalon preceded me, the muscles in her legs and hips drawing tight, slackening

7

and regrouping as she walked. The Dryco logo, a smirker (in past incarnation, I'm told, known as a "happy face") was tattooed on her right buttock; I imagined it all agloat as I returned its stare. The store manager, honoring our appointment, approached as the doorman unlocked the steel gates.

"Mister Dryden," he said, "Marvelous to see you after so long."

We'd last been there the week before. Mister Dryden bought abut sixty books a month. He thumbed them and threw them, having—his phrasing, tapping his forehead—filed them in the software bank. I was no longer sure if he remembered what he read even as he read it.

"Searching particulars?" the manager asked.

"No," said Mister Dryden, eyeing the heights of the store for crawlers attempting a sneak; I'd already cleared. "Clerk me."

"Yes, sir," said the manager, clapping his hands, speaking to his assistant. "Clerk, please!"

"*Clerk!*" snapped the assistant. A fellow with glasses approached and stood before us. I was a foot taller and forty years younger.

"Clerk here," he said.

"New?"

"I've been here sixteen years, sir."

Mister Dryden put his hands on the clerk's shoulders and spat in his face. His temperament had been uneven, of late.

"Then hop."

"Yes, sir."

We went to the businessing section. As Mister Dryden strolled the aisles, he selected his books, throwing them at the clerk, who caught them with the ease that comes with inborn talent. I wandered ahead.

Mister Dryden doubled back—inadvertently, I suspect—coming up to an elderly lady wearing a veiled hat. He coughed several times as if clearing his throat. Neither she nor her bodyguard moved. He nodded to me. I walked over and stood before them.

"Trouble you want?" asked her bodyguard, leaning against the carrel, biographies of Proust and of Reagan on the shelves behind him. "Tu concedar, chocha?"

Mine is a peaceful soul, after all, and this appeared at once as a bluff sitch, long on theory and short on practice. I looked to Mister Dryden, awaiting another nod. The bodyguard scratched his chin, staring and sizing. He looked me over like a plum for the picking; I was prepped to be plucked. To lure the rash and feckless, I wear earrings—black onyx inverted crucifixes on gold hoops. Were he to grab one he would find that my plastic ears were velcroed on. The Health Service removed my originals years before, when Enid—my sister, an Ambient—suggested this ploy. The Ambient way is to bluff, then to fool—then, if need calls, to term. In this, my way and theirs washed similar streams, though at the time I felt convinced that the Ambient life could not be mine.

Mister Dryden, who seemed—as always, now—preoccupied, shook his head. The bodyguard and I bowed slightly toward each other and then we moved along to different aisles. Mister Dryden and Avalon made for the art department, and I followed.

No one else was in there; I could let slip my clutch and viz the prints on the wall. There were gorgeous reproductions of Bacon's screaming popes; many of Goya's *Los Caprichos* in hologram; some Chester Gould panels involving Flattop. Schönberg's *Pierrot Lunaire* suffused the department's air. Avalon flipped through a book of black and white photos of nude women bodybuilders in select attitudes—sinking and drowning in thick mud, being buggered by rude savages, torched like the martyrs of Smithfield, wheelbent like St. Catherine, skinstripped as was St. Bartholomew, pierce-arrowed in the style of St. Sebastian—the photog was wild with cunning invention. Mister Dryden tossed over a volume of Arbus; the clerk groaned, snaring it. The morning light, pale and gray, washed over Avalon's face as she studied the photos, her dark eyes ashine; I thought how brown and soft she looked, where she wasn't black and leathery. I wished we could hug until we'd crushed each other's bones. She weightlifted, too; enough to stay fit for conferences.

She sidled over, rolling her tongue across her lips as if checking for flaws, showing me a print from a different book, pegged *Auto Fatality 17;* the artist possessed a keen sense of color but no eye for form. She grinned, tossing it onto the floor. Her leather moved as she did; I should have loved to skin her.

"Sonny better finish soon," she whispered to me, taking my arm. "My feet kill me in these fuckin' heels."

I said nothing. I smiled; her eyes sparkled like shattered glass, and in them I saw what she chose not yet to say. She twisted her hips, seeking comfort from her outfit. The suit rode higher in. Avalon, I knew, had come to appreciate Mister Dryden's affections—such as they were—less and less, but she had not known him for so long as I had, and so was not as well attuned to his quirks, which had, after all, become quirkier during the preceding year.

"New suit, Shameless?" she asked me. I wore a two-piece in corporate blue with faint pinstripes, not unlike Mister Dryden's. While he preferred a certain élan in the garb of Avalon, he cared little for what I wore so long as it was protective, and fit.

"Bought it last week," I said. It took me four weeks to receive it from the time I placed the order; were I not working for Dryco it would have taken ten months, and then more likely I would have received delivery on whatever had been available; no matter the size, color, or material—not always because of shortage, but generally for reason of discare. It was best to take what was given if you wanted anything at all, or so it was always said.

"You look good enough to beat," she said, winking. As she stood near, brushing me, I felt my skin warm as if I were slowly being cooked. "Cost much?"

"Fifteen dollars," I said.

"You never get blood on your suits, do you?" She rubbed the lapels between her thumb and forefinger. Her knee slid against mine, with purposeful caress.

I shook my head, attempting to think. Logic left my mind when she drew close; her touch left my thoughts agibber.

"The amateur's mark," I said.

"I'd like to get blood on his suit."

"Think he's nearly done?"

"Can't be," she said. "Clerk's still alive."

But he was done, and motioned for us to move. We reached the center desk; the store manager bounced over as if expecting to be fed a treat.

"Did we have everything you needed, sir?"

"No," said Mister Dryden.

"Would you care to special any titles?"

"Timeshort," he said, slapping his hand loudly against the counter, as if to demonstrate his existence to the skeptical. "I shop, I see to be itemed with my wants. I'll do other if you absent my wants."

"Sir—"

Avalon and I waited, yawning, while they went at it tong-and-nail. We knew he would continue to shop there: it was the place of the manager to be abused by an owner; the place of an owner to abuse. Like the sunrise, you came to expect it. The clerk's arms trembled beneath his load.

"—idiot," concluded Mister Dryden. I could not help but notice how his neck darkened as he spoke; his anger was such that I felt that were he to have continued his screed the blood, rising, would have filled and burst his head asunder, spraying forth a foamy wave.

"House charge or Amex, sir?"

"House."

"Fine. *Clerk!*" The store manager clapped his hands. Mister Dryden had accumulated an enormous stack of books; thirty dollars worth, I estimated. The clerk lifted them onto the counter.

"Look out—" said the manager's assistant, too late. One book fell onto the floor; the clerk held onto the rest of the stack. The book that fell was a leathered edition of *Last Exit to Brooklyn*. A gift, I suspected, though for whom I wasn't sure; his son, whose birthday was two days off, wasn't much for linear print.

"Durak!" the store manager shouted; the assistant slapped the clerk several times, as if attempting to wake him.

"Let's exam," said Mister Dryden, seemingly calm once again—it was terribly hard to easily discern his fury, until it alit. I handed him the book; he peered at it closely, as if deciphering subtle code. He vizzed out the window for a moment, raising eye to unjust Heaven and Godness therein. He glared at the store manager; pushed the book into the manager's chest, a heart-blow.

"Scratched," said Mister Dryden. I hoped he wouldn't take this too far but suspected he would.

The store manager eyed the book a moment, at last pretending that he had glimpsed an appropriate flaw. "Let me see whether we might have another."

"Fool," said Mister Dryden, rapping another book over the manager's head; the book split and bent. "Thank me."

"Thank you."

Mister Dryden hit him with the book again. This wasn't a professional's behavior, I thought, and—admittance—suddenly felt embarrassed to be connected with him at all; felt disgusted for having to feel such a way about him. But amateurs of any sort draw my ire deep, and he behaved no better just then than any amateur.

"Disirregardless," he said, "If this is how I'm serviced I'll spurn." He almost sounded as if he meant it.

"Please, sir—"

"I've decisioned."

"At least," said the store manager, holding his head as if quietly trying to rub the pain away, "I should let you deal with the one responsible as you see."

Mister Dryden appeared so startled as I was; this was twisting anew. When scenes such as this usually unwound, the store managers beat the clerks themselves before firing them. There was but one thing to be done if this ploy was enforced.

"AO," said Mister Dryden, staring at the clerk.

"I'll be in the car," said Avalon, turning away. I wished to take her and run, forever avoiding the unavoidable.

"Wait," said Mister Dryden, scratching at his arms; she stopped. "Safety first. Don't alone streetways." He looked at me, and nodded.

"For what reason?" I heard myself asking.

"He disturbed, O'Malley," he said, sounding calm again. "Victimize."

"No sense doing what hasn't point," I said; he would have agreed, once. "Let's—"

"O'Malley."

He knew and I knew that it was this or the gutter, awash in the millions, adrift with the chanceless, alone in the crowd.

"I don't feel that this is part of my job."

"He disturbed. Revenge me."

Freedom rings but no one answers; it was difficult to remain ever optimistic. I sighed, turning, dreamlike, toward the clerk. A job's a job, and I do my job; the work ethic, after all, made America what it is and I always found my pride in honest work. My father told me anyone could make it to the top; he was easily led, and so often seduced by other's wiles, and for the loveliest lies the deepest fondness grows. I feared, that day, that I was so close to the top as I would get, if I did not find another way, some way, somehow; a kid allowed to dust the candy in the big window.

"O'Malley."

Look your form in mirrors and run mad, Ambients say, and I knew of what was told. As he sank, I sank, and I knew I could sink no more. That morn I felt my mind shift, and at once made ready to seek other—but there was no other, nor did it seem possible that there ever would be. Take the given or lose the all; that was the way. There I stood, sans ears, sans love, sans soul; part owner, part Ambient, each together less than each apart.

"O'Malley!"

I pondered which of my suit's accessories would be most appro: the batog, the chuks, the chain, or the trunch. I estimated that my batog—two sharp sticks lashed together with heavy wire—would do. Never howitzer a housefly. Once more, I paused; my limit neared. Mister Dryden spoke.

"Don't see, muchacho," he said, quivering as if being charged. "Do."

I did.

2

"BLUE MOON OF KENTUCKY" PLAYED WHILE AVALON sipped Glenlivet through a straw from a liter. She drank heavily on conference days in hopes of being unable to recall them from month to month.

"He bleed enough for you?" she asked, pulling off her cap, unlacing her suit.

She wasn't speaking to me. Mister Dryden said nothing, nor did he watch her as she shed. He picked up the phone and called the bookstore, asking that his books be delivered to his office within the hour. The books were reshelved, he was told. He said he saw no reason why his wishes wouldn't be fulfilled as demanded, and hung up; he hung up on everyone except his father. Taking beauties from his compartment and bennies from his drawer, he washed them down with absinthe. A few snots and sniffs from the kane and he sat sufficed. Not until a year ago—after his mother died—had Mister Dryden much to do with the reckers so successfully imported into the country by his organization. Now he was always on the fly. Drug's shrouds swathed him so closely that it was as if, having been hurt and seeking protection, he chose to wrap himself so tightly in bandages that he might suffocate long before he healed.

We drove to his office, at Rockefeller Center, in the Dryco building. Army troops passed us, marching down Fifth in haphazard formation, the smirkers on their helmets bobbing as they huffed along.

"Yellowjackets," Jimmy sneered, nodding at their sunflower flakjacks. "Think they sting like fire."

Avalon donned her conference outfit, hooking up her armor, a heavy steel corselet daubed with orange trim. Daggers rose from each breastplate like exomissiles. She slid on her spiked leather bracelets, her kneepads, her elbowpads, her thick wool leggies, and her leather G-string. Finally she pulled on her tight leather mitts and her roller skates.

"You're pillowing?" asked Mister Dryden, frowning.

"Yeah," she said, oiling the wheels with a can of 3-in-1.

We parked out front, in the small street by the plaza, in front of the building. I brushed soot from my eyes as we stepped from the car; my hands were filthy from being in the air. Sirens whined in the distance. Several jets passed east, overhead, toward Long Island.

"We'll afternoon it down, Jimmy," said Mister Dryden.

"Right," said Jimmy, standing at ease beside the car. He wore a dark blue Navy bridge coat that must have weighed thirty pounds; too warm for the weather, I thought, but he wore it always. For aesthetics he'd sewn skull-and-crossbones patches on the shoulders, and a patch of the Lion of Judah on the back. His hair, knotted into thick ropes, tumbled past his neck. He wore razor knucks strapped to his left hand. Standing next to him was unsettling. I'm big, but Jimmy was magnificent; I came up to his chin. It was good to know that in theory Jimmy worked with us and not against— still, you could be certain only of yourself. Every worm can turn and strike, and it always seemed to me that Jimmy was only waiting for the moment he could keen to strike deep.

At the building's entrance, Mister Dryden shouted to a gentleman arriving, an unfamiliar face; someone's replacement. He had a compact bodyguard; they wore gray suits. This signified that he was but a boozhie midman and so could be easily replaced as the day demanded. Only owners and their immediate lessers wore corporate blue; it wasn't forbidden that others should, but to do so would be considered unmannerly at best.

"*Tom,*" said Mister Dryden. "Well-going, son?"

"Fine, sir."

Tom looked to be thirty years older than Mister Dryden.

"Conference-ready?"

"Yes, sir."

We entered the lobby, Avalon rolling on ahead, zazzing around the planters and the display cases containing Dryco-made products: electronic gear, sports equipment, art supplies, cassettes, phone systems, Army weapons, farm tools, fiberoptic line, auto parts, laserlights, robots, and plastic statues of E. Dryco—directly or indirectly, it didn't matter—controlled about 40 percent of American production and could if desired lay claim to another 30 percent.

A silk banner hung from the ceiling in the lobby, wafting gently in the AC. On it was printed the Dryconian ethic:

WORRY NOT, WONDER NOT.

We newstanded a moment. The proprietor, an old man legbent and wobbly with rickets, leafed through *El Newsweek*. I picked up the two dailies—the *New York Times* and *USA People*—and dropped the two cents in his hand. In a guarded nook was Mister Dryden's elevator. "Open," he said, pressing his hand against the printcode monitor; the door opened. We entered and began rising to the sixty-fifth floor. Most elevators had Vidiac piped in, but not Mister Dryden's; we had nothing to watch but each other.

"Basic morning meets, OM," said Mister Dryden, slipping his stance, weaving slightly, as if the increasing altitude affected his sense of balance. "You can skip. Three contractings and one intrapersonal. No shakes."

"No problem," I said. Most important business meetings I attended with Mister Dryden, so that I might lend counsel and prevent assassination. I knew so much about the workings of the organization in most areas as he did—most, but not all. Once area remained an enigma and I suspected, then, that it always would. I suspected as well that so long as it did, I would go no further than I already had; it was something the family kept tight, and underwrapped, like the crazy uncle locked in the attic room—though whatever it was, was considerably more useful than that.

"Who're you seeing?" Avalon asked, making noises with her straw and giggling, her bottle tucked in the crook of her arm. The more she drank, the stronger her accent grew. She was born in Washington Heights. Her parents were English, by way of Barbados—perhaps vice versa. Her name was Judy—Judy something; she never said what. Proxies tend to lose touch with their families during their time spent as lalas. Avalon hadn't seen hers since she was eleven; she once sent them a Christmas card.

"Pards," said Mister Dryden, chewing his lip, tapping the walls with his fingers as if attempting to send messages to the spirit world. "La Rue from StanBrand, Jameson from XBP, Timmerman from Gorky-Detroit. They're reporting me preprogram."

"Sounds thrilling. Who's the fourth?"

"Lope."

"He's a nice old man," she said. "The old ones always spend more sugar than the young ones."

"Is he still working with Intel?" I asked; Lope hadn't been by in months—working on arms deals in Siberia, I believed.

"He's working his old boys with this one. He stands to Marielize Atlantic City."

"Why?"

"We won't."

The system was simple and, unlike most systems, often worked. Mister Dryden steered the business; the computers and midmen ran it; his father owned it. His father owned many things. Dryco piefingered every major country, stuck both hands deep into America. Mister Dryden's father—the Old Man, we pegged him—was the most successful of those who had bested the Ebb.

"How long's it going to take?" asked Avalon. "I'm freezin' my ass."

"Hourish. I'm gauging that Lope'll conference today."

"I didn't think he liked violence," I said.

Mister Dryden laughed, pressing the up button several more times. "Ask Dad," he said.

In the halcyon days, in those shimmery years lostbegone, the Old Man and his wife—Susie D—controlled the most profitable recreational drug circulation network between the Americas. With trusted assistants such as Lope and with friendly competitors—those they hadn't had to buy, as it were—they directed other promising enterprises on an equally productive scale: carting

19

and disposal, active/passive pleasure provision, domestic security and international antiterror assistance, and general import-export. Even then the family was rich, though of comprehensible wealth.

"Note me, OM," said Mister Dryden. "Call a maintenant."

For years the Drydens stood firm, reinvesting their profits and growing evermore secure. Their influence was strong, before; afterward, it was complete. The administration of that day, having beguiled the nation so willfully with enthralling lies, suffered a succession of unexpected horrors, long developing and at last erupting. The panic was on; no one understood what was happening well enough to concoct a believable deceit in time, and so for a while it all came down. The Old Man and Susie D knew when to move and when to lay still, and as all began to tumble they caught, reaped, secured, and ran. Their plan worked well—for them, and for their friends. It was as if the country had been in a theater when the cry of fire rang; when all broke for the exit, they discovered that the Drydens had locked the doors behind them, and now charged all an escape fee.

"Maintenant?" I asked, "Why?"

"Speed increase," he muttered, pressing the button again.

"You're flyin' now," mumbled Avalon.

After the Long Island accident and the birth of Ambients; after the revelation of the Q documents and the loss of spirit thereof; after the economic emergency, the resulting currency devaluation, and what was called, by some, the unavoidable regrouping of structures, came the twelve months known by Ambients, and now by most, as the Goblin Year. All made up the Ebullition (another Ambient coinage that slipped into general use—though we just called it the Ebb). I was twelve, that year, unknowing of the inventiveness of my future employers; uncertain, as was everyone, of what future there might remain. My mother had been killed earlier, during a pro-life riot. My father, once a realtor, once well-off, managed to hold only one property, the building on Avenue C in which Enid and I lived, and had lived, since that time. Dad was gone in a matter of weeks; Enid raised me, having raised herself.

"I was elevatorspeaking," he said.

"Oh," she nodded. "Of course."

"I'll see what can be done," I said, knowing nothing could be done; there was nothing wrong with the elevator.

"Good man," said Mister Dryden.

Since then, all had adjusted—some more so than others. It was quite simple. The government served those who supervised the sailing of the yacht of state; the government controlled the business that controlled the government. Complex in theory, it was infallible in practice. I gather that new owners weren't much different from old ones; oldboss, newboss, as Enid put it. Live and let live was the word; so went the thought, so went the act. With useful exceptions matters ran themselves; that this did not always work to everyone's benefit aroused among the government apparatchiks no concern, brought no interpretation, produced no apology, stirred no regret. Those in control worked their legerdemain when and as they wished. It was nature's way.

"Here now," said Mister Dryden as the elevator slowed.

American society, thus, had three arenas in which all could cavort: that of owners and their servants; that of boozhies, the old bourgeois; that of what the government pegged the Superfluous. The last, like owners, paid no taxes; unlike owners, they were felt to deserve no shielding from the vicissitudes of life. Unless they entered the Army (by draft or, in the case of women, by choice) the Superfluous were underemployed. Some were useful to industry; the elderly were useful in research. All did business on the unders; many got along. There was no excuse for being poor in America; it was much easier to be dead.

"Ola, Renaldo," said Mister Dryden.

But no cynic, I; there was never a country like America in which to live.

Mister Dryden's waiting room was impressive: paneled in wood-tone, shielded from the public hall by three-inch glass; that hall's door openable only from the reception desk. A neon smirker hung behind the desk. Renaldo was the receptionist. He was once a member of La Societa Mariel, formed originally to provide its members with jobs; people helping their own, as the government always insisted. As with Jimmy, the lure of Dryco proved inescapable. *Madre* was tattooed in his lower lip; her image marred the backs of his hands. He shaved his head; he affected a bushy mustache and wore small hoop earrings. The metal plate in his skull reflected the overhead light; his head at some angles resembled an expensive kitchenware item.

"Renaldo," said Mister Dryden, "Punch up 37H, 26B, 29C, 2T. Expect them. Don't enter others."

"Toderecho," said Renaldo.

Cameras focused the doors leading from the public hall. On his monitors, Mister Dryden could see who entered, could signal by silent alarm. Renaldo kept an ax by his desk, ready for unsolicited arrivals.

Avalon and I sat on the couch nearest the elevator. I shifted as I sat so that my weight wouldn't ache my hip joint. We looked over our papers: I had *USA People* and she read the *Times*. The first three of Mister Dryden's visitors arrived and disappeared behind the office door. I studied my paper. NATION'S CRIME RATE PLUNGING WEEKLY, the headline read; in smaller type, *Slower Progress Seen in Major Cities*. The twenty-first anniversary of the start of the Russian-American War was to be celebrated this year in the capitals of both countries, from July 4 to November 7. Enormous profits for both sides had been realized during the previous quarter. Additional advisers were to be sent this year into Pakistan, Nigeria, and Costa Rica by both sides, to assist those countries' armies. Poland was again up for grabs; a settlement was made in Indonesia, good for three years. The blessing of the Russian-American War—indirectly, of the Pax Atomica itself—was that the two countries never needed to battle directly; that would have been neither emotionally productive nor financially wise.

There was other news. Britain was in good form; under the guidance of King Charles—presently occupying himself buying horses in Kentucky—and the National Front, unemployment was down to 80 percent. In Germany, President Streicher set forth new policies promising shifts in direction concerning resident Turks. Swedish destroyers shelled Oslo; another argument over fishing rights. Lucy, the last rhinoceros, died of old age in the Cincinnati Zoo. Why they called it *USA People*, I'll never know; there were rarely any in it.

Another gentleman was admitted into the office, a portly chap with neatly brushed white hair.

"Hi, Lope," said Avalon, looking up.

"Good morning, my dear," he said. "Good morning, Mister O'Malley."

I nodded. He returned his attention to Avalon.

"So well you look this morning," he said to her. "New outfit?"

"It's for the conference."

He sighed. "Take care, my dear." The first three gentlemen departed and Lope went in. Lope and his two brothers began working with the Old Man early on, while they themselves yet lived in Colombia. They assisted the Old Man in securing his own trade routes following the death of his original partners. Over the years, Lope provided great assistance to the Drydens in every way, and so came by his own fortune—his brothers proved not so efficient, or not overly so, and never made it quite so far.

"Want to rag it, Shameless?"

"Sure," I said; we exchanged papers. The lead headline of the *Times* was MOM KILLS, EATS BABY; the leftovers were photoed on page two. *Psychic Sex Secrets of the Senators*, read the second lead. The local news was nothing new. Two bombs blasted at the Trade Towers; none of Dryco's floors suffered. The Statue of Liberty's arm was blown off; there was a photo of the amputee, rather resembling an Ambient in her new-made loss. The Dow hit 500. The Army-estimated population of New York City—for all intent, the island of Manhattan—was reported as approaching four million; the National Census figure, three years earlier and as accurate today, was 450,000. The Harlem River was on fire. The Hackensack Ripper perpetrated his one thousandth outrage. A cancerous young Bengali was brought to New York on Air Force One by the First Lady; American medical care could work clock-round to save a child who, once saved, would be shuttled back to the motherland to starve.

There was national news. In Washington, vids to be released by the FBI were said to show the president engaged in what was judged a doubtful if unspecified action; the press secretary issued a statement saying that the president could not be concerned with minor domestic problems when the complexity of foreign relations demanded his full attention. RUSSIANS SHOOTING FRIENDLY SPACE VISITORS? an editorial wondered. And E, who many—the Old Man among them—called this world's true king, was reported seen in Cleveland, risen again, wan but sturdy, tramping uncertainly down Euclid Avenue. His followers rushed to that city.

A figure toting a large parcel approached the waiting room from the public hall and buzzed. Renaldo signaled Mister Dryden.

"Recon?" Renaldo asked.

"Si," Mister Dryden said. "Abiert, porfav. Momento."

Renaldo pressed the remote on his desk, opening the door. The bookstore manager smiled, wearish beneath the weight of the load. I stood and walked over to take delivery. Avalon got up and rolled over to the info desk, looking for something else to read. Mister Dryden stepped from his office, Lope following not far behind.

"Deliver now or never," said Mister Dryden. "Other work more import?"

"Our clerks are dreadfully slow, sir—"

I was reaching for the parcel when I noticed its ripped corner. A blue wire protruded.

"Down!!" I screamed, shoving the manager into the public hall, knocking the package from his hands, and further away. "The door!"

Renaldo pressed the closure as he ducked beneath a chair. Mister Dryden and Lope leapt back and dropped behind the desk. I threw myself onto Avalon; she wrapped her legs around me as if to guard my lower half. Her daggers pricked me; I didn't mind, and they wouldn't penetrate the Krylar vest I wore beneath my shirt. The bomb blasted as the suite's metal door closed.

The glass wall surrounding the door held, thanks to the wire embedded within; it webbed inward from floor to ceiling. Looking up, I saw a gaping hole in the floor outside; the hall walls smoked and blistered. Renaldo opened the door and doused the fire with an extinguisher.

"Was that the bookstore guy?" asked Avalon,

squeezing me. I had no desire to get up, leaving her grasp to risk being shattered again, but knew I must.

"Was," I said.

"Damn," said Mister Dryden, rising, peering about as if there might be more incoming. "Good work, OM. We'd termed if you hadn't spotted."

"Just what's expected," I said. When I stood it felt for a moment as if I had thrown my back out. This sort of thing, these minor disturbances, happened about once a month, always had. It should have seemed as if it would be only a matter of time before they got us, but it never felt that way—it was simply part of the job. Nonetheless, it did tend, I think, to keep us all a bit overtuned to our surroundings, and perhaps keeping so eversharp and toepoised made for some uncertainty we could have done without.

"You'll be extraed, weekend. Lope, you viabled?"

Lope arose—carefully—from behind the desk.

"I believe," he said, holding the desktop, pulling himself up as if into a life raft, "if you station someone at the public elevator to doublecheck no one could get this far."

"Fortress life isn't mine," said Mister Dryden.

"Ask for trouble, Thatch, and you'll get it. Please take my advice. On this, if on nothing else—"

"Needless. Ignorance was his, I reason." He looked irritated, and not for having just avoided being blown up. "Avalon, you? AO?"

Avalon rose, nodding. "Shameless, they're bent," she said to me, pointing to her daggers. "Straighten them for me, will you?"

"So who behinded it?" Mister Dryden asked me, looking down the hall. "Dred?"

"Too white," I said. "Not the turf." Her daggers scratched my fingers as I twisted them into place.

Throwing her shoulders back, Avalon lifted her breasts
so that I might shape with greater ease.

"A loco?"

"He'd have swallowed it, for sure. We'd be far, far
away."

"Renaldo," he asked, turning. "Mariel?"

Renaldo frowned. "Fuckin' peñejo."

"As guessed," said Mister Dryden. "A store in-
sider. Grudging." He reached for the phone, pressing
out a number. He connected instantly; his lines were
owners' lines, and always worked. You could punch in
the same number on a public phone thirty times and
get a different response each time, on those odd occasions you got through at all. Emergency lines were another thing; those were always out of service.

"Captain?" he said. "Dryden here. DIA8782"—that
was his phone code. "The big bookstore on Fifth.
Right. Hotbedded. Attack tactic tacked. Neuter and
buy. Snap it. AO." He hung up.

The Home Army always did Dryco's bidding: as did
the Regular Army, the other forces, the Senate, the
House, and the President. Of all magics practiced, the
Drydens' was the most infallible. For years it puzzled
me. Over time, by the retrieval of dropped hint and
tossed-away suspicion, it entered my head that they had
something: something picked up during the Ebb, something much more frightening in perception than it could
ever have been in use—so I thought.

"Hall?" asked Renaldo, gesturing toward the smok-
ing floor beyond the shattered wall.

"Call a maintenant."

"Coño."

"No me hoda," Mister Dryden laughed. "Lope and
I were concluding."

"In a way—" Lope began, but didn't finish.

"Ready up, Avalon."

"Fuck this—"

"No danger foreseen. A ready suffices. AO?"

"Let me get my stuff," she said, rolling into his office.

Lope moved toward the public hall, as if attempting to leave without notice.

"No exit there," said Mister Dryden.

"Where, then? Isn't the guard's stairway close?"

"That won't do. Neither OM nor Renaldo can stair you down and with the boobies up you can't stair single. You'll have to conference."

"Please, Thatcher—"

"It'll inspire. You'll brisk new blood. Viz. See."

"I won't watch. Thatch. Please—"

"Such a mari. Avalon, *prep*. We activate in ten."

Avalon rolled out of Mister Dryden's office, a thick pillow tied over her bottom as if for a bustle.

"You can't move, pillowed," said Mister Dryden.

"I'll wear what I want to wear."

"It's unsexed—"

"You're not gonna get knocked on *your* ass. Let's go."

Avalon removed her choppers and her wig, giving them to me for safekeeping. I checked her crasher to see that the full-face visor moved smoothly and then pressed it down over her head. She picked up her bat and wrapped a heavy chain around her waist.

"*Ya!*" Mister Dryden yelled, shouting out an arcane victory howl he'd developed in free moments. "Renaldo. Info to Jake. AO to concept. Kap?"

Renaldo nodded. Mister Dryden caught my glance, and winked. Something afooted. We left.

The conference room was on—was—the sixtieth floor. There was high-gloss flooring; areas were fenced and bleachered at each end for company reps and guests. Windows ran along each wall.

Conferences had been held monthly during the past

year; all top-position midmen participated. Conferences were only one of several ideas of which he'd conceived since he began spiraling down: ideas seemingly
designed to bring financial ruin and personal oppro-
brium upon his own company; ideas that, by his own
design or by accident, had the opposite effect.

As Mister Dryden's proxy, Avalon joined in only if
her assistance became essential. If called, she threw
herself in with such intensity that no one lasted, pitted
against her.

"Ready?" Mister Dryden asked Avalon; she didn't
answer.

No other companies wished to participate in his conferences, but as they were Dryco conferences, they were
unavoidable. They also proved surprisingly popular
among those owners, foreign and American, not participating. Japanese, Chinese, and Russian associates
of Dryco filled the bleachers on our side, scorecards in
hand. Most wore round their necks the low-cost dis-
posable cameras mass-produced in Switzerland, reliable enough to last a roll or two; they loved to
permanize what they saw. They always bet as to whether
Avalon's assistance would be required, and at what
point.

"How do you think we'll do?" I asked Mister Dryden.

"We'll kill 'em."

This month Dryco conferred with SatCom. Under
the rules of the game—as developed by Mister Dryden—the winner engulfed the loser, gaining control of
the loser's assets but none of its debts. Dryco never
lost; I knew that if anyone else ever happened to fairly
win, Mister Dryden could simply readjust the score and
victor anyway. No one would be left to deny it, afterward.

Lope sat by Mister Dryden, looking nauseated. Our

tigers, hopped and action-ready, rolled before our bar-
rier. The camera people readied their equipment in their
reserved spot; Mister Dryden never lost his business
sense, and so had leased the domestic rights to the Violence Channel and sold the foreign rights for theatrical
release. I sat with Avalon by the gate, giving her water,
calming her so well as I could.

"I've offered to go out in your place," I said, keeping
my arm around her waist for support. "He says no."

"Good thing, too," she said, attempting to see whom
SatCom might have brought in as proxy. "Some of them
bitches'd eat you for breakfast. Stay clear, Shameless."

Mister Dryden rapped his gavel on the podium, saying:

"Meeting, order." He blew the whistle.

The aim of a conference was to destablize all members
of the opposition so effortlessly as possible. Everyone
wore skates, and was armored, and outfitted. I believe
Mister Dryden lifted the concept from an old movie he'd
once seen, undoubtedly while kite-high. The whistle
moved them; at command they tilted full and bore.

The marketing manager of SatCom was first put in
his place. Our VP of adverts demonstrated an aspect of
the problem under review; the manager went spinning
across the floor. Once he went down, one of our exe-
cutaries brought up a point with her machete and ruled
him out of order. The debate continued. A conference
such as this really got the adrenals spitting. The average
time it took for teams to agree was four minutes; then
the proxies emerged, if needed. This meeting was hard
and had gone six minutes by the time we led.

"Oh, fuck," said Avalon, staring ahead, pulling away
from me. "Goddamnit."

SatCom's proxy rolled onto the floor.

"Close me up, quick," she said. "She'll kill everybody in the building if I don't move."

The new player—wearing skates—was more than six feet high. Her upper armor consisted of black chain mail worn over a breastplate. Long black leather leggies rose on high; her elbow and knee guards bore sharp spikes. She was nude between her navel and thighs. She carried a long mace and a broadax. Her crasher was black, too, with great horns rising from the top; on it was a grotesque face mask with eyeslits.

"You've met?" I asked.

"Yeah."

"Who is it?"

"Crazy Lola. We grew up on the same block. She's fuckin' psycho."

"How do you know it's her?"

"Look at her hair."

Crazy Lola's pubic hair was dyed blood-red and shaved into the form of a heart.

"Anything for attention."

Avalon picked up her bat and loosened the chain at her waist so that she might remove it more speedily; I'd taught her that trick.

"Scoots, Shamey."

"Break a leg," I replied.

Crazy Lola hadn't run the ground twenty seconds before she'd maced our sales manager. Our last regular player, the VP of demographs, dispatched SatCom's last executary with his kendo pole, only to skid into the path of Lola. Slipping her mace into her holster and raising her broadax, she brought the latter down onto his crasher and split his head to the chest.

Avalon shot out to great applause. The women circled warily in opposite orbits, calling each other baleful names. Then Crazy Lola charged, brandishing her mace. Avalon spun to her right and cracked Lola in the faceplate with her bat. Lola fell on her back, her crasher bent back against her head; she was on her feet again in moments. Avalon made a leisurely circuit to the side and then moved. I could barely look, but did; I knew she'd win.

Crazy Lola put away her mace and charged again, flailing her broadax in a wide circle. As Lola flew toward her, Avalon dropped to her knees and whacked her rival on the legs with her bat. The broadax shot out of Lola's hands and hurtled toward our bleachers. Most of us ducked—I, most quickly, I'm sure—but two Mitsubishi reps froze and suffered unexpected haircuts. Lope hid his eyes behind his hands; Mister Dryden grinned, nudging him.

Thrown off balance by Avalon's swing and by the weight of her own armor, Crazy Lola fell forward and slid thirty feet down the floor, Avalon hot on her wheels. Lola hadn't a chance. Avalon, holding fast to the rubberoid end of her chain, rushed by, lassoing Crazy Lola's neck and pulling the chain taut. Then, yanking Lola upright, holding the chain, beginning to pirouette, Avalon started swinging her around. She spun faster and faster; Lola, disoriented, rolled helplessly on Avalon's line. It reminded me of one of the more memorable science fair experiments in high school. When she built up enough centrifugal force, Avalon let go the chain. Crazy Lola cannonshot through a window in a rain of glass.

"Meeting adjourned," said Mister Dryden, rapping the gavel once more.

Our audience, heady with delight—save two—stood Avalon an ovation as she rolled to our barricade. I opened her visor and put her choppers in; she was shaking. She burst into tears; I don't recall that I'd ever seen her cry before, and without thinking of consequence I threw my arms around her and hugged her. She kissed me; her tongue slid into my mouth like an oyster. Mivida, I thought. My corazon. Ambients say of their loved

ones that till time's lovely end, their blood beats their
beloved's heart everafter; so mine beat Avalon's. She
returned my embrace, tightened; my chest stung with
the prick of her daggers.

"I've had it, Shameless," she whispered to me as I
held her. "I can't do anymore. I can't stand it."

"You won."

"He won," she said. "We've lost. We'll always
fuckin' lose."

I didn't want to admit it, because I didn't think it
true. "I know."

"Can you get us out of this? Any way? I'm ready to
take off—"

"You'd be guttered," I said. "There's no hope
then."

"Damn little now," she said, squeezing me. "It
don't matter. Don't fuckin' matter. I've had it. You've
had it."

"I might be able to work something out—"

"*What?*"

"I'm not sure yet. He wants to talk to me. Something's on. Don't see what yet."

"Whatever. Talk and tell me. But I've had it, whatever you do."

"I know."

"Better let go, Shameless. He might see us."

"He might," I said, not fearing. He'd been vizzing
our way, but I estimated he'd account it to the moment's
heat.

"I've had it. Never again. Never."

With little tumult and no shouting, the president of
SatCom stepped onto the floor, striding over his ex-
employees and ours, almost slipping in the wet spots.
Mister Dryden awaited, rocking forthback on his heels,
self-full enough to pop. The fellow presented Mister
Dryden with the appropriate deeds; they bowed. He

knelt down before Mister Dryden, leaning forward, brushing the hair from his neck. Mister Dryden nodded. Jake, the main office overseer, approached, withdrawing his long Kyoto sword. Jake, a real master, handled the more delicate aspects of corporate etiquette; he always wore an immaculate white suit.

He rode with us down to the lobby; he and Mister Dryden chatted on the way about King Dagobert's latest edicts in France and how Dryco reps might best deal with them, whether eyesaware or underlight. We walked to the plaza. Mister Dryden bade Lope goodbye, winking at him as well. Lope looked pale, and more than a bit suspicious. Jake went over to hang—as if it were a prized Christmas ornament—the newest trophy from one of the flagpoles. Some of the older trophies were but bony skulls; replaced soon enough, recycled into candy dishes and jewel cases and other useful objets d'art.

Avalon stepped into the car; Mister Dryden put his hand on her shoulder.

"Front yourself," he said and motioned toward me. "OM. In the back. Let's talk."

As I climbed into the car, settling in beside Mister Dryden, Lope's limo, over on Fiftieth, exploded. There was nothing to do but watch. Mister Dryden looked at the wreck and leaned back into his seat.

"Can't be too careful," he murmured, smiling. "Downtown, Jimmy. Bank me."

We drove down Fifth, past the bookstore. Flames rose like flowers from the ruins.

3

"BATBRAINED. NOT IFFED OR MAYBEED. HE'S SLIDING hard and fast," Mister Dryden said to me, attempting to explain as he drew shut the clear panel dividing the car's front compartment from the rear, turning on the bar-sink faucet so that the roar of running water might muffle our illicit chat. I saw Avalon through the panel removing her conference outfit. She put on only another wig, my favorite: the lovely light brown one with aubergine highlights. The hair glided in snakish curls beyond her waist; it was as if Lady Godiva rode the front, blowing wisdomweed from Jimmy's bowl.

"He's always been eccentric," I said.

"Eccentric is as eccentric does," said Mister Dryden, downing four pills, swallowing dry. "He's far gone now." He offered me some tablets; I declined, happy to avoid all forms of polypharmacy.

"Maybe it only seems that way."

"He's entered permanent right-brain mode. No, OM. Action's time is here."

When speaking with me alone, Mister Dryden often let slip to some degree the bizspeak that, through practice, came so naturally to his lips; obfuscation was not his intent with me, as it was with so many others.

"Big action or little action?"

"The biggest," he said, coughing. One of the tiny pills, half-dissolved, flew from his throat in midspasm and stuck to the front seat. I slapped him across the back.

"AO?" I asked; he nodded. We drove west, down Forty-seventh. Empty storefronts lined Midtown streets; vast offices blockaded the avenues. Over time an exodus of smaller businesses from Midtown—their owners frazzled by ever-increasing rent, ever-decreasing trade, and ever-present fright—swept clear the streets of the extraneous. In even the most populated buildings—Dryco's as well—whole floors sat empty and defixtured, windows sealed and trimmed with flowery decals. There was space aplenty now, though in Midtown as in much of Manhattan, no new offices had risen for two years. O contrare: those retaining possession of smaller buildings often torched them so that the ruins might fall under city ownership.

"I haven't seen him for very long periods lately," I said. "He hasn't seemed so different, the past few times."

"He gives good behavior when publicked," said Mister Dryden, taking another couple of pills to counter the effects of his coughing fit; with water, this time.

"I'm sure you've seen more than I have," I said.

He nodded. At Sixth Avenue was ABC, another Dryco holding. Immense colorgraphs of network stars hung from the tower's sides. Some wag had rappelled up and painted mustaches on several; those, and those of stars recently canceled, were being rolled and removed by workmen and maintenants.

"How batbrained are we talking?" I asked.

"Total," he said. "Ego gone wild. Paranoia. The works. Reason's headfled."

"Is he still working on those Bronx plans?"

"Exclusive. Exxing when he's saying I'm destroying the company."

I said nothing, for I had thought that was what he intended.

"Every day," Mister Dryden continued, his eyes focusing, "he secluded with Army corpsmen. Running his plans to Bronx it and leave all else waysided."

Since Susie D died, no one saw overmuch of the Old Man, who over the years had grown fond of shelter. Once a month we weekended at the estate in northern Westchester so that we might soak our souls in verdant hours and dull our sense with country air; during those visits the Old Man appeared when food appeared, and when he chose to drag us all to chapel service. Otherwise he vanished so completely as did the vice-president a few years ago. Those were merciful weekends, truly; I could spend more minutes with Avalon, serving as her guard when she wished to ramble across the estate's green meadows, for even there one-on-one protection was deemed essential, just in case.

"Maybe he's just bored and this enlivens his mind," I suggested.

"Enlivens?" said Mister Dryden. "Boils it red."

The death of his wife—it seemed to me—never caused the Old Man the unbearable pain I believe it caused his son; perhaps it caused not even bearable pain. The Old Man and Susie D were married for more than forty years, but I never saw theirs as a union forged strong through love's blasts, resembling, rather, the bond between Siamese twins: undeniable, inescapable, attached by chance, kept whole by necessity, ending only in death. An Ambient comparison, perhaps; I stand by it.

"He's moneytied us," said Mister Dryden. "Filling the Bronx's pockets. In several areas right now we've got to float fast or we'll be docklong and dollarshort. He's preventing."

"How so?"

Susie D passed into Godness's other domain during one of our weekends there, as we slept; no one ever specified what killed her, though rumors drifted like floaters down the Hudson. A coronary, we were first informed; that became a stroke a day or two later, following the cremation. The coroner's ruling was death by misadventure; that could apply to anyone, these days. During the past long year Mister Dryden had never spoken directly of his mother's death. The Old Man's words were select: curiosity, he said, killed the cat.

"Boredom has nada to do with his hobby," said Mister Dryden. "He's sunk millions down per quarter. My millions. His millions. That's the line as bottomed. Millions best spent elseways. On the coast. In Africa. In the Sydney markets. For the casinos, immediately; unless we refund, Mariel's going to move. Lope came by to brief me that he was signing over to them, since he couldn't count on our help."

"So you helped Lope—"

He shrugged. "He'd have talked. Word spreads. I've problems enough. These things happen in life."

I wondered where else they might happen; thought it was wise to change the subject and so avoid one of those things about which it was wise to worry not, wonder not.

"How many millions are involved?" I asked.

"Half our working net'll be Bronxed. Land purchase wrapped last month. Last quarter our profits downed 75 percent of last year's. It's madness. His madness.

The Army primes to push far with this. Jumps full command when his finger points. They can output this one forty years. Constructions to begin, end of the season. End of construction, when the money goes. Before I have it, at this rate.''

We steered down Seventh Avenue, reaching the Times Square Free Zone at Forty-third. As we glided through, clearing our lane, I saw Army boys frosting the wall with icy blooms of razorwire. Over the entrance was stenciled the message: *The Guilty Will Be Punished*. Times Square was Manhattan's only Free Zone; it wasn't large. At Dryco's suggestion, the Army had set the quadrant apart, though city police patrolled regularly, in groups of six. Here the uninvolved could spend their passions on harmless excitements, releasing emotions otherwise kept bottled before those in action against state interests—keen to divert such energy toward their own devices—applied more glittery methods of uncorking. Each day, each night, the Army admitted thousands, in rotation, for two-hour shifts so that all might stalk in ease, slaughtering time, frolicking beneath the advertisement's gleam, vizzing the enormous vid monitors that hung from the building façades. The zone's streets were perpetually wet; the only way to clear the area for oncoming shifts was to send through Army vehicles equipped with water cannons.

On assurance of death, 1A cars passing through the Free Zone were left unscarred; Army boys, arms linked, shielded our land, to certify.

"But the capital isn't touched," I said.

"Not yet."

"And our investments—"

"His rumors take wing and fly. Evidence grows. I suspected and as always I'm right. Land values in Manhattan dropping now. In Miami and Atlantic City. New Orleans and Sydney and Leningrad. On every coast, gracias of his wordspread. The Army wants to redivert from Manhattan to dry shore, half to Bronx and the rest overseas. Claims no sense protecting what won't last. Investments ruined and dead gone. My investments.''

Passing into the Herald Square Secondary Zone we edged through the crowd awaiting Times Square admittance. We slid by city buses chugging along, passengers fly-clinging to their graffitied hulks. Two tumbled off as we passed; a taxi swerved to run them down. At Thirty-eighth, three cabs and a delivery van had been torched by those impatient; the offenders—I surmised it was them—lay covered in the street as if to be sheltered from the sun, surrounded by Army boys. Another limo, an old Lenin, sailed by, clipping ne'er-do-wells at the corner of Thirty-sixth; they whirled and fluttered like falling leaves. Wishing to avoid Thirty-fourth Street's mania, we turned west onto Thirty-fifth, the ba-ba-da-da of "Teddy Bear" thumping along.

"We can relocate—"

"It's the interim that'll term us," said Mister Dryden. "His idea of reinvesting covers Bronx only. He wants to close foreign markets for fresh cash. Subvert all under his fear.''

"You mean about the Green? It's not even proved—"

"In his mind it is. He can't say why rain falls but he spells the weather's future. Nightmare made flesh. We'll be exxed.''

"You think he really believes it?"

"I did," said Mister Dryden, his voice lowering, "But a new thought strikes.''

We turned south onto the West Street speedway, passing the Javits Center. All along the Hudson from Midtown down, barges pulled into the rebuilt docks—some, at Dryco's request, built so high above the water that elevators were needed to uplift the freight—bringing in much of the city's imports: fabric to be reworked into clothing in the sweatshops, prepped goods ready for resale in the big stores, service equipment of all sorts for all types. Food was distributed through the Javits Center; by river barge, by train from upstate, by long trucks on their twice-daily runs through the tunnel, the produce demanded by Manhattan's throng arrived and was dispatched by the Army boys. From the buildings' ten dozen exits poured streams of trucks, vans, cars, carts, wagons, and dollies, all topfull with pickups. Near the newer part, Army trucks were conveniently parked so that the choicest items—meat, real milk, fresh fruit—could be loaded after confiscation for zone HQs. The public took what it was given—nothing unusual in that.

"What might that be?" I asked, looking into his eyes to see what might be there; seeing only the eyes of someone who had escaped from something—often.

"That his plan could be subtle. That with the Green and with the Bronx he intends only destruction. Kill what he built. What Mom built."

"Deliberately?" I asked, surprised to hear the pot kettlespeak.

"Why else?" he said, "He's done worse. Believe."

As our conversation continued, I turned to viz the river, finding nothing beneath the glaze coating his eyes, but seeing in his face—beyond the sweats and the shakes and the pallor—signs of something that troubled so deep that I began to feel I should begin to fear. Mister Dryden teetered into hysteria's edge; touchdancing the chaos astride the abyss, Enid would say.

"Why would he want to do that?" I asked, softly, so as not to further alarm.

"Paranoia strikes deep, he says. His redeeps mine twenty over. He wants to keep me from getting it, OM. I can't say why. He'll gotterdam it all."

"Have you talked about this—"

"Talk's time is over. He's ready to action me now. Any day."

"Maybe not."

"He is," Mister Dryden repeated, shaking more violently; I worried, briefly, that he'd combined his reckers carelessly, but then his flesh settled. "He wants to take me out."

"But why?"

"He's batbrained. As I said. Shooting on impulse's charge." Mister Dryden's lip was bloodied from his nibbling it as we spoke. "I'm sure he thinks he works on reason still."

"Does he?"

"As said. Talk's time is over. Big action calls."

"What action plans?" I asked.

"I suspect he feels I'm going to do something to him."

"What?"

"What I plan to do to him." he said. "I'll need assistance. Assistance most silent. Cunning calls."

Traffic slowed as we neared the Downtown Control Zone, even in the 1A lane. Inland, just before the barricade, I saw traffic stilled along Canal Street, all awaiting passage through the Holland Tunnel, the only Hudson crossing open for public use. New deflooding devices were being installed, and it was open only a few hours each day. The Lincoln Tunnel—closest to Midtown, and to the Javits Center—and the George Washington Bridge, high above water and sturdy, were reserved for Army use sole. Oil slicks on the river, combusting, flared yellow fire as I looked across the river's surface; old boxes, tires, papers, and wood drifted down with the current. The sun's light, eking through clouds, shone on Jersey City's spires, and made ashimmer the waters' ripples. As eve drew, blue lights would arise from the Hudson's silent passengers and float like balloons across the surface of the deep. No one fished out corpses anymore; they all had their reasons for being there.

"My assistance?"

"You'll recompense."

"For what?"

"I won't demand," he said, "but I will detail."

"Do," I said.

"You'll need assist, after," he said. "But that in a mo. Tomorrow we weekend, upstate. The birthday, AO?" Mister Dryden's son would be ten the next day; his son and his wife lived at the estate, for security's sake. "All sets as looks appear till night. I access you to his study. Sunday he enters to program. You rig a blast. Drape it in terrorchic. Any group suffices, though Maroon might best it. He goes in. He goes up. You're safetyplayed, meantime."

I didn't respond at once—that he slipped back into full bizspeak to outline his program, as if fearful that he might be heard, even over the water's din, even in his own car, suggested that more was up than seemed evident.

"AO," I nodded.

"You could method it," he said. "You walk the walk. You talk the talk."

"AO," I repeated. With plasticine and powder and a quartz timeset a blast was the easiest thing to rig.

"Reaction?" he asked.

"You're sure it's necessary," I asked. "No other option?"

"Nada," he sighed. "His fear grows and he sets danger for all, OM. Keep him boiling as at present and we'll be meat for the stew. If he snaps, it won't be me alone. He'll take my son. Avalon, probably. You, definitely. Set him loose on the path he knows and he could lose it all twice over. He's not above much. If he ever chose to do what he could, all'd be lost for all. Untermed, he might do it yet.''

"Do what?'' I asked, realizing what subject he neared.

"Worry not, wonder—''

"AO,'' I interrupted, seeing I'd come no closer this day; seeing that soon I might. "You mentioned recompense?''

"Certain,'' he said, the hint of a smile shading his lips. "Loving You'' started up on his soundtrack. "First, a move would be ordered. Afterward a readjustment of rank. If son becomes father, then who becomes me?''

"Me?''

He nodded. "You've valuabled yourself thirty over, OM. Time comes to take you from guarding and put you in your place. As my righthand, you know so much as I. You'd become CEO.''

"What about Jake?'' I asked, thinking of that Kyoto sword.

"His talent lies where he leaves it. Yours needs the touch of free air.''

"How long have you been thinking about this?'' I asked, doubtful still.

"Longtime,'' he said. "But the top only holds so many. Room must clear first. You'll clear. Then you'll move.''

"AO,'' I said.

"Second,'' he said, "Recompense further is already effected. A different readjustment.'' Extracting a blue envelope from his jacket pocket, he handed it over.

"What's this?'' I asked, breaking the flap's glue.

"My will,' he said, "Revised as of last week.''

It was; I recognized the signatures of his lawyers, and their holographic seal affixed at the bottom of each page.

"Clause 16A," he said; I found it and read it. I read it twice more.

"Seriously?" I asked.

"Even now, it steadies. Even if you decide otherwise in my request for assistance, you'll claim 25 percent of my holdings and future inheritances. You serve well, OM. Goodness claims those who wait."

"Even if I decide otherwise, this stands?"

He nodded. "Though if you do, and I'm taken first," he said, the hint of that smile long faded, "you may not enjoy for long. His hands could cut all our strings, and drop us in middance. Consider."

We neared our destination, the Trade Towers. Smoke still drifted near the base of the south tower, where the latest blast had occurred. Our operations were located in the north tower, as was Mister Dryden's downtown apartment. To the right of the towers, near the river's edge, stood the beginnings of the floodwall. When the possibility of the Green first showed itself, years ago, the city borrowed funds from the Old Man toward the construction of a fifty-foot wall intended to surround Manhattan. The funds were no less liquid than the waters to be fought and were mostly diverted to other campaigns. The floodwall ran only from the towers south to the Battery. Traditional American handicraft was employed in the wall's construction, and so most of it had collapsed.

"I just don't know," I said, after some minutes.

"You don't want better?"

"I do."

"A better place to live you'll have. You can move out of the freak show down there."

"I like where I'm living," I said—that wasn't strictly true, not anymore. I liked living with Enid, who liked where we lived.

Jack Womack

"I can't stand even thinking of those Ambients," he said, shivering again. "The real ones, I mean."

Mister Dryden knew my sister was an Ambient, a voluntary one; such had been reported to him many times by the anonymous wishing to further themselves.

"I'm rather used to them," I said.

"OM," he said, "You can't know how many you'll help if you do this."

"Say that I do," I said. "Someone had to take the fall. Even if I disguise it we'll be suspected—"

"They can't touch me," he said.

"They can me," I said; it wasn't the police, or the Army, that concerned us, but the Old Man's guards and supporters, who had their own interests to consider, some of whom were even more accomplished than Jake when it came to discipline.

"You'll lowlie it after, my request," he said. "Out of country. For a couple of months until we can reorganize. Fire a few, here and there."

"Still—"

"Hear my last proposal and decide," he said. "You'll need assist in this yourself, certain. Rule me out for the obvious. Trust no one at the estate."

"Jimmy?" I asked.

"More in his pocket than mine. You'll need someone lightfooted. Sharp wits about. Trustworthied. Keen to travel. One with whom you work well. With a bulb dimmer than yours, perhaps, so as not to outshine."

"Who?"

He motioned toward the front seat, looking through the clear panel. The seat was broad and the car wide; Avalon lay there, on her knees and elbows, curled up, asleep, facing Jimmy. Her bottom was raised as if for a computer advertisement. Sharp blue electric flushed my skin. Jimmy pulled our car onto the ramp leading into the subtower area, and her form was lost in shadow.

"Avalon?"

"As described," he said, no discernible emotion in his voice. This seemed entirely too much like one of my dreams; I felt my objections drifting into sleep.

"But—"

"OM," he said. "It's time for many changes. Her fondness feeds me no more. I see how you see her. See how she sees you back. Only nature's way at op. This morning I saw how you clasped, postconference. Even when eyeshut, I see."

"I'd think you wouldn't be very happy about it—"

"I'm not, on level one. On level two, as said, it's time for many changes. There's no point keeping what you haven't got."

A heavily guarded garage area had been built beneath the north tower, and we were therein admitted. Jimmy pulled the car onto the lift. At his signal, the lift rose; we floated upward, secure within our chamber.

"So—"

"She'll assist after," he said.

"In what way?"

"She'll say, Saturday, that she keens to cityshop. You'll guard. A houseguard will drive you down. En route, the setup effects. Once cited you'll contact the name I'll give. They'll exit you. Wherever you wish to vacation, you can. London. Leningrad. Zeiching. You name."

"And when we return?"

"If she wishes to stay," he said, "She can."

"With me?"

"With you."

Something roiled in my stomach as I shed all final qualms; for a moment I felt I was being eaten from within. I looked up again, at Avalon, and imagined myself with her, running down the roads. That I wished so much to be with her decided my mind and buried my soul. I can only say it was a decision to do that which you think you'd never do yourself, no matter how many others ever expected it of you—like joining the Army on whim's notion, or tossing yourself from a moving car, or blowing up the world.

"I'll go," I said. Mister Dryden smiled. The lift stopped.

"In the office I'll pass contact info. Talk to Avalon. See if she goes?"

"You think she won't?"

"See," he said. "You could do it sole, if needed, AO?" I nodded. "But then you wouldn't, perhaps—"

Neither of us said anything, for several long seconds.

"See. In seclusion. All of this is in seclusion."

"AO," I said. As we stepped from the car one of Mister Dryden's phones buzzed. I picked it up and handed it to him.

"Dryden here," he said. "AO. They imaged, then? You did? Prokashnik! Spot them twice over. My account. AO."

He hung up. I lifted my eyebrows, curious.

"Two casinos look safe," he said. "Mariel listens well some days. Especially with inspiration effected. Jake effected that." Without warning, his face downcasted.

"What's wrong?" I asked.

"We'll have to raise the boardwalk, still," he said. "Floods at high tide. That damned Green."

The Green was so arcane that even our city's denizens were struck dumb by the possibilities. The subject never arose in chat; like the existence of the Superfluous, like Ambients, the Green came up only in discussions of problems for which the ever-inventive young would probably find a lasting solution. The debate was hampered in that no one agreed as to what the Green would involve.

AMBIENT

The weather had been peculiar since I was a boy. The temperature in New York, these days, rarely dropped below forty—though the previous June there'd been a one-day blizzard—and though it averaged sixty to seventy year-round, on occasion it had gone so high as one hundred and fifteen. Deserts expanded worldwide; in the American west, the Dust Bowl brushed the skirts of Dallas and Chicago. Once, during a trip to that latter city, I recall standing with Mister Dryden on the ninetieth floor of one of our buildings, watching through the window a broad brown band writhing along the horizon's line; the state of Nebraska, rolling up like a rug.

As American grainland vanished, so Canada's and Russia's grew, and so from those countries our wheat arrived to supply our stones. The Siberian growing season lasted eight months of the year, lately; for eight months of the year, too, it snowed in Sydney and along the southern coast of Australia. Ten months of the year, along the Pacific coast, it rained, a cool, perpetual drizzled fog. The last time Mister Dryden and I were in LA the rainy season was off; a thermal inversion had set in. The air was so thick you could nearly roll it into little balls.

And so far as anyone admitted, and so the Old Man believed, the sea would rise five to one hundred feet in five to one hundred years. No scientist would, or could, explain precisely what was going on; at heart, everyone, I believe, suspected that someone else, somewhere, for some reason, was doing it all deliberately.

Not all of New York would sub, according to the Old Man's experts; the Bronx and much of upper Manhattan would forever rise above the waves. The Old Man planned for the building of his new city, fresh and shining-bright, on the golden-green hills of the Bronx—of which, that day, he owned 100 percent of the land.

Visions come sometimes to my sleeping eyes; once I

beheld one of the city of Old New York, one hundred—
maybe five—years hence, a Venice on stilts: cobbled
docks extending out front the tenth floors of the most
attractive skyscrapers; gondolas plying the gray currents,
down the watery boulevards, in morning's mist—the towers still habitable, high above, and the old horrors way
down below the ocean. Mister Dryden, even early on,
had no faith in my vision, and laughed the time I told
him. He said I was a hopeless romantic. Perhaps. Some
dreams fade like cheap dyes, bright at first wear and drab
thereafter; unlike their dreamer, my dreams never ran.

For that afternoon's remainder, I stayed with Mister
Dryden as he went about, checking what he thought
needed checking. Through the Dryco bank—Chase,
obtained like so much else, during the Ebb—Mister
Dryden, and Dryco, and the government could weigh
in balance the daily worth of most of the world's
nations. Since the days after the Ebb, when all countries' banks began working with paper commodities
rather than paper currency (the debts could never have
been paid otherwise), Dryco had held a close grip on
each and all, for no other reason than that Dryco owned
so much of every sort of thing, everywhere. The Old
Man devised this barter system, or so he claimed; more
likely it had been Susie D's toy; she was always more
apt in those fields. Mister Dryden effected and programmed the weekend details: diamonds from Mandela
would ship to Amsterdam in exchange for chips from
Frankfurt; Malaysian lumber would sail to Tokyo in
exchange for denims from Quito; from Canada's mines,
bauxite was to go to Zeiching and Shanghai along with
American Pepsi-Cola, both in trade for Vietnamese
TVCs that would later make their way to France, in
exchange for champagne soon to be guzzled at Mister
Dryden's Westchester table. As we were at war with

Russia and its allies, all trade with them was carried on only during the first half of the week, through a different exchange.

I checked in with the Market about certain of our holdings. Some delay occurred in my obtaining info. Two hours before, at the conference's conclusion, SatCom disappeared from the big board, and all stocks held by other companies and by striving midmen suddenly became Dryco property—for Dryco was not a member of the big board, or of the exchange; the Old Man never trusted the Market, he said. Once the last suicides had been carried out, my info cleared quickly, and I found what I needed.

Around four I approached Avalon, wishing to talk.

"Here?" she asked.

"Too many ears," I said, looking toward Mister Dryden. "Down a ways."

We made our way to a lower floor, to the Central Data Processing Department on the fiftieth floor. As we stepped out of the elevator, we clutched each other for warmth, for the AC was powerful on that level. As we walked into the main office, our breath escaped from our mouths in clouds.

The office was full. Processing midmen—women, mostly—once worked at home, doing piecework with small terminals. After much thievery of time and material, all Dryco computer ops were required to work at the office. The staff worked in thirty-two hour shifts; on average, they received forty cents an hour after taxes as overtime pay.

"Where d'you want to talk?" Avalon asked me; she'd borrowed Jimmy's coat and buttoned it around herself. It reached the floor.

"Down at the far end. Away from them—"

"They can't hear," she said. "They're not paying attention, anyway."

I rubbed my hands together, warming them; wishing I could rub them against Avalon. Each processor sat in a small cubicle, their eyes focusing the CRTs hanging on the walls before them; each wore headphones so as to hear their terminals—number eights—as they punched away. A red light flashed over one of the cubicles. One of the office maintenants rolled over and unlocked the stocks that held the young woman's feet. It guided her across the room, toward the lav; her white cane helped her in tapping out the way. The system had flaws; some employees went insane—they were fired—and some grew blind—the ones whose fingers slipped were given Braille keyboards, at cost.

"What's the deal, then?" she asked, after we reached the far end of the room. I told her what he'd told me.

"What do you think?" I finally asked.

"Sounds wonderful," she said, not smiling.

"Yeah—"

"Sounds like smoke and words," she whispered. "And a whole pile of shit underneath."

"I don't think so."

"I don't trust him," she said.

"I know."

"You do?" she asked. "Why?"

"I've known him longer. He was talking me today as he used to."

"Making any more sense than he has lately?"

"In some ways."

"Ways that help you," she said.

"That help us."

"Seem to, don't they? What if this is just to set us up for something?"

"Why would he do that?"

"Why's Pops do things the way he does? Why do either of them do anything the way they do? They're both fuckin' crazy."

I still hated to admit it, for whatever reason. "I know," I said.

"And you think he's less crazy than his father?"

"Look," I said, "Weren't you just saying a few hours ago how if I didn't do something, you would?"

"Yeah."

"What?" I asked. "What'll you do?"

She leaned against the wall, folding her arms across her chest. "If he's out to take us," I continued, "he will, one way or the other. But we'll be together. Right?"

Her eyes brightened; I decided to be more overt than I had been—the time seemed so right as it ever would.

"I love you," I said. I'd never said it before to anyone but Enid; had felt it for Avalon since the moment I first vizzed. "If he's leveling, then we'll be doing AO for a time. If nothing more. Both of us."

She nodded, and let her arms drop to her sides.

"Whatever happens, we'll together. Do you want that? If you don't—"

At once she put her arms around me, clamping me tight. I felt the bones in my back pop as she squeezed. I brought my hands to her face, stroking each side.

"I don't trust him," she said. "We better ready to run."

"We'll run together."

"Ready to kill, Shameless," she said. "Ready to die."

"Together," I said. "You'll go?"

"Detail it," she said. We walked back toward the elevator, all proper and business-pure. Into her ear I whispered her cues. Red lights went off at each end of the room, and maintenants rushed to lead. Saturday, I thought. After tomorrow's long hours we should never part alive.

4

BEFORE I LEFT I CHANGED CLOTHES, PUTTING ON MY highlace black boots, dark pants, a sweatshirt, and over all my Krylar coat. Signing out at eight—Mister Dryden and Avalon kept to their downtown apartments, on the one hundredth floor, and so my shadow could safely stray—I picked up my check and walked out. There was extra this week; not so much as I would have wished—it never was. I made $4,000 a year working for Mister Dryden. Enid and I, who owned one small building between us, by law paid the highest percentage of property tax. It was judged a great incentive that the more buildings you owned, the less tax you paid. Last year our property tax ran $1,800; take so well electric bills, cable bills, phone bills, food . . .

As an owner's protégé, my personal taxes were nada; boozhies shelled the funds that kept the wheels rolling over all.

There was a Chase on Chambers Street, near Centre;

I went in, sliding my card into the machine, and waited for a response.

"Good evening, Mister O'Malley," said the voice; bank voices—number sevens—were sharp castrati sopranos. "Can I help you?"

"Deposit."

"Code first."

I pressed out my code with care. If you miscoded while transacting, the machine electrocuted you. Chase claimed that, for the public, the printcode was still in development.

"Good evening."

"Night," I said, leaving. Near the night courts, off Foley Square, was a Dogs Я'Us that kept the late hour so that lawyers and juries might larder their maws. I fastfood it only on payday; at least my Drydencard exed me from the 30 percent VAT added to all goods' retail cost. Dogs Я'Us, safe for all, used only organic additives in its wares; you could be sure of what they held even if you couldn't choose the breed. I usually stand by an unexciting diet: fruits and veges, tolerably safe if soaked for several hours; bread bought from kosher bakers and thus free from unnatural carcinogens. On occasion splurge became a must. I ate five wienies. Three eleven-year-olds served up; the girl wore manager garb. Her wedding photo hung over the counter; the couple, in full dress, stood by the sprout bar, hard by the plastic Happy Dog figurine.

I moved along up Centre Street, satisfied. A block up was the Tombs, packed with disparos: Dreds, Mariels, Maroons, problematics, foreigns, and all of like ilk. In the buildings' heart was Wonderland, where, I was told, the choicest cases were taken. I knew little more, then.

The smog was nearly translucent. I passed through the checkpoint at Canal Street. A sanitation truck roared

Jack Womack

through the barricade behind me, rushing down Canal.
It stopped at Bowery; the driver raised the truck's bin
and dumped its load into the street. Hundreds of bags
burst, hitting the ground. The driver returned to his
starting zone. Trash pickups in the Downtown Control
Zone and in the abutting Secondary zones were recycled over the wall, in the Loisaida Twilight Zone, the
barrio de noch, my neighborhood. It was easy to get
into a Twilight Zone. The official name for such an area
was an Enterprise Zone, but no one who live in them
called them anything by Twilight Zones.

I stepped through previously recycled garbage as I
strolled Canal, garbage scattered further by tads pluck-
ing deposit cans, hoping to turn them roundo, penny
for ten. At Mulberry I weaved north, pushing through
the crowds, scooting past the clunkers scuffling the
streets; once such a mobile home was obtained, a family could drive a Twilight Zone indefinitely, taking turns
at the wheel, stopping only to tank and tum. I knew the
streets by rote; none bore street signs. A stranger might
be lost for days, though the locals would surely spot
him long before.

Merengues blared from a thousand boxes. Droozies
(the Druzhinas—local vigilante units who, in zones,
parceled order as they saw fit) had stripped a young
girl, shaved her head, and, having daubed her in tar,
trounced her with long poles. Consorting with Army
boys, or so suspected; that was the usual treatment for
such dalliance. There'd been a blast farther up; smoke
dyed the air brownish-blue. Folks perused the bodies
in the street, retrieving what might later prove usable.
Someone from on high lobbed a chunk of concrete; it
bounced off the hardhat I wore down here. Knees buck-
ling, I moved along, suspecting no personal animosity.
Ahead, youths lithely sprang through a restaurant window, followed by additional youths swinging bats,

56

pipes, and old parking meters. Losing their quarry, they upended pedicabs and trampled the riders. Their colors announced them as members of the Law's Long Arms. An old Pontiac scraped along the street, hauling produce from the Javits Center. The car was tireless; the women pulling had a rough time of it. Nearby, two rascals wedged a boy into a crack between two buildings and took turns playing Johnny-in-the-pony. At the corner of Grand, a woman straddled a man lying in the walk, caressing him repeatedly with a hammer; her point seemed moot. I paused to give ear to two accordionists playing Stravinsky's *Rite of Spring* and gave them each a nickel. One put the change into a plastic capsule and swallowed it, so that it might be recovered safely, once home. I always went through Chinatown, walking from the Tombs; when stalking time settled, it was the safest route.

An Army truck bashed through the crowd, lights on and sirens roaring. The Home Army boys never patrolled Twilight Zones in standard fashion; they'd sooner go into Long Island. Antiterror units came in periodically, for gaiety, and for the touch of the multitude. The truck stopped; soldiers stood up in the back.

"*Bailé!*" they drawled, firing into the people.

I dove into a nearby doorway, estimating I'd be missed. The soldiers shrieked like ghosts as they reloaded. I edged my head past the corner of the door and looked out. The wire shirt beneath the truck had pulled away on one side; someone so observant as I tossed in a mollie. Seconds later the truck hurtled into the air, crashing in flames on a group holding the corner of Kenmare. Those troops who survived were extracted from the wreckage by samaritans, and torn and shredded.

I ran down Delancey, a wide street lined with buildings' dry shells. The Brooklyn sky was deep red; the towers of the old Williamsburg bridge far away shone bloodish in the reflected light. I heard shouts; the truck blew.

On Eldridge Street I slowed. Nobody lived here, not anymore, not even squatters. Hanging from the sides of buildings were bloody-boned remains, left as warning. The Moonboys, an undernourished contingent, controlled this area, but they knew me, and if any prowled nearby, they must have supposed it not worth giving greeting. Haphazard blockades of cement blocks, boards, and barrels still filled the intersections, tossed across by citizens long lost. I walked the street's middle, whistling "Big Noise in Winnetka," avoiding open manholes and excavations. There were no streetlights in our zone—they brought good money as scrap—and it was a smoggy night, but I pulled my flash and had no trouble. I passed the hull of a century-old synagogue; every inch of it was graffitied. There were the usual tags, obscenities, and political messages: U S OUT OF NORTH AMERICA, NO FUTURE, MY RIGHTS OR I BITE.

A better-lettered sign stood in the midst of the street, placed by the Army years before. *Don't Touch Anything*, it read, *It Could Kill You*. Smudged handprints nearly obliterated the warning.

I climbed over heaps of debris where buildings had fallen into the street. Near one heap was a skeleton, lying languidly on the pavement, as if awaiting the next course. Feeling my high school soccer-team days again, I booted the skull down the street; ran and booted it again. It went for point against an empty hydrant; startled rats scrambled for cover. Two copters whipped over, all searchlights on, their pale beams piercing the smog. Someone had dropped off a city bus further along; it lay on one side, blasted and burned. HAVE A NICE DAY, its destination sign read.

Heading east on Houston Street, I entered my quarter. People crowded the streets once more: residents of every creed and color, Ambient throughout. I walked north on Avenue C. My part of the neighborhood was safe as could be; our Droozies kept a pretense of order in the area, and Ambients tended not to injure others reasonlessly—though when they had reason they were the most dangerous opponents of all. As I walked through, I felt the sustaining comfort of being in the place where I had grown up, knowing all and having all know me.

In lieu of streetlights, trash can fires, supplied and fed by the block associations, cast warm orange light through the haze. Our building was at Avenue C and 4th, two five-story tenements joined years before to form one. We had abandoned the upper three floors; nobody around here could afford to rent apartments no matter the charge, and landlords weren't esteemed no matter who they were. I'd blocked the windows of our building, and sealed the upper stairway, but bargain finders had still snuck in. The last time I'd looked, it appeared that much of our roof was out on indefinite loan.

Enid and I lived on the second floor. On the ground floor were her two small businesses; Ambients were born entrepreneurs. One was a nickelodeon, the Simplex, a rep house showing classic films on vid. The screen was of unbreakable thirty-foot liqrystal that she'd obtained in trade for our father's old leather coat. The sound wasn't marvelous, but you could usually hear something. You kept your feet propped unless you wished to feed the rats. The marquee was unlit, but I knew what was playing. This week's bill—subtitled in Spanglish—was *A Clockwork Orange* and *The Wizard of Oz*, favorites of the heartyoung nostalgic.

The other business was her club—hough, Ambients

called it—Belsen. It catered to Ambients and lovers of
Ambient music. Ruben and Lester, the bouncers,
greeted me as I entered. Being Ambients, they dressed
as if Halloween Carnival went on year-long. Being Ambients they would have been hard to miss in any season;
Ruben had no arms, and Lester had no body below the
navel. Their agility was so great as the average Ambients'. If any customer grew testy—except during
Happy Hour—Ruben loosened them up with his hobnails; then Lester leapt on and windsored. Lester was
quite the sweeter of the two; he wore a black reverse
Mohawk and a domino mask with sequins, the kind
Woolworth's sells. Ruben, whose hair was uncombed
blond, wore a discarded camouflage jumpsuit, obtained
when he had discarded the former wearer. Inverted
crosses hung from their ears. Ruben and Lester were
lovers, which, though no longer illegal, was frowned
upon among non-Ambients.

"Hi-de-ho," I said. They grinned.

"Who hangs and how high, O'Malley?" Lester asked
me.

"Skyhigh," I said. "How's biz?"

"Bloody fucko."

"Enid near?" I asked.

"To the clouds she rolled," said Ruben, gesturing
upstairs. "Margot atow. Persuading what she lists."

"Spin and wheel with little diddle," Lester laughed.
He reached up, pulling himself onto a stool one-handed.
His arms were big as my legs.

"*Little* little."

"Margot lowlying still?" I asked. Margot was Enid's
lover. She bartended three nights a week. Except for
Ruben and Lester, Enid never hired any but women,
notwithstanding that discriminatory hiring was illegal.

Ruben shook his head, tossing his cigarette to his
mouth with a quick flip of his chin. "To sight your

ragged puss in glory grand," he laughed, "to taunt
your mind with apish tricks."

"Wonder and glory," I sighed.

I sat at the bar, nearly ordering my usual—a Pepsi—
then, changing my mind, ordered a triple gin. I hadn't
drunk alky in years, but that evening I wished to bib-
tuck my mind a spell. The bartender, a young black
women whose right hand consisted of two thumbs
joined at the shoulder, was new; except for Ruben, Lester, and Margot, there was constant turnover in the
hough. Ambients tended to circulate in ease if not care.
She knew me; she waived payment. I left her a penny
tip anyway; the glass was clean and unbroken, and she
hadn't thrown it at me.

Over the backbar was a scrawled poster listing coming attractions.

TOMORROW
ANN FRANK/BATTERED CHILDREN/
MULTIPLE BIRTH DEFECTS

SATURDAY
CELESTIAL PALSY/IRREVERSIBLE BRAIN DAMAGE/
ZYKLON-B

The club was closed on Sundays.

At the far end of the bar gathered a pride of transies,
resembling proxies at first viz. Their dresses, their hair,
makeup, and forms approximated. Transies were unique
among voluntary Ambients in that they chose to add
rather than subtract. Those who could bribe it had T
and A augmentation; no one became a transy who
couldn't bribe it. Having done so much, they retained
their artillery, to flash at the uninitiated. They made
love only to each other; posed and preened for all.

I wasn't sure which band prepared to play; Ambient

bands were as one to me. This outfit had a one-armed bassist. They stumbled over, untuning their instruments. I drank my gin quickly, hoping to exit before midnight. The band introduced themselves by throwing a table into the audience. They began bashing the first song; a composition of their own, I suspected. The audience thrashed about, hopping up and down, smashing heads together, clapping stumps, flapping flippers, bouncing from side to side, wailing and baying and howling for the moon. Ambient singers are prone to tonelessly shout all lyrics at voice's top; this fellow was of the traditional school. Two-thirds of the way through their first number of the clock read midnight, and Happy Hour began. The red lights on the ceiling flashed and the sirens blared. I gulped my gin and made for the side door. The audience pulled out their toys and began to play. The chainsaws were revving up as I ran to our apartment.

At the top of the stairs, I stepped over the homebodies who had bedded near our door; they were called such because their bodies were their homes. There were seven in our hall. Many places provided floor space for them—even the Army let some spend each evening in Grand Central, perhaps a thousand, by their count. The official government tally, much lower, enumerated only those who died before morning.

I unlocked the five locks on our door, then the two on the gate, and went inside. I relocked the locks and slid the gate shut and put up the police bars. Enid was there, watching TV; Margot lurked unseen.

"Hi-de-ho, Seamus," she said.

"Ola." Something about her was different; for a moment I couldn't tell what. "You painted your nails."

"Finified bright and embaled dark," she said. She'd painted them black; they'd been red. Enid, tired of her head simply shaved, had six months earlier wheedled the Heath Service—she'd gone to high school with a doctor in the appropriate field and had something on her—into implanting nails, points up, in her scalp. There were seven great spikes above her forehead and fourteen smaller ones scattered over her skull. Officially the Health Service refused to treat Ambients, much less offering to adapt those who wished to become such.

Enid's presence awed the most jaded. She was my height—six three—and not dissimilar in bulk, for she had worked with weights since she was seventeen. Tonight she wore a black blank tee, her spike bracelets, and pink tanga lacies.

"They're you," I said, sitting beside her, kissing her cheek. Stuffing oozed onto the floor from the sofa as I sat; a rat pattered off to the kitchen as if to bring me my slippers. I removed my hardhat and my boots and pulled off my ears, laying them carefully on a nearby crate. Enid gave me those earring for Easter, three years before; I was quite protective of them. The throb of the drums and the bass and the chainsaws resounded through the soles of my feet; I lolled to the lulling sound of breaking glass.

"Fizgiggling and wandering far, I viz," she said. "How does downstairs go?" She was drinking from a bottle of Stolichnaya; she drank two quarts a day.

"Bloody fucko, I'm told."

"Beat me. Pestered full and joyful?"

"Looks that way. Little bitty surly one near?"

"Don't meanmouth," said Enid. "You think her such a whipperginny. Consider her mode."

"Dreadful thought."

She looked at me, quizzical. "Does alky wash your mind?"

"I had one drink?"

"Tu?"

"None other. I left when Happy Hour got under. Idolators fawning the great bore me."

"Eyeing you guzz would appall," she said. "Stolly?" she asked, waving the bottle.

"I'll use a glass, thanks."

"A *glass*!" she laughed.

"Try it," I said, "You won't break so many teeth."

She tossed a lamp at me; I brushed it away, walking to the kitchen. In that room's dark I heard the voice of the refrigerator: *Door ajar. Please shut.* The door was not ajar, but the computer—a number three—couldn't know; dust had gotten in the chips. Thousands of times, day and night, the refrigerator cried *Door ajar, please shut.* We never had appliance money, and so could afford neither new refrigerator nor repairperson. The voice was pleasant, and the sentiment inoffensive; you got used to it.

Getting a glass from the cupboard, I brushed away the roaches and rinsed it out. I looked out the window; through the smog I could see only the warm glow of fires. As I left the kitchen, a tremendous chunk of plaster fell from the ceiling. There were gaping holes in every room of the apartment where the plaster had been shaken loose by the vibrations below, or where our small roomies had chewed through.

"What sore-eyed sights so dearlynear," I heard, reentering the living room. "Long steeped in urinals, flecked roundabye. How runs this eve, mewlypuke?"

"Amazing," I said to Enid, staring at Margot, who had come in from the bedroom while I was in the kitchen. "You didn't move your lips once—"

"Sizist," said Margot, addressing me; her contratenor rang like clanking iron. "The mouth gapes wide and drops the brains away."

She lifted herself onto the sofa, snickering at me. On hobnail Margot was about three foot nine, an achondroplast: a dwarf, a born Ambient. She wore a shapeless blazer with the buttons and sleeves ripped off, and a tee that read ELVIS DIED FOR SOMEBODY'S SINS BUT NOT MINE. Her pants—cut off above her ankles—looked to have been yanked from a corpse.

"Control your manikin, Enid. People will talk."

"True tones told in dulcet crystal," said Margot. Enid handed me an untapped bottle. I filled my tumbler, and drank.

"Cheers," I said.

"Fuckall," they said.

"Rolling soon?" I asked Margot.

"Rolling raw to rock away," she said. Margot packed a swordstick four feet long; she used it as a staff. Around one wrist she wore a pink leather bracelet beaded with razors. Her black hair was cropped close, except in the front, where it hung over her face in long dreads. She'd recently filed her teeth into sharp points. I didn't dislike Margot, but she could be overly candid in her expressions toward me. "As we cats awayed," she said, "how then did piglet play?"

"Well," I said. "And now expecting a nice, quiet evening in casa."

"Opt for pleaz and not for pain, eh?" she said, hopping off the sofa, grinding her heel against my foot. "Losient."

"Pick on your own size," I said.

Margot balanced her cane across her shoulders, her stubby arms outstretched. "Your mind sets a great sail burstfull with wind."

"You'd look lovely crucified," I said.

"How the thickened plot."

"Lay no blows, my loves," said Enid, intervening. "So cruel to each and all."

"Relax," said Margot, smiling. "With rude children only games entrap."

"Good eve," I said, taking my place on the sofa. Enid stood to see Margot out.

"You're off?" she asked her.

"To skim the wide surf," said Margot.

"Have fun," I mumbled.

"Again this way you will?"

"Again and ever," said Margot. "To the gone world till then."

"You'll go how?" asked Enid.

"On angel's wings," said Margot, "with angel's feet."

Enid bent down to kiss her. Margot lifted her head in caressful submission; nicked a small slice from Enid's cheek with her razors. My sister shivered with delight. "Merricat," she whispered.

"Cuddles," said Margot, her voice raw with throat's lust. Enid began unlocking the door.

"Bye," I repeated.

"Order your house, gullyguts," commanded Margot of me, smashing a favorite vase of mine with her cane. She twisted through the opened door and was gone.

"Till tomorrow eve," shouted Enid down the hall. After she relocked she came back over, took my hand, held it, and squeezed it hard.

"A long time of it?" she asked. "You're wearish to my eye."

"Just an average day," I said. She laughed, lighting another cigarette; no one but Ambients smoked anymore, not even the Old Man. The untouchable caste of American smokers never extended to American producers of tobacco; smokestuff could be exchanged for so many useful things from countries whose health concerns were less exacting. Tobacco's sale was again legal in America, but the national habit had been fairly broken over the years. There were still private antitobacco groups in existence—their favored mode of reprisal be-

ing, upon sighting a smoker, to squirt lighter fluid upon
the offender and torch away—but you would never find
their reps in a Twilight Zone.

"What have you been doing with yourself?" I asked.

"Nada fatal," she said. "Kept a coil in the hough a
time. While the bands delivered. Margot ticed me off
and away. Subtlelured. We played bedwedded brides in
Heaven's soft arms. We ingled and tongued, unblushing
and hellraked."

"Sounds like joy over joy."

She sighed, and smiled.

"Anything on TVC?" I asked.

"Overload. Flip your fancy if you list."

We had a 1:25 Cinescope Sony. We rarely used our
unit's VCR; we could rarely spare money for tapes, and
the ones used in the theater didn't fit. I took the remote
in hand. With Citicable we received nineteen channels.
Enid had it tuned to one of the vid channels, the limited
one that on occasion played Ambient groups; there were
three vid channels besides Vidiac. I started punching
through the stations. "I Love Lucy" rerun. Basketball
game; the Hanoi playoffs. Movie, *Devil Bat*. Variedade
from Cuba. "Leave It to Beaver" rerun. Movie, *Sound
of Music*; to save time for commercials, all the songs
had been cut. "Twilight Zone" rerun. News program
from Japan. "Amos N'Andy" rerun. Health network;
a doctor detailed the dangers of the nonessential am-
putation. Movie, *Godzilla Versus the Smog Monster*.
"Dobie Gillis" rerun. Static. "Honeymooners" rerun.
Weather channel.

"Return to Lucy," Enid said. We sat there, drinking
and watching. TVC shows had commercial breaks every
three minutes, and so it was hard to make any sense of
whatever plots there might once have been. It was always disquieting to watch those old shows, even when
they were colorcoded (they never got the color right—

for example, I could not see Fred Mertz wearing purple pants) and transferred to digital tape. I regretted not having more of a choice in TVC viewing. There were seven other special channels, showing business reports, art programs, classical music and opera performances, ballet and modern dance events, graybearded British comedy and drama shows. Only owners and thrifty, pretentious boozhies had money enough to obtain those channels. The Drydens never watched them; if they watched TVC at all, they watched the Violence Channel. That was strictly controlled, so as to shield from the owners' impressionable youth ideas for acts that they hadn't yet conceived by themselves. Porn channels, like the magazines, no longer existed; under the Equality Acts ours was not a society to favor the exploitation of women over any other group equally available.

"What sinks your lids so low?" Enid asked.

"Nothing. I'm just tired."

"No yielding when you're fishyeyed," she said, again watching the screen, zapping repeatedly to savor the color's shifting murk. "No lipsalve spent. When you guzz over the flow will spill like Serena itself."

"Nope."

"Does the pain burn diamond sharp?"

"No pain yet in what isn't hurt."

"Did something implead your name too near?"

"His waiting room blew. It drew close."

"Was la puta laced?"

"Avalon, mayhap?"

"AO."

"Wasn't even hurt. Her skin unblemmed."

"Sauce for drake's duckling, then," said Enid.

"Much was on her mind," I said.

"Not her alone and sole. You're under shrift to her wet scent til the walls pour warm and steaming."

"We may be going away for a while."

"To pass this way again?" she asked. I didn't respond at once. "Seamus?"

"Of course."

"So deep in mystery you tread. May we hear?"

"In a while."

"Say what upsets you so," she said. "Your dreams?"

"No worse than ever."

"The nightmare rides you hard, but at morningshade you're left whole and freshly dewed. What else bends you twice?"

"Nothing."

Enid punched off the TVC; she looked troubled. "Then bed and bideaway if words fail," she said. "Care's nurse calls loud. Sleep in easeful dream."

Enid and I understood one another perfectly; Ambient speech, like everything, grew on you. To set themselves even further apart Ambients at an early age had developed their own cant: a little Spanglish, some obsolete English; whatever slang they liked or developed on their own. The raison d'être for Ambient speech was that only in word and not in image could true beauty be found, and no inherent horror could ever disguise or disfigure it. Even the uninitiated found the phrasing musical.

Enid picked up her bottle, I lifted my glass, and we passed into the bedroom. I took off my clothes and sat down on the bed. When she disrobed, I turned away. Since she'd had her breasts removed I'd had difficulty vizzing her with her shirt off; the doctor—the same one she'd known, who'd implanted the spikes—had, upon being requested to do this as well, left enormous scars. Enid was just as glad.

To be an Ambient was sometimes unavoidable, never illegal, often disturbing, and always subversive. The original Ambients were those children born to parents living on Long Island twenty-some years before. Of those originals there were fewer than three hundred, but even before the faithful began to join them, there always seemed to be many, many more.

Had it not been for the accident . . . on that windy day snow fell like ash over most of the island. In its wisdom the government assured those penultimately affected that there was small chance of lasting effects being suffered. The innocents went about their lives after that for a couple of years, and then new effects, everlasting, set in. First, across the island there emerged from troubled wombs Siamese twins, dwarves, giants; the armless, legless, noseless, earless; children with quiet twins forever nestling halfway into their own bodies; living snakes, prancing imps, the ill-mixed and unmatched; albinos, popeyes, dogboys, harelippers, gator girls, seal women, and elephant men. Under the old Famplan, abortion was—and is—punishable by death; there was nada for the parents to do but have and have at, as the government kept tight eyes on them all the while. Not long after, the second effect occurred; the parents' cancers began to blossom, flowering as if in a hothouse.

The dying parents gathered up their different children, fleeing into the city as so many began to leave, where they found acceptance if not solace; the government that demanded their birth felt it needless to concern itself with their life. So as their parents died, one by one by one, the young marvels bonded fast; through attendance at the schools their parents devised for them, they all knew one another, and they were all fabulously bright. By the time the last parent died, the progeny's group was formed; their own name given by their own.

Enid—like me—was born full-formed in the city, but there were many among the city's disconcerted who saw in Ambients a chance to add their support to the statement already made; Enid saw early. By altering the body in unappealing ways and thus becoming voluntary, the non-Ambient might not only find kinship but could as well demonstrate the iniquity of a society that forced one to do such. I am not much for dogma, myself.

"Is your fat tongue yet loose and flapping?" she asked, pulling her sheet over her.

"Not so much," I said; my glass was empty.

"Beat me. Dim our dark room, grace."

I switched off the light, laying down on my side of our beds.

"Speak. My ears hear my copesmate's cry."

"I've a proposition offered," I said.

"That yields such suck to sorrow? What gives?"

"Mister Dryden wants me to kill his father."

"Such prospect pleases?" she asked, breaking what silence had settled. "Assayed by the signs you viz?"

"I told him I would."

"Paused on the blade of the knife?"

"Yeah."

"You can't hack and slash till bitter end, Seamus."

"I think I'm too preoccupied right now."

"With?"

"Avalon."

"She loves the smoke yet hates the fire?"

"Oh, no," I said. "She's willing to help."

"What ills, then?"

"I'm scared for her. For both of us."

"Beat the bush and snatch the bird. It's sure she's a big, big girl, brother-o. Handling herself should go natural."

"AO."

"Sight your own risk first."

"AO," I said again.

"What afears you most, then?"

"A lot. Everything."

"And this eve you feel to be strewing moss over still rocks?"

"In a way."

"So overslip till morningshade," she said, kissing me goodnight, careful not to poke me with her nails. "Toss it high and glory."

"All right."

We lay down, my head on my pillow, her head on her block of foam. She'd tried styro, but tired of pulling it up with her whenever she rose or turned. The room was hazy; my eyes stung and burned. Smog crept through the hole in the bedroom ceiling, over our beds. I made a note to myself—again—to nail something over it. Before I slept that night I spent boozhie notions, thinking to myself that, as it had gone, no matter how well I did, it would never be so well as it should have been. That it would now be seemed—possible, endearingly possible. My pain slept before I did. Ambients rejoiced that these were the last days, wished and prayed that they were, and would have given over their souls to whoever wished to keep them if in so doing an end might be delivered to the world that ran raw around them. I didn't mind, so long as it was done right.

5

I DREAMED OF AVALON, AND OF MYSELF; WE SAT IN A
dark green gondola floating down Fifth Avenue, through
a fine mist that speckled our skin. An unseen boatman
steered us. We stopped, drifting silently; Avalon
speared fish in the water: shiny bream, turbot and sea-
robin, bass, blue, monk and weak. A crowd on one of
the high bridges between buildings above quietly ap-
plauded. She brought one wriggling to her mouth; bit
off its head. I dreamed.

When morning showed I arose, brushed off the soot
and looked through the window bars, pushing aside the
old newspapers we used as drapes. I was bonestiff, and
felt I'd been starched. The sky was overcast again; a
glorious day were it to rain, though then the streets
would flood. The Serena—mild evening drizzle that
passed over, most days—helped; only on rainy days did
the air clear enough so that breathing didn't cause you

to feel your were participating in one of the more stren-
uous Olympic events.

"Light?" Enid murmured, rising slowly, as if from
a swamp. She shook her head; bits of foam drifted to
the floor. "Time?"

"Ten. Rise and shine."

"Fuckall," she said, sitting up and lighting a cigarette before her third breath left.

"Shine," I said, "Not whine."

Enid reached into the bed, extracted an old newspaper from the mattress; torched it with her lighter and
threw it at me. I stomped it out. Suspecting further
comment would pass unappreciated, I broke for the
door and went down the hall. I examined the locks on
the front door, determined that no wanderers of the late
had tried to check in as we slept. I switched on the
TVC; the news was coming on. The screen was filled
with computer-coded blurs and smears of color; after a
moment it coalesced into the form of an anchorperson.
You couldn't tell any more whether the anchors were
real or not, it was all so smoothly assured.

For breakfast I rehydrated some seaweed and sautéed
it with parsnips in a margarine sauce; Margot had made
off with much of the food during the week, and so I
made do. I popped a straw into a box of Pepsi and
drank it as I ate, and watched the news. The anchor
was midsentence as I upped the vol.

"—fierce fighting reported along the Zaire border.
In Libya victory was claimed—"

Enid emerged after so long, wearing a pair of my
pants and a tee on which were imprinted the words
CULT FIGURE. She gargled with a new bottle of
vodka. She drank as if someone might steal it from her
before she could pass out.

"Thirsty?" she asked, waving the bottle before me.

"Bite your own dog," I said, that morning feeling no desire for alky.

"Out the wrong side you tumbled." She grimaced. "Too much life too with it too soon." She moved over to the stereo, banging into the furniture as if playing dodgem-cars.

"If you'd deafen this early," I said, "might we hear tunes recorded in a recognizable language?"

"Bloody bloody balls."

"—that killed the senator and six Health Department officials during yesterday's Human Life Day celebration continues to reverberate—"

A roach scampered across the sofa arm, attempting to sidle by me. I was reaching out to flick it when a stupendous roar boomed through the apartment; for a second I thought a raid was going under. The roach disappeared, as if vaporized. I looked over; Enid hopped along with the music she'd turned on. At intervals her motions reminded one of rhythmic movement.

"How does it kill the rats?" I shouted.

"Que?"

"That noise. Will the rats bleed to death or are they just sterilized by it?"

"—police say the bloody trail of the Ripper leads to this abandoned trailer parked on a Hackensack landfill—"

"Sounds as if they're pushing the singer's head through a Dispoz," I remarked; she smiled.

"I'm hearthappy. Margot gifted me last eve. With pleasure pure and lilting smiles."

"—speaking from the Hall of Nixon in Zeiching—"

"She's so thoughtful," I said. "Where'd she dig it up?"

"Courtesy Grassy Knoll cassettes."

"Has this group a name?"

"Nad. The bassist was in Theory of Hell. Our hough they once graced, begoneaday."

"—stated in the Bull that only God can decide when children are to die, and therefore, that child abuse centers in Switzerland should be banned—"

"No workaday today?" she asked, her stomp unceasing.

"I'll need to leave around one or so," I said.

"To set sail your deeds over bitter water?"

"We'll be going to the estate."

"For two days gone?" she asked.

"Longer."

"—said the successful treatment of little Tamoor demonstrates—"

"What wind, then, shall stir your hair?" she asked, turning down the stereo. "When the moon stares down in deadlight where will you wait to gaze?"

"I'm not sure. Europe, probably. I think Leningrad."

"Your mind's set?" she asked. "No ho your art?"

"No ho," I said. "I told him I would."

"Actions decide. Words stick fast in lie's mire. Where will your actions lead?"

"—in denial, the president said that all the cameras show is what they chose to see—"

"Somewhere better, maybe."

"My suspicions wail and make wary, Seamus," she said. "I eye you and I viz a puss long soaked in brine. You cleave yet to speak?"

"It'd do no good."

"So you say. AO. Go as you list, then. I go as I. Margot and me skim Brooklyn shores meantime, before Sunday service."

"Why?"

"To meet and greet. Your fear fools will tread us?"

"It's dangerous over there, Enid—"

"And my concern buys less for you?" she asked; she was mad. "Off we each to the gone world. You viz my need. Blind me as to yours. Fair's unfair, Seamus."

She was right. I still didn't want her to go to Brooklyn, though she, and most Ambients, often did.

"You never tell me why you go," I said.

"For we'll ever return," she said. "Can you promise like truth?"

I shook my head. There were reasons that bridges and tunnels to Long Island were sealed; reasons for mines to besprinkle the East River, the Sound, and the ocean immediately south. Queens and Brooklyn were treated as extensions of Long Island; the Army was at war with Long Island, and Brooklyn was considered the city of the dead. During the most troubled time of the Ebb, during the Goblin Year, the government formed the Home Army from the old National Guard, sending troops wherever disturbed masses needed minding. Long Island's citizen, not forgetting the accident some years earlier, proved not so keen about such assistance as most people in most places thought it best to be. From Brooklyn, now, most of the terror groups operated as well, sending forth citizens in night's dead to strike Manhattan again and again. That anything remained in Brooklyn, or in Long Island—and much did—caused illimitable annoyance to the Home Army. Fresh units went in monthly; nightly bombing runs continued without cease. The war had lasted fifteen years and would likely last fifteen more.

If Ambients were hooking into anything over there, none of them—not even Enid—ever told me, so I suspected that they weren't. But, after all, I wasn't an Ambient, and so wouldn't have been told. I had a hunch why they went there, just the same, and for whom they forever searched.

"You're right," I said.

"Tell all if you can," she said.

"—looking for a short-term Manhattan loft, saying the energy level here is fantastic, and that he can't wait—"

"I'll speak. Your advice'll be good to hear."

"Beat me," said Enid, sticking her elbow between the window bars and rubbing away dirt in a slow, sweeping motion. She looked at the dark gray sky once her view was clear. "Rain away all. Wash and be done."

"It's eleven A.M.," the anchor said, fixed and grinning. "Do you know where your children are?"

"Shop with me, Seamus, before you away. Things we wish will wait no more, whether you wait to use or not."

"All right."

We donned our ankle-length Krylar coats and, going downstairs, found Lester and Ruben hosing the club. Drains in the floor let the water flow back into the tank, where it could be refiltered. We told them we'd be traveling. Lester smiled (showing the glass stones in his broken front teeth), snared his dagger, and bounded up the stairs to keep guard. His enthusiasm was infectious; I felt new lightness in my own step. Ruben and Lester lived in a small space behind the club; it was more reasonable, and cheaper, to give them that than to pay them salary—90 percent of which would have been lost to taxes, for by receiving anything they would be considered to live in the midmen bracket, and thus liable.

"Something I have for you, if you wish to skip light with such jabbernowls. Kick memory and stir when we pass back."

"Beautiful day," I said as we pushed into the street, wondering what she had for me. A fourth-floor resident of the next-door building dumped the contents of her chamberpot out the window, missing us; she hurried off for more.

We moved uptown, toward Sloan's. The crowd wasn't bad; we stepped from the sidewalk only to avoid mounds of rubble, or where holes had been left, dug deep by scavengers of old pipe and wire. Rats scurried with pigeons and sparrows amidst the feet of the crowd. I held a scented cloth over my nose and mouth to muffle the odors; Enid claimed to be used to it, but she smoked so much that if she retained any sense of smell, it was entirely atavistic. We were lucky, in one way, living here; Loisaida was so full of Ambients, and in such disarray in comparison even with other Twilight Zones, that the most hard-pressed boozhie wouldn't approach. Our stores and our neighbors remained our own.

"So liptight and woeful," she said. "Such drawn eyes. Speak, then, What concerns so?"

"I've worries about this," I said.

"Porque?"

"It's such a troubling plan that he has," I said. "Something's off."

"Plan's plain as I viz," she said. "Drop the golden oldie."

"What if it makes things worse?"

"For whom?"

"Me," I said. "Avalon. Everyone."

"How?"

"I don't know."

"Why beef doing the do? Your feature attraction, isn't it?"

"But the Old Man never did anything to me—"

"What has he done for you?" she asked.

We passed myriad vendors; those of the outback, not of the city, might call them colorful. Their wares were spread along the sidewalks, lying on rags and on yellowed newspapers. For barter there were reckers of all

79

kinds, knives, bolts of burlap and of polyknit, pocket computers, battered furniture of worn wood and split plastic, counterfeit lottery tickets, every size of battery, paste jewelry, bathroom fixtures and good copper pipe, aud and vid cassettes, portraits of E painted on crisp black velveteen, and back issues of *National Geographic*. In food stalls, and from portable hibachis, others hawked fried things on sticks; clouds of acrid smoke wafted from their grills as if from a crematorium.

"That's not the point," I said.

"What is the point?"

"Why do something that causes no good?"

"Chary thing to hear your lips drop. Where is this good to be found so freely?"

"Somewhere—"

"Answer here, then. What do you get for the use of your hands?"

"I'll be in charge of the company," I said, "and Avalon will be with me."

"You'd wish other?"

"The same," I said, "in a different way."

"Your fears whelm over for love of your owners?"

"No."

"What will they obtain? One shuffles off the coil—"

"The other inherits the blessings."

"Deserved?"

"I suppose so," I said. "But I'm not sure."

"Have his senses bid long goodbyes, as you say?"

"He wasn't always like this, you know. Just in the past year—"

"The snow drifts thick?"

"Two rhinoplasties he's had. You could make a tea service out of his nose."

AMBIENT

"Why then toil for his betterment? In just admiration of his holy glory?"

"No. We've got to have money, Enid. Godness knows your businesses don't bring enough in—"

"Ah," she said. "Then for the long long green and a better's taste."

"Yes."

"A taste better fitting our own soft mouths?"

"Of course."

"And your tidbit's mouth so well?"

"Yes."

"Is it for her rather than you that you ready for this?"

"For both of us," I said.

"Both?"

"For all."

"For her," said Enid. "As said, sight your own risk first. In her paw would you lay your soul? Do you fret that if you do she might leave you noddypeaked and bowelfettered?"

"She wouldn't do that," I said. "I trust her."

"And what of your owner?"

"As much as I can."

"How far could you throw, then?"

"Far enough," I said. "It's just hard to tell. I have to run on hunches and guesswork."

"His plays might miss the cushion?"

"Maybe. He's been so off and running for so long."

"So if the young one troubles so well," she said, "overthwart him. Nail and faretheewell."

"It's the Old Man I'm supposed to—"

"Double their trouble. Carry off and pash them. First the one, second the other. Squeeze their sheets and have their drippings warm."

"It's not worth it," I said. "Slip doing that and I'm in the street. If I'm unlucky."

"If luck shines?"

81

"I'll be dead."

"Beat me. What else to do?"

"What I'll be doing."

"If luck yields you'll be off no worse than most."

A middle-aged woman slipped at the edge of an excavation and tumbled in. The rats set upon her before she could be dragged out. Everyone listened to her screams, and watched.

"So worse is most that nothing bears so little bad. If loss nears, Seamus, then lose all and be proudfull."

"If that comes, it comes. I wish—"

"Wish and wing away. You could Hamlet for age over age," she said. "Hear me now before you pave your dark road, thripping fingers to perp and blast. My brother's soul I feel my own. Your power is mightier than your sword. I've seen all. In light you insinuate smooth. At dark's need you take your tyrant garb. Let your inside traipse limber. Earplay the life and list to other options. Time irons all and the pieces drop like maydown. Destiny's book is unreadable but you can steal the lines ahead. If triumph comes, use gain to good effect. Salve the lost and damned in New York's stews. Flea the owner's ear. Lift their dresses high and rip their oysters' pearls. Be the Naz and still spend your biscuit in your honey's little pot."

"That'd be the best," I said, thinking of Avalon; however it went, we wouldn't be apart. If I had to leave Enid, though—"But I'm afraid it'll slip through my hands if I try."

"Then take hands and grab," she said. "Even romance has a room if a house is there to hold it."

We kept walking. At 12th was a small Ambient iglesee; the inverted cross hung over the door. In the window was a ceramic Jesus: he lay on his back, his arms outstretched; his wrists and legs bled, the hump between his shoulders was scored and diced, his head was bloodied, his guts poured out his side. A broad grin calmed his face. Regular services and weekday affairs took place at the iglesees; one Sunday each month—the one upcoming would be this month's—all Ambients, original and voluntary, met at a place they called Under the Rock. I knew where it was, but had never gone there, for those meetings are offtouch to non-Ambients. When I first heard of the place, years before, I wondered about the name. *Upon the rock shall the church be,* said Enid, *and under the rock will be we.*

Only Catholic churches and Ambient iglesees served the purposes for which they were consecrated. I remembered when there were many churches. Bad judgment by past government leaders caused them, long before, to push through the acts that sanctified America as a Christian nation in law so well as in spirit a year before the Q documents were revealed.

The Q documents—discovered by a team of Israeli and American archaeologists—were the long-lost original gospels. They detailed how Jesus, a trusting sort, was hired by Pilate to spread confusion among warring Jewish factions; how Judas found out and so betrayed his betrayer; how Jesus, pulled from the cross in time's nick by those wishing to use the affair for their own effect, recovered and was by accident seen by his horrified followers; how some of his followers were so horrified that they wished to kill him—again; how Jesus escaped with his wife, Mary Magdalene; how he died, at an advanced age, somewhere far from Gethsemane. You can infer the rest.

The documents were examined by all concerned until it was admitted that there could be no doubt. My old Catholic church, troubled by its own problems, felt that the matter certainly warranted further investigation in the future. America had little time to live fully as a

Christian nation before the Ebb fulfilled itself. Only vaguely did I recall posters in the subway, put up by churchmen: photos of log-stacked Auschwitz victims, the message below reading *Accept Christ And Live.*

When we reached Sloan's we bashed through the curbside crowds, busy victoring the spoils from the street bins. We passed the barriers setup to thwart food rioters, went through the metal detectors, and at last received a basket in exchange for our deposit. Enid ran down the aisles, dumping in horrors galore: Slurpies, Sugar Tarts, Whoopies, Stickies, and a brand of candy called Braineaters, which came in the form of jelly-filled skulls. I picked up a few apples and oranges, fresh from Spain, which at least retained the skins in which they had been issued. To keep our buys separate I stuck my fruits onto Enid's nails.

"We need toilet paper," I said, realizing as I said it that I supposed mine would be supplied elsewhere for awhile.

"The tile is free for all to peel."

She threw a loaf of Softee bread into the basket; it bounced out, as if trying to escape. We caught it near the dairy aisle.

"I've a bizarre idea," I said.

"Que?"

"Why don't you buy something healthy?" I said, looking over the colorful labels and shiny bags in the basket.

"Porque?"

"Variety," I said, picking up a bag of Sugar Chips and shaking it; it rattled, as if filled with tacks. "It wouldn't kill you."

"Why enact what hasn't conclusion?"

I convinced her. She picked up a box of Soyream and a block of Kraft Dairy Solid. She would even have gotten a carton of eggs, but this month's New York delivery was consigned by the government for our Italian friends, or friends of theirs, or friends of someone's. There were other things needed, but the store was out; no matter how much of anything came into Manhattan, it was never enough.

Supplied, we aimed for the exit, returning our basket before we entered the line. The mob resembled rush at the barricades, but our line was short; we reached the cashier in less than half an hour. The market had Vidiac; a bank of monitors hung above the checkout aisles, but I didn't watch. I thumbed papers in the nearby racks. There was a useful article detailing how vampires might be distinguished, and thus avoided, in the work place; another entitled IS YOUR SPOUSE A REINCARNATED SEX KILLER? with the True Story of The Hackensack Ripper As Told By His Ex-Wife From Beyond The Grave. *Tiempo*'s cover article concerned the coming food explosion—sounded unpleasant—and, past the features, several news photos—thus allowable—showed dead young women decked in lingerie.

"Oneseen, allseen," said Enid, glancing over my shoulder. "Man's pride dulls all." She tossed back the copy of *McCall's* she'd been looking over; FORTY THINGS TO DO WITH MACARONI was the lead article.

Once we were rung Enid laid out two dollars; we stuffed the goods into the bags we'd brought. Our trip home was calm; we didn't talk. My mind drifted off to be with Avalon, and I counted the minutes till I'd see her again.

"No visitors?" I asked Lester, when we returned.

"No blood," he said, extending one arm, balancing with the other.

"I didn't ask that," I said. "You'd have licked it up,

anyway." Lester smiled, and bounced down the stairs. We went inside.

I didn't have to leave just yet—it was only past noon— and so I soaked my apples and oranges, having plucked them from Enid's head, carefully dropping the fruit into the sink one piece at a time, so as not to splash out overmuch water. Enid turned suddenly, as if she'd been slapped.

"Memory returns," she said. "Tarry a mo. I've an add to your repertoire."

She ran back into the bedroom. My refrigerator consoled me.

"*—door ajar. Please shut. Door—*"

I took out the apples and oranges, dried them, and slipped them into my Krylar coat's pocket. Enid returned, carrying a new button-push chainsaw that was no more than a foot and a half long.

"I'm not going dancing," I said.

"Court and tease, then," she said. "On off's chance."

"It's rather puny, isn't it?"

"But marvel." She held the chainsaw away from us, turning it on. As she pushed the button the saw shot outward, tripling its length as it roared away.

"Cunning," I said, impressed. "A bit overmuch for what I expect."

"Then in event your expectation adjusts. Carry, for me if you will."

"What if it goes off accidentally?" I asked. "I could lose something."

"As you could if you don't tote it," she said. "The safety's on, till yours goes off."

"Where'd you get it?" I asked, noting the file marks obliterating the serial plate.

"A friend whose fingers burned with it. Encloak it in your wrap."

"All right. Gracias, Enid."

"Por mivida," she said, slipping it into one of my long coat's inner pockets. "Seamus?"

"Yes?"

"I spec we'll glimpse sooner than you see," she said. "But—"

"I'll be back in a couple of months."

"If but in other shape we ever clasp again," she said, "My blood beats your heart allafter, everafter, till time's lovely end. Take as you will."

She kissed me; her spikes scratched my forehead. I didn't bleed much.

"Too early on the light aroused," she said. "Left me drumbling poor and undermeal. I'm to bed and bideaway till eve crawls up dark."

"Take care."

She walked back into the bedroom, shedding her clothes as she went. Before she went in she bent over to pick up one of her bottles. I smiled as I looked at her massive gray flanks, thinking of Lucy, the late rhinoceros. She'd be fine in my absence, I knew, and so I worried about her not at all. Only Enid had kept me straight and narrow, made me continue school, found the funds that allowed me to do so, stood by me at every time of pain. But her life was hers; mine was mine.

As I went downstairs I readied myself; I walked out, heading over to Third Avenue. Jimmy always picked me up on the north side of the 14th Street barricade, before we cruised uptown to pick up Mister Dryden and Avalon. I'd be the last one in the car today, it was so late.

The guards at the barricade's pedway looked to be vets of the Brooklyn campaign, judging from their mien and their insignia. When I showed them my IA card they waved me through, sans exam, sans questioning.

Just outside, some Army boys took turns raping a woman; one standing near appeared to have rigged a reproduction of his unit's insignia from a coat hanger and held the decorative end over a fire. I turned my head, so as to pretend I hadn't seen. Jimmy stood by the car, watching; when he saw me he waved.

"Hop in," he said, looking up at the sunny gray sky. I slid in beside him, nodding to Mister Dryden and Avalon who were in the back, seated some feet apart. We took off, aiming toward Broadway. Most of our trip passed in silence, as if by speaking we feared we might break our bond and spoil our luck. On occasion a few words slipped out, as if to increase tension.

"Anything but party this afternoon?" Avalon asked; she lay curled up in the back seat's corner. Mister Dryden sat in the seat behind me, playing a game—to have judged from the beeps, and lack of dialogue—on the IBM.

"Dad'll want to sport after."

"And chapel?"

"You know Dad," he said.

Midtown and Times Square and the Clinton Twilight Zone were as they ever were. After we entered the Upper West Secondary Zone at Sixty-first, surroundings felt busy but not so tenuous (the ridge east of Broadway, further up, was high enough to remain above the water, it was believed, and so remained better kept). At 120th West Harlem began. That Twilight Zone ran to 181st; there, the Inwood Secondary Zone—boozhie-laden, like the Upper West—picked up.

At 119th, Jimmy patted my arm and motioned beyond the exit.

"Bullyrige it looks up there," he said.

Between 120th and 135th the subway became an el. Youngsters had derailed the train. The Demon Lovers, likely; they'd divided the area since domesticating the neighborhood Droozies. Jimmy and I lifted binocs so we could viz more clearly what was downcoming. Half the cars remained on the trestle, half hung over the side. The front car lay crumpled in the intersection of Broadway and 125th. Members of the gang scampered over the sides of the cars, tossing in mollies, ducking as they blasted. Others ran through the cars still on the track, greeting those who hadn't escaped.

"Duppies look like roaches, don't they?" said Jimmy. He turned on the broadcaster, tuning what might be heard on the train's intercom. The automatic recording played, saying, "there is another train just behind this one. Step lively."

Army vehicles positioned, rocking the train. As the fires climbed up the cars, the bright graffiti blackened; flashes flew up with each blast like sparks from a fireplace log. Only the need for reliable public transport kept trains running; only in Manhattan, only during the day. The fare was high—a quarter—but I doubted that anyone paid, not anymore. I never went in the subway; trouble finds you well enough without your looking.

"Overmuch warifying. Boys too blueswee and jangbang with vex. We'll take Henry," said Jimmy. "Belt up."

We belted, and we turned onto 120th; Jimmy switched on the electroshield. We passed Riverside Church and Grant's Tomb, dark and battered in the afternoon haze. Handy, unoccupied structures were often used by the Army boys for target practice.

The drive up Riverside was uneventful. Residents of West Harlem needed fuel too badly to live with the comforting sight of a forest at riveredge, and where once a squirrel could leap from limb to limb for blocks without touching ground, stumps replaced trees and stews replaced squirrels. As a teenager, I remembered hearing stories of the Naturals, who, it was said, lived in the park, having turned against civilization as they found it, living off whatever or whoever might be caught. They were said to wear cloaks of thorned shrubbery and masks of carved tree bark. All romance, after all, one of those tales you grow up hearing—such as how blind alligators swim through the sewers' murk, or that if you piss on the third rail you'll be electrocuted, or that most of the homebodies once had money in bushels. Certainly not; only the ones living before the Ebb.

Driving beneath the Army-green girders of the George Washington Bridge, watching the great flags hanging down from the arches billow in the breeze, passing the broken stubs of the toll booth plaza, we reached the Saw Mill Parkway, which was under Army guard. In lieu of conversation, I turned on the radio, dialing to WINS news. Israeli settlements on the Persian Gulf were shelled by Iraq. Tass reported that the Czara and the Politburo met to discuss the growing demand among the Russian people for vid channels of their own choosing. An unconfirmed report from the White House listed the security adviser missing and unaccounted. The president's Food Commission reported that hunger in America had been eliminated among those who hadn't starved. Dryco had done its part in the past to accomplish that goal. Parcels of supplies had been airlifted to starving farm communities in Indiana at the Old Man's request nine months earlier. That the supplies consisted of surplus diet pills, laxatives, and pictures of E was noticed before takeoff. Not even the Old Man's foes claimed that the huge boxes were deliberately dropped into the midst of the crowds; they were.

After an hour—it was just past three—we turned off the parkway onto the estate road; the guards saluted as we passed. The estate stretched from the river several miles in and several miles up. There were forty-five buildings on the grounds besides the main house and the chapel. Guards, relatives, friends, tutors, proxies, lalas, visitors, and hangers-on stayed in the other houses. I even had a house provided for me on our weekends. Mine had fourteen rooms; I'd never seen half of them.

"Dress," Mister Dryden said to Avalon. He seemed eager for fun. She put that wonderful wig back on again; slipped on a pair of black stilettos and pulled on a heavy white ribbed sweater. It covered her to the tops of her thighs.

"Wifey ought to like this outfit," she said.

"She won't notice."

"You could set her on fire and she wouldn't notice. But I know who will."

"Birthday boy?"

"Uh-huh."

"Father equals son," Mister Dryden said, smiling.

We drove by the airstrip. The Old Man retained four jets, refitted Boeing 837s. Neither the Old Man nor Mister Dryden flew much anymore; it was too easy to take a plane down. The copters, big black Sikorsky autogiros, were also there. Tucked in one of the hangars was the Old Man's first airplane, a prop job he and his first partners had bought in Boca Raton, in the days before he'd even met Susie D; some wit, years past, had scrawled *Rosebud* across the nose. The airstrip's radarscopes were in constant operation; if an attack was launched by anyone other than Russia itself—not likely—exos would take all intruders so well as most of the neighboring property. A starscope searched the skies hourly for flying saucers. The Old Man faithfully believed a Church of E precept that, upon his return, E would come to earth in some sort of flying saucer, accompanied by a retinue of, in the Old Man's phrasing, "space critters."

The Old Man loved security. A twelve-foot stone wall surrounded the central estate. The grounds were further protected by razorwire, searchlights, alarms; by wolves; by machine-gun towers spaced every five hundred feet along the walls. Copters flew over every five minutes clockround. There was a small gauge railroad running undergrond from the estate to the Dryco building in the event that a hasty escape became necessary—it never had, and doubtless never would.

"Approaching, Martin," said Jimmy, speaking into the intercom as we ranged. "I and I and three."

"Roger."

When this had been a public road, Mister Dryden enjoyed switching the road signs, setting up impromptu demo derbies among travelers passing near. Some time ago the Old Man requested of the Army that the road be closed to nonstate vehicles. There weren't many country drivers nowadays, for safety's sake; near the cities, apart from estates and those areas under Army patrol, all rural pastures and havens were infested with rogues and footpads and highwaymen. There were fewer cars, too, that could safely drive so far as this: most new American cars—made, like so much, under separate but equal Russian-American production (Gorky-Detroit in the case of automobiles)—were traded to Europe and Japan, to countries no longer producing steel or no longer having access to the ore fields of Canada, Brazil, and Siberia. Only owners could afford and obtain new cars. Many in America had automobiles, just the same; there were thousands in the cities, all in use (there had been an oil glut for years) and none newer than twenty years old.

We drove through the gate. The driveway was a mile long; you could see the house halfway up, standing alone on the hill, shining white, illuminated from without at eve. It was built in old Long Island style, though larger: boxy, multilevel, enameled and polished, with long pipes of chrome and walls of glassblocks; with many, many mirrors.

We pulled to the side of the house. From the summit, on the patio, I looked off down the green lawn, through the fir trees, across the wide lake, over the meadows, and saw the Hudson River coursing by the Palisades. Looking in the city's direction, even from this distance, I could see the black-yellow haze that settled over New York every afternoon. Before so many furnaces had been reconverted for the use of coal, the smog hadn't been so noxious. Now most eves were so black you couldn't walk a block without resembling a miner by the time you reached the corner.

Avalon and Jimmy got out of the car, walking to the house, down the slate path that would round the swimming pool. I watched her walk; the longest strands of hair tickled at her rear, her ankles wobbled in those hooflike shoes. At the head of the pool, between the columnades, the statue of Prometheus from Rockefeller Plaza lolled, watching leaves drift across the water's surface. The Old Man collected bibelots in these quiet years. The Public Library's old lions protected the gate leading onto the cricket field, where Jimmy and the estate security enjoyed Sunday afternoons. The Pulitzer fountain, once situated before the Plaza Hotel, served as a birdbath in a court to the south. Atlas shouldered the world near the barbecue pit. The Old Man would have moved the Brooklyn Bridge to the estate if he had a river to put below it.

"Nice to home it, eh?" Mister Dryden said, smiling. I nodded, and thought of how much plasticine I'd need.

6

"THE MAYOR, HE TRIED TO SUCK ME INTO BUYIN' CEN-
tral Park last month. Told me his new projections
showed that most of it would stay above ground," said
the Old Man to a friend during the cocktail hour. He
drank his usual, Jack Daniels—one of his smaller companies—and bottled spring water. " 'Like the tree-
tops?' I asked."

"Like how much did they look to pocket?" asked
his friend Carlisle, another of the old entrepreneurs.
Carlisle, since the Ebb, had owned much of the American chemical industry, courtesy of the Old Man's lar-
gesse.

"Fifty million," said the Old Man. "I said you take
that fifty and you pound it up your ass one buck at a
time with a jackhammer. Shit."

"Park'd be a hassle," said Carlisle. "Lots of lumber, though."

"It's always pissed him off that he had to sell Van

Cortlandt Park so cheap. Not to mention those other deals I cut. He knows I got his balls on my keychain. Just wants to raise a good kitty for himself for when he retires and moves back to Havana. I told him Manhattan'll make somebody a good aquarium someday but my money's goin' into the Bronx. Safe, high, and dry. Fuckin' yankees always fuckin' think they can fuck you over.''

"I hear you," said Carlisle, who was from White Plains.

"No way," said the Old Man. "*Nobody* fucks me over."

The Old Man was bigger than his son, long-boned and wiry; dressed old-money style—sneakers, jeans, and tees sans comment. He often wore one of those green Chinese caps; on his the red star was replaced by a smirker. He tied his white hair back in a severe ponytail. The Old Man was born in North Carolina into a family not particularly known for anything, or so he claimed. Over the years he'd changed his name to fit the sitch as it arose, at last settling on Thatcher Dryden, Senior, not long before the Ebb. Nobody remembered his original name, he least of all.

"Five o'clock," he said, glancing at his old Timex. "Let's get rollin'."

Many of the Old Man's companions, and their wives or proxies, turned up that afternoon to help celebrate his grandson's tenth birthday; they'd all be flown out that night, Mister Dryden let me know. There was Carlisle; Turnbull, who was in munitions; Willetson, who specialized in robots and maintenants. Also MacIntosh (coal), Samuelson (automobiles), Parker (computers), and twelve others, former entrepreneurs all, all now running somewhat more stabilized industries than those in which they were once most active. Most of them, for various reasons, had also changed their names over the years.

The four house guards—Barney, Biff, Butch, and Scooter—came with us. We walked to the chapel, a small building boasting a Wrenish steeple. The chapel, built of pink Italian marble left over, I suspected, from some Roman bordello of Mussolini's day, stood a thousand feet or so from the main house. We passed the garage, which held thirty cars. Jimmy was inside, working on our Castrolite. The Old Man owned thirty cars, mostly blat from Gorky-Detroit: Redstars, Lenins, Zils, Marx deVilles. He also had several timekeepers: an Olds Rocket 88, a black '49 Mercury, a '57 Chevy, flame-decked across the hood, a purple and yellow Hudson Hornet, and a beautiful old green Cadillac which he claimed once belonged to Jerry Lee Lewis.

We trailed Barney and Scooter; the Misters Dryden walked ahead of Avalon and myself. The youngest Dryden and his mother—apostates—remained at home. A patrol copter dipped over the trees; caps flew off and their wearers bounded after them. During the ruck Avalon took my hand. Her breasts swung beneath her sweater; the long brown hair she wore fluttered in the now-gentle breeze.

"How're you doin'?" she asked.

"Low-key," I said. "Everyone was certainly quiet on the way up."

"I know," she said. "Felt like I was in a casket on wheels. Fuck if I was gonna say anything."

"Not with Jimmy there—"

"What about Jimmy?"

"Mister Dryden's sure that Jimmy's working cover on us for the Old Man."

"That's interesting," she said.

"How so?"

"Pops thinks he's running cover for Sonny. Hush,

Shameless, we're here." She let loose my hand; the feel of her skin still warmed my palm. We entered the chapel's threshold. The minister greeted us, resplendent in his gold suit, glowing like a dashboard saint. Avalon sat between father and son; I sat behind them. The others tumbled slowly into the pews. The chapel had salmon-pink stucco walls threaded with gold, offset with dark oak woodwork. The interior remained shadowy within—little sunlight eked through the abstract patterns in the bulletproof stained glass—and one's eyes adjusted but slowly in the gloom.

The minister stepped to the altar, beginning the ceremony; the organist tootled softly. The service was patterned—possibly by accident—after the Mass; there was an introduction, a kyrie, an invocation, a blessing; all but Communion, which was pointless in either event. Mass was easier to sit through without laughing. When I was young I went to Mass only under threat; these days I went by choice, sometimes, for the ceremony. It is more impressive since they began giving it solely in Latin. That was one of the changes thought essential by Pope Peter after his ascension to the chair, after the murder of John Paul, after the discovery of the Q documents, after the papal seat was moved to Zurich. It was reasonable that Godness should use a language that none of Its followers understood.

The minister reached the penultimate stand and deliver.

"All the world's a stage and all the men and women merely players," he called; we responded. Tears softened the Old Man's eyes. Avalon yawned. Mister Dryden scratched at his skin.

"And now the stage is bare," said the minister.

"I'm standing there," we replied.

"With emptiness all around."

"Are our hearts filled with pain?"

"Shall I come back again?" He paused, and then: "Tell me," he said, "Are you lonesome tonight?"

The organist laid his paws on the buttons, banging out "Big Hunk O'Love." We opened our hymnals and made joyless noise. The minister raised his hands in supplication; turned to face the altar and the statue of E. The statue began revolving as we sang; to see it left one wordless. It was a life-size simulacrum of E, feet spread manfully, microphone in hand, wearing tinted glasses and a spangled jumpsuit with high collar and cape. An eagle was reproduced in rubies—many rubies—over the stomach. On the wall behind the statue was a colorgraph of E shaking hands with Nixon; the One and All circumspect, he whom my parents called the Great Satan cold with smiles and delight.

"Adios," said the minister, tossing his scarf into the congregation. No one moved until the Old Man looked to see who had been blessed; then everyone lunged to grab it.

"Like E," concluded the minister, "let us leave the building."

The male Drydens had belonged to the C of E for so long as I had worked for them. The group's central belief and ground of being—I had doubts, frankly, but claim no expertise on dogma—was that E, dropped off by Godness, walked with man for a time and returned to other spheres when man proved callous. E would return one day—Judgment Day, I believe, to lessen confusion—and lead his people to a better world. How the Old Man's world might improve remained a mystery of the faith.

We returned to the main house for dinner. At dusk the sport would begin; once finished, I could start my work. On the way back Avalon caught my glance, smiled, and turned away. That look assured me that I would do all that needed doing.

Once out of sight of the chapel, everyone lit spliffs and tossed down reckers. At the house, the Old Man returned to his Jack Daniels. He was fond of remarking that he'd never used drugs but had only supplied the demand according to free market dictates. Even now the circulation of kane and other reckers accounted for a good percentage of Dryco exchange, notwithstanding that such drugs were illegal. The government—at Dryco's urging—made certain such laws stayed booked, to ensure healthy profits.

I strolled through the living room as everyone prepared to dine, eyeing the surroundings for signs of anything untoward. All looked as ever; the long white couches stretched along the walls, the low tables gathered their daily allotment of dust. There were few books in the room, or anywhere in the house; the Old Man was of an illiterate generation. No art hung from the walls; a large portrait of Susie D looked out from above the fireplace. Terribly cenotaphic, I thought, though had they wished to do so at the time, she could have been cremated in it, so huge was its vault. I stared at the portrait for a moment, remembering her, standing in awe of how closely the painting showed her as she was: short, squat, cold, and scheming. She'd never said two words to me in eleven years, feeling it beneath her to acknowledge help; any help. I think the only person she trusted—and he, not overly so—was Mister Dryden. The painting showed her sitting, fists clenched in her lap, her trousered leg tossed over one arm of the chair, her hair in a gray crew cut. One suspected that she was to the Mack truck born, but became somehow sidetracked, and so wound up here.

We ate in the dining room, the largest room in the house. In the center of the floor, surrounded by large soft cushions, was a wide white panel. Biff pressed a button; the panel sank through the floor to the kitchen below. Once loaded by the maintenants, it again ascended to the dining room. As all toppled down onto the cushions, the Old Man blew his whistle; the tasters entered the room. I lowered myself carefully, to prevent my knees from going out.

"Gimme the lowdown," he said to the tasters, who tried everything. The Old Man ate fried chicken, mashed potatoes, white gravy over bread, and sweet potatoes; Mister Dryden picked at raw steak and raw onions; the rest of us eyed a variety of colored things in interesting shapes. The tasters stayed upright, gave approval, and waddled away.

"I could stand hearin' a few tunes," said the Old Man, motioning to Scooter. "Slap somethin' in the tape deck, would you?"

Music resounded throughout the high room, music from the longaway: songs by Buddy Holly, Roy Orbison, the Band, E himself. The Old Man reclined on his cushions, holding his drink and—his phrasing—a big old chicken leg. His lalas comforted him; they had perms and painted nails, were heavily made up, and wore tiny red panties with black zippers running down the front. They were about nine years old.

"Sex. Drugs. Violence. Rock and roll," said the Old Man, raising his glass. "Something for everyone."

"Toast the birthday boy," commanded Mister Dryden. No one demurred.

"Where is he?"

"Boy!" the Old Man yelled. "Get your ass out here."

At the entrance to the dining room appeared Thatcher Dryden III. Since the days he'd attempted to strangle his first-year tutor, we'd all called him Throttler. He sauntered to the table with his usual panache.

"Ho," he said, flicking out his switchblade. "Let's cut."

"Seat yourself, boy," said the Old Man. "You're missing your own party."

"Hi, Stella. Hi, Blanche." The Old Man's lalas smiled at Throttler, blushing so red as their undies. He pinched them; they wiggled. "Unhand, gran. Lemme roll and thunder."

"Hell, no," said the Old Man.

"Strazh, Dad," he said, pointing the blade at his father. Mister Dryden beamed. Throttler reached across with his blade and speared a sweet potato. He bit off half and then spat it onto the white panel. "Terminate," he said. "Weenies we want." He sat down by his mother and kissed her on the cheek; she didn't seem to notice.

"Well," he said, "go on."

From where I sat what I saw of Avalon was lovely but expressionless. She lay on her stomach near the fried chicken, facing away from me, her long legs spread out behind her. Her sweater pulled over her bottom as she reached for food. Mister Dryden sat beside her, idly fumbling his fingers between her legs as if searching for something out of reach. She paid him no mind, and I felt no jealousy; he seemed to be doing it out of habit more than anything else. His wife and son faced him across the panel.

It was uncommon for Mrs. Dryden to dine in company anymore. She was about five ten, and couldn't have weighed more than eighty pounds. Gossip I overheard implied that wives of other owners considered her paunchy. Owners married only so that they might have legal heirs, but few owners had heirs of any direct sort; their wives were remarkably thin and, because of it, remarkably barren. Mrs. Dryden had fulfilled her duty when she was younger, and a hundred-pound tub.

Mrs. Dryden wore shades—it was impossible to gather at whom she was looking—and never spoke. The last phrase I heard her utter was some years before, idle muttering about the help being allowed to sit in the same room as she. Periodically a tear rolled down her cheek; the drugs made her eyes water. Her hair was swept above her head, held in place by a gold tiara. She wore a brocaded purple caftan with long sleeves and so many jewels as the statue of E. During dinner she motioned toward her works; Throttler pushed up her sleeve, took the hypo, and filled her up. I remembered when she hadn't done drugs. She and Mister Dryden met while he was at Yale. She'd attended Wellesley. Like all owners' wives, she didn't work.

As we ate, the strains of "Love Me Tender" came over the speakers. The Old Man's eyes misted. He began to frown and shook his head, as if he'd gotten a chunk of hot sweet potato caught in his throat and wanted to draw attention to that fact. He readied to reminisce, and we all knew about whom. We heard the story he prepped to tell perhaps six times a year, for so long as I'd worked for Mister Dryden.

"Did I ever speak of the time I met E?" he said, lifting his eyes upward to assure himself that we paid attention. "While he was on this earth?"

We shook our heads, muttering; stared into our plates.

"Forty times overtold, gran," blurted Throttler, slipping his hand down the back of Blanche's panties. The Old Man looked at him, his eyes encrusted with benevolence's paste, ignored him, and continued.

"When I was sixteen," he said, "Me and some old boys headed out to Oklahoma that summer to see 'bout gettin' jobs workin' in the oil fields useta be out there. Stopped in Memphis on the way to spend the night. We drove over to Graceland to see if He was home. There was a few guards and a buncha people hangin' round outside the gate. It was fuckin' hot. Boys I was with

102

wanted to go back to the motel. I said I wanted to stick around awhile. Couldn't say why. Just did. They left. Said I could walk back to the motel when I got tired. Dumb fucks.''

Mister Dryden slid forward, closer to the food, closer to his father—he never tired of hearing this tale—pulling himself over the cushions as if through the trenches.

"I sat down on the curb there. Funny thing. Longer I stayed the more I wanted to stay. Night came and most everybody else left. After so long even the guards shut the gates and went into their little houses. Started rainin' fuckin' hard but I couldn't leave, somehow. It was like God's hand was holdin' me there so that I might stay and meet His son. I musta looked like a fuckin' asshole, though, cause by that time I was soakin' wet.''

A certain air about Mrs. Dryden made us suspect that she had relieved herself. Barney came over, stood her up, put her over his shoulder, and carried her upstairs to her room, where the maids could clean her and put her to bed.

"A big old black car pulled up 'round midnight and I waved. The car stopped. I walked over to it, stood there by the side. The lights inside came on. The window rolled down. Inside there it seemed the most lavish thing. Two big old boys sat next to Him, pointin' guns at me, just in case, I figured. It *was* Him, in there. He was a glory to behold. He wore dark glasses and a dark cape covered His raiment. In His hand He held a long silver flashlight. His hair was black as a raven's wing and swept back. He turned and looked at me and then spoke.''

He paused, waiting to see if we remembered our cue. "What'd he say?'' half of us asked, loudly.

" 'Gettin' wet, aren't you?' That's what He asked me. I said yeah. He smiled and there was a glorious

103

look to His face. There was a big bag of cheeseburgers on the floor of the car and I was hungry and I almost asked Him for one but I didn't. He asked me my name and I told Him. He nodded and reached out His hand and took mine. As I held it for that moment I felt the electricity go right through me and all the power of God. I saw He had a gun pointed at me, too. Even God can't be too careful, you know. He said don't do anything I wouldn't do, brother—"

"And I haven't," Throttler interrupted, appearing overly gleeful. The Old Man stared at him for a moment.

"And I haven't," he went on. "They all said goodnight and rolled up the window and drove in. Gates shut and I just stood there in the rain. It was obvious He was filled with the glory of the Lord—"

I'd paid closer attention to the Old Man this time, attempting to discern signs of impending madness. He sounded no more irrational than he ever had.

"—though if I didn't know better, I'd of sworn He was stoned."

Avalon rolled over onto her back, and closed her eyes as if to sleep. Her sweater pulled up in front.

"Then I left. I like to think I followed His wishes as He asked me to. You know, had Jesus been real, and if he'd been in the same situation as E, he'd have done it all the same way."

And vice versa, I supposed, picturing E in that jumpsuit, crucified.

"Where's the cake?" the Old Man suddenly asked, as if returning from an unexpected trip.

"It's ready?" Throttler asked, looking up.

"Better be," said the Old Man, pressing a button. As he lay back, his lalas dived for him. Again the panel descended, bearing away dishes and half-eaten dinners. One of the guests nearly tumbled in, chasing the last crumbs on his plate. Dinner ended when the Old Man finished. When the panel rose once more it bore a six-foot-high cake of memorable form: a combination of Graceland and the Tower of Babel might be the most accurate description. Ten candles rounded the dais on which it sat.

The Old Man rubbed his hand over Throttler's hair, as if trying to wipe something off. "He's a good li'l feller."

"Wish it, son," said Mister Dryden, smiling again.

Throttler blew out the candles one at a time, so as not to strain himself.

"What'd you wish for?"

"A copter," he said, eyeing the cake. "This tried and passed?"

"You don't eat the cake, boy," laughed the Old Man, "you eat what's in it."

The top of the cake popped open; a lala leapt up. She was fifteen or so, and naked. The effect didn't come off as intended. Halfway through the opening her hips stuck; she struggled helplessly as all silently watched. When at last she pulled herself free it was with such effort that she lost her balance, sliding down the side of the cake head first. She rolled against Mister Dryden, getting frosting on his trousers and shoes. He jumped up and kicked her in the stomach, then drew back to kick her again.

"Stop it," yelled the Old Man.

His foot landed again; she doubled up, holding her sides.

"You dumb fuck, *stop it*!" screamed the Old Man again, rising suddenly and taking hold of his son's arms. "She's Throttler's present, not yours."

There was a dull throb at the back of my neck. I excused myself and left the room. I could have blinded myself to anything, were I to see it often enough.

In odd moments I'd gathered the material I needed to complete the morning's project, and so I knew I could spend time late this evening assembling and rigging the timer as I wished, once I was in my room in the main house. I went to the garage to see how Jimmy was coming with his adjustments. He was attaching a new headlight onto the left fender as I walked in.

"How's it going?" I asked.

"Not so bad, man. How goes inside?"

"They're playing with Throttler's present."

"Yes, man. Saw her when she come through. Nice bungo-bessy, sure."

I heard wild laughter, and a steady chant of approval, and her screams.

"Sound like he took his free grind ticket, man."

"I suppose."

"Now he bust the double figures, he be bullyrige like his father, ta raas."

"Or worse," I said, trying not to hear the sounds within. "You having any trouble there?"

"None I can't fix," he said, "Unlike some."

"What do you mean?"

"I mean Boy Dryden, man, and I mean his father, too. Walk blind like they do and one day they walk one step too far."

"Could be—" I said, trying to spot his stance, seeing if this was but a lure to lead me out.

"Boy Dryden especially," said Jimmy. "Knows he spin too fast now. Don't want Papa to pull out his bag of tricks."

"Tricks?"

"You know, man. What he keeps so tight. His snake in the rock. Shark in the water."

"I'd keep still for the moment, Jimmy—" I said, hoping to draw a response.

"I be no penny catcher like they gather, man. I be

here to drink milk, not to count cow. I and I will come forward soon, irie? Big tree gonna fall hard one day."

"May be."

"He rax up plenty great, man. Boy Dryden be scared over. If I be that man I be scared too. There be much confusion before Babylon falls, the Lion say. Much fullness brimstone from Jah on high. Much fullness for him."

Throttler walked out, slipping on a tee that said *Surrender Dorothy* across the front. I heard stirrings and soft conversation from within, as if from a dream; they prepared for the evening events. The Misters Dryden first emerged, shotguns loaded. I think little of guns, usually; an amateur's tool. Guns had been outlawed for so long that they would seem obsolete but for the fact that the Army—amateurs all—finds such use for so many. Owners, of course, may own guns; for protection, and for sport.

"Let's roll, O'Malley," said Mister Dryden.

Biff and Scooter led the group; I walked behind the Drydens. There were fourteen players. The women never participated, nor did the children, not even Throttler.

"Good shootin' weather," said the Old Man.

"Get much this week?" asked Carlisle.

"I honestly don't know," he said. "Haven't looked yet. Hope so."

It was a leisurely stroll, some three-quarters of a mile, to the playing fields, through shady groves of evergreens, fresh and sharp-scented as a Christmas-tree lot, past a small pond edged with cattails, by a red gazebo tucked in a bosky glade, through a stand of weeping willows. The wind blew gently and the songs of birds serenaded us as we trod along.

"You see the latest Gallup?" one of them said. "The president's got 91 percent preference."

The Gallup in question enlisted the opinions of twenty-three people, including both Drydens.

"Way ahead of whatsisname. This election's safe."

They always were.

We reached the range, a long meadow between two wood lots. Fifteen guards were positioned at the far end, near some shrubbery; I knew that a haw-haw ran behind them. Each guard wore a gray Sherlock hat; each shouldered a long knobby club. The quarry lurked in the bushes nearby. The Old Man walked over to the gamekeeper, who wore a bright red cap so as to avoid falling prey in moments of excitement.

"What came in, Titus?"

"Had trouble with the shipment, sir," said Titus, nodding toward a white semi parked on the field's edge. "Packed sardine-tight. Smothered, every one."

"Shit," said the Old Man. "Round up some replacements?"

"Yup. Fresh vanload. Plus the one sent down."

"Sounds good. Everything set?"

"Yup." Titus clicked on the tape in the box he carried and, following Mister Dryden's request, "All Shook Up" began playing.

"Spread out, everbody," yelled the Old Man. "When I give the high sign, move forward at a steady clip." The players aligned themselves at the head of the meadow.

"Ought to play sometime, O'Malley," said Turnbull.

"You know that boy," laughed the Old Man. "He ain't much for sports." He raised his arm over his head, shouting: *"Yeee-hah!"*

The band trotted across the meadow. The guards thwacked at the brush with their clubs. Figures leapt up, peering about, running like hellbats, hoping only that they might be overlooked. There was so much chance of that as of the president being Republican.

"Asked 'em if they wanted to come to the country," Titus said to me. "They did."

Twenty-six trophies danced through the dark. All were naked: black, some of them, and some Asiatic; the rest Latino. Before she went down I saw the lala who had rumpled Mister Dryden's suit.

"*Yee-Hah!*"

They preferred children; there was less to clean up afterward.

7

BEFORE I TURNED IN, NOT LONG BEFORE MIDNIGHT, I set the alarm and prepped my material. The study was on the first floor, near the foot of the central stairs. Mister Dryden assured me I'd have no trouble getting in.

Had the alarm not sounded at five, rousing me from my depths, the dream I suffered just before waking would have been lost in sleep's successive hours. I dreamed I walked along the seashore. In the distance, near tide's reach and breaker's grasp, I saw something struggling. Running down, arriving in a trice, I found Avalon, lying naked on her back, her arms and legs buried in the sand. She looked at me, silently pleading for help; she couldn't get out. I pulled her free. She took my hand, led me up the beach, far from the ocean. She lay down, drawing me toward her, pushing my head between her legs, and shoving my face against her quim. I kissed. She grew, or I shrank; at once all around

110

was dark and wet. Unable to pull my head out, I struggled, but only worked myself in further; she grasped my legs and quickly pushed me in. It seemed a marvelous way to drown. Suddenly I saw her from above as she lay on the sand, her teeth ashine as if set to bite. She stood, walked to the water, swam past the waves, dived and disappeared. I awoke, sweating and shaking, wanting her all the more.

I dressed and gathered my toys. The house was dark as I crept through the hall, gliding silently down the stairs. I pressed my fingers to the study door, and it opened. No bell rang, no light flashed; I stepped inside, closing the door behind me. There was vague illumination within the room, coming from the fish tank built into the far wall. Steel shutters covered the room's two windows; no predawn light filtered past. In seconds my eyes adjusted. There was much to see. Hanging on either side of the fireplace were the Old Man's honorary degrees, his business awards, his civic trophies, and governmental citations. Near the mantel, on the right, was Mister Dryden's first award, given the year he was graduated: the certificate announced him as one of the Jaycee's Ten Most Outstanding American Young Men. Over the fireplace hung the Old Man's portrait, done when he was Mister Dryden's age; but for the color of his hair, he looked the same now. Framed photographs lined the mantelpiece, showing the Old Man with, among others, the present Czara of Russia and the last ten American presidents, five of whom had been assassinated, one after only two months in office.

On the wall opposite was his forty-eight-inch TVC monitor. Between the windows were rows and rows of tattered record albums, preserved still. Across from his desk were three black file cabinets, always locked. His desk was perfect for the need at hand: the top was wood, neither too thick or too thin; high enough in the central part that the user's knees would not brush against it, low enough so that nothing attached underneath could necessarily be seen. The blast's force would go outward and upward, toward the seated—toward the Old Man.

Placing it was pie-easy. I stuck up the plasticine—enough to take that half of the room, to be sure—set the timer for one P.M., when Mister Dryden told me the Old Man would be in there alone, pressed in the wires and it was done. The timer would survive the blast; on its surface I'd scratched the insignia of Nouveaux Maroon, the Haitian group—Barney, Biff, and Scooter were all former Maroons, led into the Dryden web with the standard bait. As house guards, Mister Dryden suspected they'd be perfect scapes.

Before I left the study—it hadn't taken five minutes—I looked at those file cabinets. They, too, were made to survive; whatever they held would rest fast so well. Afterward, I thought, I could at last discover what the Old Man hid there, and how by it he traced his dancer's steps. I had inklings, knew that on the day the markets crashed the Old Man was in Washington with the president. Hours later, attempting to escape, the president was pulled from his copter and lynched. Whatever they'd discussed, only the Old Man knew. I had learned from Mister Dryden that in those cabinets were papers he'd secured while all was fluxed; papers he'd never since let stray far from reach. There'd be time aplenty to overlook those, I thought, and so I let them be. Pulling the door tight, I stepped into the hall, heard the lock click shut behind me.

Dawn neared now; morningshade lightened the hall at the apex of the stairs. As I passed Avalon's room I noticed that the door was open; I looked in. She lay on her bed, on her stomach, her legs covered by the sheet, her buttocks rising high. For a moment I felt stricken;

I'd seen her naked limitless times, but knowing that soon she'd be with me, and coming upon her so unexpectedly, set my heart to bursting. I neared the bed after entering her room; I knelt beside, vizzing her lying there, hearing her breathe, watching her shift gently as she dreamed. Her choppers sat in a glass by the bed, fixed and grinning. Slowly, more carefully than if I were attempting to defuse a blaster, I reached out my hand; my fingers shook as they approached the small of her back and the deep valley below. But I could not touch her, not yet; not as she slept, so absolutely unaware and so seemingly helpless. It would have seemed too akin to rape; I lifted my hand, knowing that at this time the next morning, in Leningrad, I could safely place myself against her. Standing, I stepped away, slipping once more through her door, silently returning to my room.

Resetting the clock's alarm for ten—standard rising hour at the estate—I went back to sleep, dreaming no more. When ten came I rearose and headed downstairs to breakfast. As I came into the dining room I saw that Avalon, the Old Man, and Mister Dryden were already there.

"Thought you'd need rest," Mister Dryden muttered to me as I placed myself beside him. I smiled. Breakfast was always an intimate affair; including the tasters, and Stella, and the four house guards, there were only eleven of us.

The Old Man was looking over various maps and graphs, spilling jelly on them as he ate his eggs and toast.

"Check this out now," he said, flipping a drawing with attached printout over to Mister Dryden. "You'll have a new city apartment in a place like this."

Mister Dryden picked up the sketch, stared at it for a few moments. It showed a U-shaped, six-story apartment building, with a garden court guarded by two stone lions, tails erect. The stained glass windows along the ground floor nicely offset the bright yellow brick.

"Where I am suits," said Mister Dryden.

"Won't when water starts pourin' through the windows."

"On Fifth I'm thirty floors above. At the Towers—"

"Look at that place, will you? Architect says it's exactly like it was in 1928."

"Including satellite dish?" asked Mister Dryden; it was red with white trim.

"If there'd been dishes in 1928 I'm sure they'da been just like that."

"Easy entrance frontways," said Mister Dryden. "Risks inhere to city life, but—"

"Between the hollyhocks and the zinnias," said the Old Man, gesturing toward the garden's flowerbeds, "the mines."

"Tell the gardener."

"Apartments like this'll be built and rebuilt all up and down the Concourse," said the Old Man. I suspected that Mister Dryden's might be the only one equipped with rocket launchers. "The new Fifth Avenue. Streetcars'll run down the center median. Buses along the side. 1A lane down the middle, as always. Stores'll rent out south of 161st. Bloomies, Saks-Mart. Only the best."

"What's a streetcar?" asked Stella; her purple eyeshadow matched the bandanna she wore tied round her waist like a chain for the smashing.

"It's like a—" The Old Man paused, his descriptive powers for the moment lost. "They used to have 'em in San Francisco. Before the quake." Stella, obviously unenlightened, let it drop.

"Pass the bacon," said Avalon, stretching out her arm to receive.

AMBIENT

"Choose other," said Mister Dryden, who kept clear of fried food.

"Pass the fucking bacon,"Avalon said; I did.

"You had to blow up Lope yesterday?" the Old Man asked, with that wonderful shift in direction that kept dinner conversation so unpredictable here. Mister Dryden seemed uninterested; his coffee broke in waves within his cup as he held it.

"Our help was unforthcoming," he said. "He prepped to Marielize. Tragic but essential."

"Marielize what? Atlantic City? What'd he have to say about it?"

"They shove four Boardwalk casinos now. Fronted clear, no trails to or fro. They put the knee in another four."

"Now how do they do that?"

"Standard. Blasts, kneecaps, kidsteals, wifekills. Two weeks ago they rambled the night manager at Caesar's and stumped him handsaw style."

"They're uncivilized, all right," said the Old Man. "That's why we signed the truce with the bastards. They're too fuckin' wired to deal with. What'd Lope propose to do that you disagreed with?"

"To fund them steady. To steal baby and bath."

"So?" said the Old Man. "Let 'em."

"We need our hand there."

"Boardwalk's underwater at high tide now."

"Prop, Dad. The Green's all prop. Dark and black. Property doesn't negate."

"Does when it's at the bottom of the fuckin' ocean."

"The line's bottomed," said Mister Dryden. "You know their weeklies. As stands we sit and give. Mariel takes. We get nada."

"Don't need it."

"Nada funds that could keep you Bronxing."

"Don't need to sink money in new aquariums. There's plenty yet to cash in."

"Not overlong," said Mister Dryden. "We can't Bronx it much longer."

"The fuck we can't."

"But Atlantic City is—"

"*Shit*. If Lope's boys want it, if Mariel has it, it doesn't mean horseshit to me."

"Mow or be mown, Dad. Money them now and we'll spend later."

"Will we?"

"I say gut it and I say rollaway."

"You don't dig, son. We'll be Bronxing long after we're both gone. There's buildings up there you couldn't build now even with my money. A brand new city—"

Mister Dryden rested his head in his hands; by his pallor I could guess that he could need refreshers, soon.

"Trees along every street, son," continued the Old Man. "Give Bronx forty years. There'll be more money comin' in than a thousand accountants could steal. It's a big dream, sure, but a solid one—"

"An insane one," said Mister Dryden.

The Old Man stroked Stella's legs, sat on his pillow, and stared at his son. "And I suppose you'd say the dream's crazy as the dreamer?"

Mister Dryden said nothing.

"I'd hate to hear accusations 'bout *my* sanity comin' from a hophead like you."

"*Errored!*" Mister Dryden's knuckles whitened as he gripped the pillows on which he lay.

"Lately all you been doin's sittin' around replacin' the land's fat with your own. If you weren't shittin' your pants all the time about somebody gettin' something we don't want for prices we won't pay you might get something done sometime. But no, you just sit on your ass, doin' reckers, fuckin' around—"

116

"Trying to keep the company at peak roll—"

"I don't know about that, son. Just don't know at all."

"Know what?"

"Don't know how much longer I can keep a hophead runnin' everything," said the Old Man. "I just might have to start gettin' more involved with workin' that day-to-day shit again. I'm startin' to think all of this might be havin' a bad effect on you."

"You're speaking both sides now—"

"Yeah, I might just have to realign things. Set it up so you won't have so much pressure on you. Make it so you won't have to do anything more complicated than takin' a shit. You think you can handle that?"

"Fucking old—"

"Probably not. Well, I think I can handle everything else. Been years but an old dog doesn't forget his tricks—"

"Tricks he never knew."

"How's that, son?"

"Mother'd do the tricks," said Mister Dryden. "And you'd beg the scraps—"

They each looked ready to go at one another; I readied myself to move. Neither had weapons more sharp than forks or butter knives in reach, but those could be enough if aimed properly.

"Can I go shopping?" Avalon asked suddenly, interrupting, wiping egg yolk from the corners of her mouth. "I'd love to hang around and watch you two go at it all day but—"

"Course you can, darlin'," said the Old Man. "We always work out our disagreements better in private anyhow. Don't we, son?"

Mister Dryden's eye flickered toward me, and then to Avalon again. "You'll need guarding. O'Malley. Shield."

I nodded, and stood. Breakfast broke up; the white panel lowered to the kitchen below. Avalon went upstairs to change. As I stood in the front hall waiting for her return, Mister Dryden came up.

"Are you all right?" I asked.

"See my meaning?" he asked, shaking his head. "Batbrained. Absolute."

I agreed, thinking it safest to so do.

"We'll continue in the study," he said. "I'll exit pronto, sure, beforehand."

"Good."

"All set?" he asked.

"AO."

"Know the spot?" I nodded. "Six weeks hence," he said, clapping his hand on my shoulder. "Fun it up."

Avalon descended the stairs, all vision and delight. She was wigless, and wore a chartreuse sweater, over-the-knee brown boots with flat heels, and buttock-tight Pretty Poison jeans. She clutched her large shoulder bag against her right side.

"I got my money," she said, patting her hip; that she could have fit anything into her pockets was surprising. "Ready?"

"Set."

We strolled out as if setting forth on a spring cruise—we were, after all. Butch waited outside, standing next to one of the older cars, a dark blue Plymouth that I believed Mister Dryden learned to ride in. We climbed into the back, pulling the doors shut. As we drove down the drive Avalon pressed the button that raised the shield separating our compartment from the front.

"Why isn't Jimmy driving us?" she asked.

"I told you Mister Dryden doesn't trust him," I said. "I think he wants to keep him in sight."

"What's Butch know?"

"Nothing, I gather. He'll drop us off in time to be called back up here."

Avalon smiled, resting her hand on my knee. I stroked her long fingers.

"What about luggage?"

"There're suitcases for us on the plane." We were to take a Dryco jet from the Aeroflot terminal at Newark, nonstop to Leningrad.

"Where are we staying once we get there?"

"One of Gorky-Detroit's reps keeps a dacha twenty miles out of town. I'm told it's very nice."

"We won't be in the city?" she asked. "I get enough of the fuckin' country over here. We should go to London."

"Too many riots," I said. "You'll be able to shop, don't worry."

Butch eyed us through the rearview; I surreptitiously moved her hand away from my knee. She, as subtly, replaced it. For a moment, I wondered our compartment was tapped; it seemed unlikely. None of the older cars had bugs as standard equipment and I didn't think that either Dryden would have bothered to have Jimmy install one.

"You'll keep warm," I said.

"You'll keep me warm," she said, inching her hand higher up my leg. We turned down the road leading to the Saw Mill. Not until our feet trod Russian ground would I feel absolutely certain, or absolutely safe; still, I was with Avalon, now and hereafter, and all that I'd had to do was kill someone against whom I had nothing personally, someone who might have done something to someone sometime. I put my arm around her waist and moved closer, forcing my mind to stray to where it should.

"Have any trouble this morning?" she asked, her voice lower. Butch had turned on the radio, and it was

119

hard to hear her over what, at first listen, seemed to be static, but after prolonged exposure revealed itself as one of those songs writ by chip and program.

"No."

"Why didn't you get into bed with me?" she asked.

"When?"

"This morning," she said. "I guess it wouldn't have been so safe, but still—"

"You were awake?"

"Of course. Cold as Pops keeps that tomb you think I usually sleep without covers? I wanted to attract your attention—"

"You did. When'd you wake up?"

"When you went downstairs. Why'd you just look at me?"

"I was—" Her eyes fixed me again; snake for the bird, as Enid would say. "Seemed safer to wait."

"I suppose. I'd have had to stay quiet. I hate that," she said, frowning. "You set the timer correctly?"

"Of course."

She smiled; slyness washed her features. She stroked my chin with her fingers.

"Didn't shave," she said. "Nice."

Had the panel separating our compartments been opaque I should have taken her down to the floor just then.

"When was Pops going to be in there alone?"

"One P.M." I said. "According to Mister Dryden."

"That's when you set the timer for?"

"Yeah," I said. "He was going to be in there, too, earlier."

"They'd both be in there right now, right?"

I looked at my watch; it was a few minutes past twelve. Their fights never lasted longer than two hours.

"Uh-huh," I said. "Still arguing, I'm sure."

She took my wrist and looked at my watch, pressing

the readout. She raised her arms over her head, stretching.

"They've finished," she said.

"I'd doubt it," I said. "Probably good for another half hour or so—"

"Not anymore."

An Army billboard, barely seen as we whisked by, ordered all to recycle all in the event there wouldn't be any more. Someone, probably Army boys dead with boredom, had fired a tank blast through the center of the notice. I looked at Avalon.

"What do you mean?" I asked.

"It went off five minutes ago," she said. Closing her eyes, she rested her head against my shoulder.

"I set the timer for one P.M."

"I reset it for noon," she said.

"When?"

"After you went back to your room. This morning."

"I locked the study door."

"I've known the code for a year," she said. "Pops liked to afternoon it with me, sometimes. We'd meet there."

No matter how frightened I felt, I knew it wasn't so much as I should be feeling.

"Why?" I asked.

"You look funny," she said. "Are you feelin' all right?"

"I was. Avalon, why?"

"It'll work out better this way," she said. "If it works. I think it will."

"Why?" I shouted. Butch eyed us again, but didn't slow. "Avalon, tell me you didn't. Please."

"I did," she said. "Look, they're both crazy, and Sonny was going to come out shining clean—"

"Don't you realized how much trouble'll come down?"

"You couldn't see it like I could because you worked for him too long. You'd always think he was your buddy no matter how big a fuck he was. You're blind to it. He was fuckin' psycho, Shameless. You wouldn't admit it even if you could."

"He wasn't," I said. "Not that much—"

"He was. He'd have turned on us one day. Mark me."

"I don't believe this," I said. "I don't. I really don't."

"You'd better," she said. "Look. He did me shit the whole time. Just like he did you."

"It was going to change—"

"You admit it," she said. "You really think he'd do what he said he was goin' to do? You really believed that?"

"He wouldn't have lied to me about this—"

"He wanted your dirty work and that's it. I don't think you'da been zeroed because of it later on but you can bet it wouldn't have done you any good."

"What good's this going to do? They'll all be after us now. His people and the Old Man's."

"Sonny doesn't have any people on his side. You and me and Jimmy. That weaseleye Jake. That's it."

"But he could have thrown the Old Man's people off—"

"Nobody would have figured out he was behind it?"

"They couldn't have *done* anything. If he's dead he can't confirm or deny. So now they'll have to pick somebody. Who's handiest?"

"Men never think proxies are smart enough for this sort of thing—"

"It's not going to work like you think it will," I said. "They're going to want to know why we're leaving the country, don't you think?"

"They'll find out Sonny made the arrangements himself, right?"

"He didn't make arrangements to have himself blasted."

"We'll deny all," she said, laughing. "You don't even realize the best part of this."

"I don't know *how* I missed it," I said. "What?"

"With Pops dead," she said, tossing her legs across mine, pinning me to my seat, "who stands to inherit?"

"Mister Dryden. But thanks to you, he's—"

"Dead. Who stands next?"

I said nothing.

"I know he showed you his new will," she said. "You forgot to tell me that, by the way. But I've seen it, too. Twenty-five percent you get, right?" I nodded. "So do I."

"That means—"

"We control the estate," she laughed. "We own the company."

Sometimes something happens that gives you all of death's responsibilities with none of its benefits. I covered my face with my hands.

"It doesn't strike you that we had a perfect motive, then?"

"Sure it does," she said. "But the only person that knew about it besides you was Sonny, right?"

"And my sister, and the lawyers," I said. "You, obviously. Obvious enough for them to figure."

She sloughed it off. "Their word, our word—"

"Their power—" I said.

"Our money—"

"We're in trouble, Avalon," I said. "It's not going to work."

"Why not?"

"You think we'll ever see a dime, now? If we're not *caught*, that is? We may as well sit back and watch the

123

lawyers parcel it out over our heads. They'll keep it in court forty years—"

"What if we get away, though?"

"How?" I said. "We've got to figure out something fast."

"Shameless."

"We'll be nailed," I said. "They'll take us here or there. They'll—"

"Shamey, listen."

"What?"

"We're they, now," she said. "See?"

There was nothing to be done as we hurtled toward New York. Through my mind I chased possibilities.

"Maybe they weren't killed," I said.

"You don't think you set it up right?"

I knew I had. "Do you think you might have accidentally disconnected it?"

"No," she said. "It was placed sure when I left it."

"Maybe you set it for midnight instead of noon?"

"Course not. That little light comes on for A.M. I'd have seen it."

"What if they left the room?"

"Maybe they did. But if Sonny didn't get it and then it went off an hour early—"

"He'd think—"

She nodded her head, slowly. "If he's not dead we're in real trouble."

"He probably is, though," I muttered, reassuring myself with thoughts of his demise, hoping now for what I had despised the thought of, moments before. Perspective, you might call it; another one of those things you found yourself getting used to after so long.

"I think you're worrying to much for nothing."

"I doubt it," I said. "I just wish you'd said something first—"

"So you could try to talk me out of it?" she said.

"If you're going to do something, do it right. That's what I've always thought."

"What if you do it wrong?"

"Then do something else," she said. "Quick."

We said little, then; sat quietly, holding each other. There seemed no way that we could leave the country, under the circumstances; even if we weren't stopped beforehand and somehow made it across the water, we would have to spend our remaining days in Russia, unable to return—in so much danger there as we would be here.

As we drove down the Henry Hudson, passing under the bridge, a darker realization came to mind.

8

"AVALON," I WHISPERED.

"What?"

"One of two things has happened."

"What are you talking about?"

"Either the blast went off," I said, "or it didn't."

She stared at me, uncomprehending. "Makes sense," she said.

"If it did," I said, "then they must be lowlying. They haven't shortwaved Butch."

"Maybe the thing's not working?"

"It is," I said. "Butch was going to be called back up there after he dropped us off."

"So what do you think's going on?"

"It must have gone off," I said. "You wouldn't have disconnected it, the way I set it up."

"I know," she said. "So?"

"So they must not have been in there. Or maybe just the Old Man was in there."

126

"Or Sonny."

"If Mister Dryden went, they'd have called Butch. In which case—"

"Things are either going as they should," she said, "or no one termed and we're not suspected."

"Sure," I said. "Mister Dryden would either tell the contact to send us back once we got there, or we'd go on to the airport as planned—"

"Unless that's what they want us to think," she said.

I sighed. "We might be walking into it, if they suspect. Butch wouldn't have to know."

"We're almost there," she said, "What're we going to do?"

"Let's earplay this," I said. "Viz what goes."

We were to meet our contact at Broadway and Thirty-fourth, near Macy's. Mister Dryden had not said who the contact would be, or what he or she would look like; only that we would be recognized. Under the circumstances that was no longer a comforting thought. As the car entered the Herald Square Secondary Zone I leaned over to Avalon and whispered, "It's not worth testing. Let's not stick. We'll head down. They won't come looking in my neighborhood."

"Let's get Butch to take us there."

"That's not what he's expecting," I said. "He'd have to let them know where he dropped us. It'll raise suspicion in his mind."

"How dangerous is your neighborhood?"

"Safer than this."

As Butch pulled the car alongside the double-parked trucks, a cyclist, zazzing past, bumped into our rear fender and nearly pitched head-over-bars into the street. Avalon and I jumped, fearing we'd been attacked. The cyclist rolled his bike past us—not easily, as its frame had been bent in the collision—and, when he reached the front of our car, lifted the bike above his head and smashed it down against our windshield. Seeing that he did our car little damage, while further destroying his own toy, he began screaming at us and stuck his head through the front passenger window. He continued screaming as Butch raised the window, entrapping his head between the unbreakable glass and the door frame.

"Need any help?" I asked. Butch demurred. "We'll get out here, then."

I opened the door; Avalon and I exited, sliding on whatever slipperiness lay in the gutter. Butch pulled out a long lead pipe from beneath the front seat and began beating the cyclist over the head. The windows on the passenger side darkened as he brought it down again and again.

"Let's get the fuck out of here quick, Shameless," said Avalon, wrapping her arm around me. "I hate crowds."

Thirty-fourth Street was the busiest in the city, especially on a Saturday afternoon. In most of Manhattan it was difficult to drive; along 34th it was nearly impossible to walk, so teeming were the crowds. From north side façade to south side façade, the only clear spot in the street was the 1A lane, lined along its length with two-foot-high spikes, each concrete-set three inches apart; even that lane was busier here, for Army vehicles heading to the Javits Center passed down it without cease. Army studies demonstrated that regular lane traffic here, at any hour on any day, moved along at less than one foot per minute.

"Let's walk east," I said, holding her close to prevent her being swept away by the crowd. "Then down through Murray Hill. It'll be the easiest, I think."

To gain most productive use of space, most stores along 34th displayed their wares *al fresco*, continuing their aisles—shielded from the weather by awnings once bright-hued, now soot-smeared—several feet out onto the sidewalk, leaving off only where the peddlers set, crowding the curbs four deep. Additional Army studies showed that Thirty-fourth Street was the only place in Manhattan where, on average, street traffic outpaced sidewalk traffic. Slowly, carefully, we began elbowing and kneeing our way through those prepped to barter or haggle or rob. This sort of mob troubled me most of all; in moving, one was sure to somehow offend, and such insults were not passed over here.

"O'Malley," I heard someone shout.

"You hear that?" Avalon said, pushing by a woman dragging along a baby carriage; it was loaded with wilted produce.

"Keep walking," I said.

"I'm trying," she said.

"O'Malley."

I steered Avalon off the curb, attempting to get us across the street so that we might make our way down a block or so where the crowds would thin. A cockfight was being held just off the median between Broadway and Sixth; a ring stood round to bet on the outcome, to see which bird would move toward greater victories and which would provide soup for twelve.

"O'Malley!"

Someone was getting closer, coming up behind us, and I preferred to avoid. Avalon and I came to the unbroken rows of cars in the street and began climbing over, stepping onto bumpers, crawling over hoods where we had to, ducking back as cyclists sped between the cars, whistles ablow. I lifted her over the spikes at the 1A lane and then leapt over myself. A halftrack rumbled toward us as we cleared the opposite line of spikes. Agonized cries arose over the hubbub. We looked away as two young women and an old man were pressed flat; the vehicle rolled on, leaving its red carpet behind.

"O'Malley!" the voice repeated, "Stop!"

We reached the south side of the street, pushed our way past the Herald Center, slid through the lines awaiting admittance into the ground floor's Army recruitment center. Ten stories up, along the building's cornice, on continuous run, passed the message SEE NEW YORK WHILE YOU CAN. I saw a Seventh Avenue bus steering downtown, pulling to the curb near us.

"Stop!!"

"What'll we do?" asked Avalon.

The bus stopped; passengers tumbled out as new ones pushed in, leapt on, clambered topside.

"Get on," I said, shoving her forward. "We'll outdistance and get off. Breakaway then. Hurry."

Avalon and I were the last two to force ourselves inside before the door shut. We were held tight between passengers on the higher entrance steps and the door, our arms squashed against our sides, our legs pinned to where we stood, our bodies molded against one another as if forming a vacuum seal. Had we been able to breathe it would have been quite arousing to be so near her. Something clawed at my back; turning my head, I could see a man running alongside the bus. His arm was caught in the door but he obviously wanted to keep his place; he jumped nimbly over potholes, sprang high to avoid other vehicles. The bus stopped suddenly and he was crushed between two postal vans. The bus crawled a few feet further, pulling to within six feet of the curb; the doors opened.

"O'Malley," Avalon wheezed, "Get out! This is fuckin' awful—"

"Too late—"

Dozens of people packed onto the bus; I felt my feet leave the floor as we were rammed along. The driver seemed unconcerned with taking fares, stared idly ahead, chewing on a toothpick. We found ourselves within the front quarter of the bus, held so tightly as if we'd been dropped into cement. By removing seats from buses the city had been able to provide surplus room for additional passengers.

"Stept'rrr'd'gm'pl'z," the amplified voice of the driver crackled: the quality of sound coming over the speaker suggested someone calling for help, while sinking in a fen, welded within an oil drum.

"Fuck—" Avalon said; we were separated during the last onslaught. "I'm suffocating—"

"Hold on," I gasped. Someone prodded my side with an umbrella; there was still no way I could raise my arms. I wasn't sure how far we'd gone; so many passengers hung on the outside that it was impossible to see past them. The bus lurched again and stopped. Another shipment jammed inward.

"O'Malley," Avalon screamed, "Help me!"

Only her head was visible; she drifted slowly away from me as if toward a whirlpool. In the center of the bus the crowd became more liquid; I leaned forward, certain that I wouldn't fall. It was almost possible to swim across.

"Help!!" Avalon reached out her hand; with enormous effort I threw myself forward, seizing it.

"When I stop," I panted, seeing that she was level with the side door, "Dig out. Push. Shove. Just get out."

"Yeah," she said.

The bus stopped; a hiss suggested that the unseen door to our left was opening.

"Now!"

One of my feet brushed the floor; I used it to propel myself forward. Avalon was out; a heavy man blocked my exit as he attempted to sneak in.

"Move," I shouted as the doors began to close.

"Fuck you," he shouted back. I knew this would go nowhere; with my free hand I reached up, digging my knuckles into his eyes. His great weight wedged the doors apart; as he fell back I plunged out with him, into the street. The bus pulled away, blowing vast black diesel clouds over us.

"Shamey," Avalon said, rushing over to help me, "are you all right?"

My suit was torn, beneath my long coat. One of my shoes hung halfway off my boot. Avalon's face was scratched, and her boots were scarred and scuffed. Her jeans were damp with fresh stains, and her sweater was yanked up over her breasts; as she began rolling it down, she looked at me oddly, and screamed.

"You're hurt."

"No, I'm not," I said, feeling my face, attempting to discover what had happened, wondering why I hadn't begun feeling the pain. "Am I?"

"Somebody bit your ear off."

Raising my hand to the side of my head, I discovered a sorrowful absence. "It's gone," I said. "My ear-ring."

"What about your ear?" she asked. "It's not bleeding yet."

"It won't bleed," I said. "They're fake. I can get another ear—"

"I'll get you new earrings. Come on."

"Enid gave them to me—"

"Where are we, anyway?"

"Seventh and Twenty-sixth. Just outside Chelsea. Come on."

With our Drydencards we had no difficulty entering the Chelsea Secondary Zone, our bedraggled look notwithstanding. Chelsea, boozhie-crammed, was a dreadful area awash with those lured to Manhattan by organizations such as Dryco, all hypnotized by the

132

promise that for a few well-suffered years here, one's driven path to glory in other, more settled regions of the country might be made all the more sunwashed— so long as the visit was survived, certainly. To supply the whims of the neighborhood residents, innumerable booties filled Seventh Avenue's storefronts, each good for about three months' existence—until the fad died or the rent raised. We passed restaurants providing naught but confections of bêche-de-mer and seaweed; stores selling nothing but one particular item: lamps or signs, shirts or knives. At Sixteenth, just before the barricade separating Chelsea from the Village Control Zone, was a large antique shop whose sign proclaimed it as the largest vendor of Nasty Nineties furniture in New York.

We walked the length of Fourteenth Street east, crossing through the barricade at Broadway into the East Village Secondary Zone. We were in that but shortly; at Third, we reached the wall surrounding Loisaida and went in.

"This is what it's like on this side?" Avalon asked. She seemed nervous, though it was difficult to read her features as dusk drew deeper.

Ambient graffiti was etched into the side of an abandoned building at Tenth Street: GODNESS LIVES— DO YOU? We continued along; many people were having dinner at that time of evening, and so the streets were not so crowded as they often were. After so long we came to my building. The unlit marquee showed the weekend features as being *Children of Paradise* and *Jules and Jim*. During our walk down and over I'd kept sharp eyes apprised; no one seemed to have followed us, whether on foot or in car. The gates across Belsen's door were unshuttered; we went in.

"Lester?" I shouted; there was no one in the foyer of the club, and the lights were down within. Through the tobacco smoke I distinguished several vague forms near the bar.

"Ola," Ruben said, emerging from the haze. His shirt was off; he looked as if he'd been cleaning something, judging from the dirt smudging his shoulders and chest.

"Enid or Margot about?" I asked.

"On the other side still," he said.

Avalon stared as Ruben lifted one foot to his mouth, extracting his cigarette so that he could speak with greater ease; he tapped its ashes away against the side of the door.

"Back this eve?"

He shook his head. "Spilling charms yon and hith. At play with Brook's babble. Tu corazon?"

"Mi corazon," I said, holding Avalon tightly, as if fearful she might try to dash away. "We'll raise and close. If lozels prowl near—"

He nodded. We walked to the stairway and went up, picking our way over those encamped in the hall. I unlocked the door and we went inside. Avalon stood motionless in the center of the room, as if overwhelmed.

"You live here?" she asked.

"You get used to it."

"This thing got any bugs in it?" she asked, pointing toward the sofa.

"None that bite," I said. She frowned, but sat.

"Got anything to drink, Shameless?"

"Vodka. Pepsi. Want a glass?"

"Vodka. And a glass if it doesn't look like the rest of the place."

"Here," I said, recovering a bottle from Enid's stock. She took it from me and gulped a long one. "Don't worry," I said, "we'll be safe here until we figure out what to do."

"We must be on the takeout list now, on any score," she said.

"Join the crowd."

"What's going to happen to us, Shamey?"

"Let's just take it as it comes," I said, for the moment unwilling to even try to think of something.

"Is everyone down here like that guy—" she began to say; she suddenly jumped, as if she'd been pricked. "Somebody's here."

"Where?" I whispered, looking around.

"Listen. I heard them say something."

I listened. The only sound I heard was *Door ajar. Please shut.*

"That's the refrigerator."

"Oh," she asked, relaxing, taking another guzz. "Are there a lot of those freaks down here?"

"There're a lot of people like that down here," I said.

"I heard your sister's like that," she said. "Is she?"

"Enid wasn't a born Ambient," I explained. "She chose to be one. She's not exactly like them."

"Looks more normal?"

"In a sense."

"She chose to be one of them?"

"Yeah," I said.

"Why are they called Ambients?"

"Because they're forever all around." That was how Enid put it.

"Who came up with that name?"

"They did."

She shuddered. Her eyes drew quietly shut as she sat upon the sofa.

"Tired?" I asked. "Stupid question."

"Can I use your shower?"

"Sure." We had a pump and tank in the basement; bought a week's supply at a time. Even if water had been still provided by the city to our zone, there were no pipes other than the old main sewer lines through which it might be run, and there were none of these near our building. "Try not to use too much water."

"I won't," she said. "Where's the bathroom?"

"In there. Be careful if you sit down."

"Why?"

"Rats crawl up through the pipes sometimes."

"You tried poison?"

"Things aren't that bad yet," I laughed; so did she. "There might be a towel in there."

"Might be?"

"I usually drip-dry. Enid keeps a pile of dirt to roll around in." She looked as if she believed me.

"Be out shortly," she said.

She closed the door behind her and started running out the water; she flushed the toilet twice. I supposed I could catch rain water in tubs and filter the larger impurities. I went into the bedroom and took a few minutes to nail a blanket over the crater in the ceiling. Climbing down, I looked over the stacks of old books that Enid had gathered over the years. She, like most Ambients, read anything they could find. Visible titles included *Anomalies and Curiosities of Medicine*, Bolitho's *Camera Obscura*, *Human Behaviour in the Concentration Camp*, Nash's *Unfortunate Traveller*, *Perverse Crimes in History*, Fort's *Lo!*, and *The Greening of America*. I returned to the front room. Sitting down, I switched on the news.

"—burned and raped before being—"

I watched for a time. The president and First Lady left for Camp David for their monthly vacation, having sent condolences to the security adviser's widow. A witch was burned in Ohio. In Japan a defense plant leaked cumulonimbus clouds of azure gas; forty thousand died. The anchor raised her eyebrows, as if she was in on the joke.

"Coming up next," she said, "Cattle mutilators—friend or foe?"

There was a commercial for Russian fur jackets; first you saw the furry little animals and then you eyed the peelings. Then came a campaign spot: a long white beach, a calm sea, the president and his dog, Freedom Fighter, jogging along the sand; a folksinger sang of the joys of American mornings. It wasn't the president, of course, nor his dog; both were actors. The president, when outside, was always surrounded by a phalanx of Secret Service agents.

Lastly a different spot came on, a public service message. The first shot was of a little boy shooting up; his finger quivered as the rush hit. There followed a scene of a crone thrashing a toddler with a long stick; blood flowed from his nose and ears. Then there was footage of a middle-aged man raping an eight-year-old girl; she screamed in pain. Fade to black, and the message came up:

KIDS

Black, medium hold, and then:

KEEP YOUR HANDS OFF 'EM.

A repeated buzzing and bumping ran out downstairs; it sounded as if they were cutting off their limbs with clippers. Dire screams snagged my attention. I got up and looked out the window to estimate the turnout; the crowd was usually large on Saturday nights. Dozens of Ambients queued outside. The evening fog was light. A dark car was parked across the street. The shadows within were lit by the dash's pale purple illumination.

137

I was fairly sure that the auto was a Redstar. I moved quickly to another window, turning off the TVC on the way; from my new vantage point I saw that the plates were 1A. It was past eight; at this hour one began to ready the cudgel even without such prompting.

"Avalon?" I asked, speaking through the door, over the roar of the water.

"Yeah?"

"I think we're under watch."

"There's something out there?" She shut off the water.

"Yeah. I'm going to turn out the lights."

"Aren't the drapes closed?"

"They are now," I said, pulling the newspapers across; it might make them more suspicious to see the apartment darken, I thought, reconsidering.

"Why haven't they come up here yet if they're after us?"

"They're waiting," I said. "Maybe."

"Waiting for what?"

"It's terror," I said. "They're trying to scare us, I think."

"Sounds like they're doing a good job. If they were after us, wouldn't they be up here already?"

"They wouldn't get far at night down here and they know it."

"Crossing the street?"

"They'll wait until morning," I said.

"Who do they sacrifice downstairs?" she asked; with the water not running it was easy to hear the ruck in the hough.

"Volunteers." I looked out the window again, turning back a corner of the paper. They were just sitting there.

"You ever talk to your sister about me?"

"Yes."

138

"What's she think of me?"

"She forms hasty judgments." Waiting till we bed and bideaway, perhaps. Perhaps not.

"She's older than you?"

"Four years."

"What does she look like, anyway?"

"She has style," I said, "but she's taken. Has a girlfriend."

"What's her girlfriend like?"

"Precocious."

Avalon opened the bathroom door, stepping out; she was naked. She stood in the doorway for a moment, outlined against the light, her body steaming as if fresh baked.

"When I'm wet I can't get my jeans on," she said, walking forward. "Not that you've never seen everything I've got. Not that you weren't going to see. You mind?"

"Uh-uh," I said, staring at her.

"They still out there?" she asked, leaning forward, peering out from beneath the newspaper.

"Of course."

She raised up and came over to me, twisting her arms around my waist. "What'll happen to us, Shamey?"

Her skin comforted my hands as I patted her. She was soft as fog, and I feared that, somehow, she'd disappear as soon, while I wasn't looking.

"Something."

"You think they're alive or dead?"

"No idea. Whichever way it went, I think somebody wants to talk to us about it."

"You think we'll be all right?"

"Maybe."

"Shameless," she said, holding me more tightly, "you think about me when I'm not around?"

"Always."

"You wanta sleep with me tonight?"

"Yes."

"You've wanted to a long time, haven't you?"

"Since my eyes first vizzed."

"You talk funny sometimes," she said. "Like you did in the bar downstairs. I always wanted to sleep with you, too. You just weren't in the job description."

"I guess I am now," I said. "Unless we've been fired."

"So fuck 'em," she said. "Fuck me first."

Romance's room, in our house, was down the hall. I picked her up and carried her into the bedroom.

"You sleep in here?" she asked.

"Yeah," I said, pushing aside plaster chunks with my feet as I made our way across the room.

"Where's your sister sleep?"

"In here."

"Really," she said as I set her down. She noticed a pool of dried blood on the floor. "Heavy period?"

"Had company drop in about two months ago."

She flung herself onto my bed face down, parted her legs, and, raising her bottom, moved it in slow circles. It seemed to me that her smirker tattoo glared at me, as if condescending to my presence.

"Do me double," she said, laughing, her face pressed against my pillow. "I'll suck you dry."

I found myself short on repartee under the circumstances. She rolled onto her back, looking up. "Why's a blanket nailed to the ceiling?" she asked.

"To cover the hole."

"Where'd the hole come from?"

"That's where our company dropped in."

She nodded, as if any of it made sense. She stared at Enid's block of foam but said nothing. I took off my clothes, feeling it very strange to undress before a woman who was not my sister. Avalon raised her head, vizzing me up and down.

"I've never seen so many scars," she said.

"I get around."

"What's the long one running down your shoulder from?"

"Bayonet."

"The big one in your shoulder?"

"Hatchet."

"That one?" she asked, pointing.

"Cigarette."

"You don't smoke."

"Enid does."

I got into bed with her. "You nervous?" she asked.

"Yeah."

We were busy for what seemed to be hours. Avalon had a vivid imagination and reveled in the perverse.

"You like it?" she asked, after some passage of silence. We'd not been interrupted. I nodded.

"You're shivering. You cold?"

I shook my head.

"Scared?"

I didn't answer.

"Was that your first time?"

"No," I said, adding, "Kind of."

"Kind of?" she laughed. "Who with before? Lalas?"

"No."

"Neighborhood girls."

"Kind of. I never did much—"

"Don't you like girls?"

"My work kept me so busy—"

"You sound like Sonny now. This isn't better than work?"

"Much better."

"You sweat like a hog," she laughed, rolling against

141

me, pressing her face against my chest, biting my nipples. "I love it."

"I'm glad." I dipped my fingertips into the nubby furze at the base of her skull. "You can let your hair grow out now."

"I like it this way."

"Whatever. I didn't mean—"

"I think I do love you," she said, very softly. "This is kind of new."

"I love you," I said. "I love you so much."

"Scared?"

"Yes," I said.

"They still out there, Shamey?" she asked. "Go look."

I pulled myself up and walked to the window. It was late; Ruben and Lester were dragging off the unclaimed. "Yeah," I said. "Maybe I better try to contact tomorrow."

"We better stay awake," she said. "We might have to make a speedaway."

"Unless they kill us first," I said.

"They won't," she said. "Come back here. I've got to do something to keep from fallin' asleep."

"I'm sleepy," I said, climbing back into bed beside her. She eyed me for a moment, her face shining moonbright. She pushed me onto my back and climbed aboard, grinding against me, her strong thighs crushing my hips as she leaned forward.

"Rape me," she said, her hands circling my throat.

9

WE LAY LIKE KNIVES, BLADE TO BLADE; CARE'S NURSE called and we answered. During the eve a new dream alit me: Avalon and I drifted into the sky through the hole in the roof, borne gracefully toward something like heaven; a copter buzzed near, rousting our apotheosis. I awoke; my eyes unglued. The Serena had come during the night. Waves of black water baptized us. I took the high ground; Avalon washed out with the tide.

"O'Malley!" she shouted, hitting the floor. She splashed to a gentle stop against the wall.

"Rise and shine," I said.

"Those guys still out there?" she asked.

"Fit and ready to play," I said, seeing from the window their dark car's rain-spattered gleam.

"How many are there?"

"Three," I said, stepping into my trousers.

"Recognize 'em?" she asked, pulling on her sweater.

Jack Womack

"Internal security, maybe. Or Home Army. Down from Midtown, likely. It's a big car."

"How big are they?"

"Very."

"Help me get my pants on, Shameless," she said, lying on the floor, lifting her legs. It was but a few minutes before we had her jeans yanked up so far as her waist. "Gimme the pliers," she said, sucking in her breath. "In my bag." I passed them to her before she could turn bluer than her pants. Seizing the clasp with the pliers, she pulled her zipper shut. I knew that there were proxies who had the Health Service remove part of their small intestine during the required ovariotomies so that they might wear tighter pants, but Avalon had never been so diligent.

"What'll we do?" she asked as I helped her stand.

"Watch them."

"Watch?" she said, peering out. "Look."

I did; three got out of the car and started walking across the street, as if aiming for our building.

"Rent's due," I said, stepping back.

"Want to meet 'em here?"

"I'd prefer not to meet them at all. We can get out before they can get up. Come on." I tossed her one of Enid's more subtle jackets—one of bright magenta leatherette—and I pulled on my own Krylar model. "Put it on and let's go."

"Where are we going?"

"Out. Follow me. Don't worry."

We stepped into the hall; I heard Lester arguing downstairs. Suspecting that he and Ruben could detain them long enough, I locked up, turned and shoved in the door of the apartment across the hall. Dad had evicted the building's squatters when we moved in here. The tenants left, this apartment had been locked and had not been entered—no need—until the moment I

144

broke in. The rooms were as they had been left when I was still young; only where some of the ceiling or the walls had caved in was anything disturbed. Dust and soot lay over the old furniture and on the floors, several inches deep; the spiderwebs were laced like spun cotton. The only light that came though the dust-opaqued windows—those left unblocked—was pale yellow-gray.

"Nobody lives in this whole place but you two?"

"Above the first floor," I said. "Ruben and Lester live behind the club."

"Why'd you pick this place?"

"We inherited the building from our father."

"Why?"

"As an investment."

"He was serious?"

"It was all he had left," I said, "He always said you couldn't go wrong owning New York real estate."

"What happened to him?"

"I don't know," I said as we came to the apartment's bedroom. The doorknob fell off as I turned it, and I pushed the door open. "He disappeared one night not long after we moved down here. Somebody might have pounced him outside. We'll never know. I don't think he ever got used to things. He was a worldly man, but it was a different world—" I shattered the window facing the airshaft. Both of us sneezed in the thickened dust as the falling glass stirred the sediment. The building next door was two feet away; the window across was already broken out.

"You know where we're going?" she asked as I helped her across the sill.

"Sure," I said, crawling across. The building over was in excellent shape; there was a floor at every level. Once we reached the roof we could dash across and clamber down to the next street over, away from our friends.

We ran up the stairs. When we reached the fifth floor, we stopped to catch our breath; one apartment lacked a door. We looked in.

"Shameless," Avalon panted, "what the fuck—"

A fellow in the apartment had hung another one from the ceiling; the dangler was draped in chains and resembled a chandelier. The fellow standing flogged merrily away with a long braided whip. He looked up, hearing Avalon's voice. Distracted from the moment's heat, he turned and ran toward us.

"We're bigger than he is," she said as we ran up the stairs.

"I don't care," I answered, crashing against the door that led to the roof; it fell away. We lost him, a few buildings over. We missed the roof's weak spots as we ran; he stepped onto a sag. The sound of crashing reached our ears as he plummeted through the floors. Slowing our pace, we made our way along. With short leaps at appropriate intervals, we reached the other side of the block.

"Down that fire escape," I said. "Be careful."

We climbed down, Avalon going first.

"What street is this?" Avalon shouted up to me.

"Avenue B," I said.

"This thing keeps shaking," she said, clutching the railing.

"We're lucky it's here," I yelled back. Fire escapes hadn't been required for years, having been long ago ruled an infringement on the rights of property owners; when old originals were scavenged, they were never replaced. Rusted support bolts pulled from the crumbling wall with our every step. "Throw yourself out of the way if it goes down."

The fire escape shook like a Vibrabed; a rumble— the sound of bees aswarm, and nearing—grew louder. When we reached the second floor landing we discov-

ered that someone had borrowed the ladder to the
ground. The fire escape kept moving even after we had
stopped, and from its shuddering bones rose an unpleasant creak.

"Jump," I said.

"Where?"

"Garbage," I said, hurtling over the rail; Avalon
wasn't far behind. We just hit the stack of bags at which
we'd aimed.

"You all right?" she asked as she stood up.

"Yeah," I said. "We need a plan—"

"Look out!" she screamed, throwing herself across
me; we hit the ground again. In my confusion I marveled at her passion's wildness; then her true motive
showed. The fire escape, weakened by our prancing,
dropped from the building, bringing half the structure's
façade down with it; I was reminded of vids showing
icebergs breaking away from glaciers in the cold south
seas. Screams filled the air as the innocent were
crushed. We were showered only with brick dust; for
long moments we lay there, attempting to recover.

"You still all right?" she asked.

"Barely," I said. "How about you?"

"Great," she said, coughing and brushing dust away.
"Fucking great. You were saying—"

"A plan," I repeated, rising. Uninjured passerbys
were at work pulling the shoes from the feet sticking
out of the bricks and iron.

"What?"

"We've got to act nonchalant," I said.

"Nonchalant," she said, pointing down the street.
The black Redstar turned the corner onto B, entering
the narrow street's heavy traffic.

"Follow my lead," I said, taking her hand. An old
man with a bag of candy bars attempted to sell us one
as we passed. We stepped beside a food wagon; a

147

woman there sold lumps of akee and chunks of ice soaked in coconut milk.

"That's our only choice?"

"It'll have to do. Let's go." We edged between a fruit cart and a peddler hawking wallet-sized calculators.

"Looking nonchalant," said Avalon. The Redstar came closer.

"Naturally," I said, "But be ready for anyth—"

The grenade fired from the Redstar hit the woman's cart; coconut ice fell from the sky like hail.

"Move!" I yelled, and we ran up the street; a block ahead, a cab had paused, stalled by the passage of people walking across. At once I saw what to do and nodded to Avalon; she'd already seen. She ran around; hopped into the front passenger seat. I rushed over, opening the driver's door.

"Sorry," I said, heaving him into the street. Another missile shot past us, hitting a restaurant across the way. I was sure that this bunch had to be Home Army undercover, for their aim was so bad. As I sat behind the wheel, it occurred to me that there might be a problem, but I had no time to fret. The cab was an ancient overdubbed Mustang with what I thought was a shift and clutch—driving was something I never had to do in my daily work.

"Get outta here, Shamey—" Avalon shouted. I judged that if I worked the pedals like a bicycle's we might move, and so began jerking the cab ahead. Lurch, jump, stop; lurch, jump, stop. By accident I slipped the shift into the right gear and we took off. Another blast sounded behind us. The path ahead was reasonably clear; the crowd scrambled to get out of our way.

"Come on. O'Malley, drive!" Looking in the rearview I saw the boys coming furious-fast in their Redstar.

"I'm trying," I mumbled, attempting to shift into another gear; the car's engine groaned, and we swerved into a clump of peds that hadn't yet found security, bowling them over; it didn't seem wise for us to stop and offer apology. At Eighth Street I turned left; our car wasn't picking up speed.

"You know how to drive a shift?" Avalon asked, calmly.

"I've watched Jimmy," I said.

"The limo's automatic."

I pulled, by accident, onto the sidewalk, avoiding a ditch, and we smashed through a cluster of street vendors, scattering their wares. We almost stalled; awful grinding noises came from the shift as I tried to force it into place.

"You know how to drive?" Avalon asked.

"Sort of—"

"*E!*" She reached out, grabbing the shift knob. "Move over," she said, scooting over, taking the wheel. "Get," she said, lifting herself past me. "I can't drive sittin' in your lap." I pulled myself over to the passenger side. In admiration I watched her rush through the gears.

"They still back there?" she asked; we took off through the old park and then down Ninth as if we'd been kicked.

I looked. "Forty back," I said. "They're crossing the avenue."

"What avenue?"

"A. The exit's at Third and Fourteenth. Let's break and fly uptown."

"Why?"

"They won't shoot at us in Secondary Zones," I said. "I hope."

We reached Third in a matter of minutes. She cut right over-fast, bumping over a shallow excavation, skidding onto the sidewalk, then pulled the car back into the street. A kid stepped into our path, pulling his box behind him on a wagon of rude construction. We didn't hit him but we did hit his box, scattering the components. Speakers and knobs rained onto the sidewalks. I felt sorry for him, remembering the box I'd had as a child; it took me two years to steal all the parts.

"When we get up there," I said, "drive onto the sidewalk. It'll be easier to get through the ped turnstiles and they aren't that well built. There should be room enough."

"There'd better be," she said. "Duck under the dash."

We were going forty or so, approaching the barricade. As I dove to the floor I saw the Army boys raise their rifles; massive steel plates sprouted from the street's roadbed, looking like flowers blooming. Avalon held tight to the bottom half of the wheel as she slid down in the seat, keeping her foot full on the gas. The windshield shattered under fire as we hit the turnstiles; we kept going.

"Keep going straight," I shouted. I rose and looked behind us. No one fired at our pursuers; they rolled down the 1A lane as if going to a funeral.

"Shit," Avalon said, slowing as traffic thickened. "I don't know how Jimmy does it."

Traffic was quite heavy in the Murray/Gramercy Secondary Zone, and we had to go much more slowly. We'd gained enough distance to have left the Redstar ten lengths or so behind. She pulled the cab ahead as she could, scraping along, stopping two or three times in every block; our followers, luckily, had to do the same. It seemed safer, just then, to stay in the car and not stop to run for it.

"Something burning?" I asked sniffing the air.

"The car," she said. "Musta knocked something loose when we crashed through. We gotta do something quick."

Wispy smoke drifted from beneath the hood as we passed Thirty-fourth. Our stalkers neared and attempted to pull closer to us; an Entenmann's van blocked their approach. They were so near that I thought I might be able to size them onceover better. I was more than surprised to see one of the lads ready his bazooka.

"Floor it," I shouted. Avalon roared ahead, pushing through a break in traffic; the van that saved us shattered as it blew, spraying dessert fragments blockwide.

"I thought you said they wouldn't shoot at us up here."

"They're not supposed to."

Avalon pulled in front of another cab, cutting it off. "*Culo!*" the cabbie shouted as we passed. "Fuckin' asshole!" Speeding up, he rammed against our side with his cab.

"Fuck off!" Avalon yelled back, slamming back against him. The smoke coming from our engine grew darker, and richer. The boys behind us fired again, blasting the attack cab.

"They're going to get us, next—"

"Maybe not," she said. "Look." After Thirty-seventh Street, Third Avenue had been closed to traffic; there seemed to have been a blast from a different source. Glass rang like wind chimes as it showered the street from above; black smoke billowed from what had been the penthouse of Conbroco. Strikes were common enough in Secondary Zones; this event was no more than a hiccup, and the blockades were haphazard.

"We can get through, I think."

"I got an idea," she said, breaking the police barriers. "I saw it in a movie, once."

"What movie?"

"Robert Mitchum was in it. Drug runnin', I think. Out in Kentucky or Tennessee somewhere."

Cutting the wheel, she simultaneously stepped on the emergency brake. It might have been a good idea had we been driving a different car. We spun in a tight circle in the middle of Third; I knew how Crazy Lola must have felt. Following our whirl, I judged that the plan was to take off in the opposite direction, but when she hit the gas once more we slipped into reverse.

"Hold on," she shouted, shaking the gearshift; it wobbled loosely, as if unattached. Shooting backward at twenty per, smashing the barriers at the far end of the blast zone, we entered traffic less heavy than that through which we had previously driven, coming to rest against a storefront on the west side of the avenue. The boys in the Redstar sighted and sped toward us, apparently certain that head-on would do us fine.

"O'Malley," she screamed, seeing them near, "get out."

"The door's stuck," I replied, pushing. She started shoving me as I shoved at the door. I looked up. A Fun City tour bus filled with business travelers (required by their employers in the outback to see New York and be grateful) turned a corner, blocking us off as it paused to let traffic move ahead. The Redstar—a solid, plated vehicle—struck the bus broad. The bus tipped slowly toward us; the passengers within surely wondered if this was part of the tour.

"Got it," I said, feeling as if I had broken my shoulder. The door swung open; we fell out. The store against which we'd crashed was some sort of booty; we pulled ourselves inside, finding that the gates were open and the entrance unlocked. The bus fell onto our cab; a clerk within the store leapt forward, pressing a button to raise the store's steel shield. There was time enough for it to rise halfway before the vehicles blew.

We were flung to the far end of the shop, sailing down the side aisle's floor as if on a slide. The shield fell inward; the store's fixtures tumbled. The blast's wind spread the fire throughout the front half of the establishment; sprinklers showered water over us as the alarms rang. We suffered nothing more disabling than lacerations and minor burns. Opening my eyes I vizzed what at first I took to be the crushed plaster chest of a mannequin. A charred *I ♡ Love New York* banner was wrapped around her waist.

One clerk survived, emerging stealthily from behind the former checkout. He looked at us through the black smoke and hazy rain. *Forget your receipt,* the register repeated. *Don't forget. Your receipt.—*

As we ran out onto Forty-first Street, a fresh Redstar turned the corner toward us.

"Well?" she said. "Now?"

"In here," I said, rushing across the street as I took her hand, dashing between cars. "Quick."

At Third and Forty-first was a grand old hotel built in pre-Ebb heyday. Its mirrored skin shone scarred gilt; raw plywood covered half the windows. A sign near the lobby entrance announced the arrival of the Beach Boys for one week in the Metrolounge. I suspected we could avoid our latest fans by cutting through the lobby. We flashed the guards—pox-scarred fourteen-year-olds—our 1A cards and were allowed in; we maneuvered into the atrium.

"Should we run?" she whispered.

"No," I said. "Those guards are paid to suspect. The little bastards all use superstars." I referred to the razoredge pentagrams they tossed to deter. "Look as if we're meeting someone."

"Here?"

Judging from the crowd the place remained popular. Eighty tons of marble covered the atrium walls; graffiti intensified the stone's natural patterns, close to the floor, where inscribers needed not to stretch that they might scrawl and carve. The twenty-story escalators—none working—resembled girders dropped accidentally from above; the hanging gardens had hung and gone to dust; colored lights made cheery the trash clogging the fountains. Pigeons fluttered through the atrium's free air and caucused on the floor; their guano whitened the balconies. Vidiac played over half the monitors; on the others, the images rolled and flapped as if for art's sake.

"Business trade stay here, probably," I said, peering about.

"Let's get out of here, Shameless."

"There's probably an exit this way. Let's check."

In public buildings public space was yielded to the use of public organizations; here, the Army and the Health Service were boothed. Recruitment posters plastered the Army's, crying for Manhattan's youth—those sans connections—to register and so be drafted: *It's Fun. It's Easy. It's Duty. It's Law.* Above each health booth's counter was a reproduction of a painting of E, his eyes shut, begarbed in white, on one knee, touching his left hand to his brow as if he had reached the chorus and forgotten the words. In his right hand he held an embryo: A NEW LIFE MAY BE IN YOUR HANDS, the sign above read, STOP BABY KILLINGS. On the counter of each health booth, below the painting, were jars. Within the jars, floating as if on summer breezes, were aging fetuses, each thrusting tiny fingers toward the guilty. Capital offense or not, the law had never been so effective as wished; in private hands, where, as the government decreed, problems were best solved, there were always wire hangers and chemical solutions. The Army and health booths went well together: one planted, one harvested.

"Shameless—"

At the end of the hallway was a sign identifying the subway entrance. A familiar sound hissed behind us. The missile launched misfired, striking the health booth; it flared, misting pink. A hotel guard tossed a superstar, hitting a stroller close by in the face, slicing dead through.

"Subway," I said, reaching the stairs.

"Is it safe?" The railing broke away as we grasped it; we slid down the stairs. Recovering, we leapt the piles of trash lying underfoot, splashed through puddles of urine, zazzed past the token booth. The clerk shouted at us from behind his lucite shield; we vaulted the turnstiles. Dashing to the platform, we saw a train at the wait and jumped aboard as the doors clanked shut. One of our pursuers, closing in, jumped after; he screamed like an angel as he fell beneath the wheels. We made our way to the last car, knowing that it would be the emptiest.

"Now where?"

"We're on a downbound train," I said, "So—" The train whipped along at five or six miles an hour.

"What's the next stop?"

"Fourteenth, I think."

"Where we started," she sighed.

"We can relax for a few minutes," I said.

We were not alone in the car. There was a pair of midmen, forced for whatever reason to rough it; a gent in a green shirt who tugged at his ears in sequence, repeatedly—they bled; a nondescript, asleep on the floor, whom some had used as a lav; several homebodies, their savings resting in bags between their feet. One fellow, not poorly dressed, sat down the way, calmly throwing up over his pants and shoes. Most of the windows in the car were broken out, only half the lights worked; we kept to the far end of the car, away from the others.

"Better than the fucking bus," Avalon said.

The door to the next car slid open and six young women—four black, two white—clad in ripped fatigues entered; each wore a black fez. They lugged lengths of chain; one shouldered a long spiked pole, at the end of which was impaled a dead rat.

"They don't look like they're up to good, Shamey," Avalon said, "And this fuckin' train is just crawling."

"Ignore them," I said patting her arm. "I'm sure they beat the fare like everyone else."

The leader—lanky, and wearing aubergine shades— stopped near the puking gent. For a moment she eyed him, and then she pulled out her pick and jabbed out his eyes. He stopped throwing up; as he lay on the floor, they freely gave him the boot.

"If need be," I murmured, "can you take the two small ones?"

"Easy."

Shades conferred with her companions; I saw her jacket's colors. They belonged to one of the more problematic gangs, the Whispers of Love.

"Yo," she said, nodding toward us. She smiled; several of her front teeth had been withdrawn.

"Easy action here, sis," said another.

"Surprise them," I whispered from my mouth's corner. "Always works."

They sauntered over, dragging their chains behind them. The little ones appeared to be twins. An exceptionally ugly one tailed; at closer viz I could tell that half of her nose had been bitten off. The one toting the rat lay down her stick as she neared. The one bringing up the rear was sumo-size, carrying an iron pipe. They clustered around us, laughing. The rest of the car emptied.

"Honey, you come down here just to see us?" Shades asked Avalon, tightening her grip on her chain.

"Bitch, what'chu doin' with Percy here?" asked Ugly.

"He look like what the rat drug in," added one of the twins.

"How come you so quiet?" Shades asked. "Boyfriend here wantin' you to behave yourself 'round us nasty girls?"

"Don't fuck yourself over him, babe, you want him, you can have him—"

Ratgirl lit a match and flicked it on me. I brushed it away and smiled.

"Too cool for that, motherfuck?" she said, flicking another at me, which I also brushed away. Ugly reached down, pulling Avalon up by the front of her sweater.

"Let's fuck, bitch. Girl to girl."

Avalon twisted away, turning around as she did. Ugly seized her arms and jerked them behind her back, bending her over until the wall of the car. They noticed the split in her pants and laughed all the louder.

"They was ready, girl—"

"Fuck, yeah, if we hadn't showed they'd be on the floor now."

"Got a sweet ass," said Ugly, ripping Avalon's pants further open and digging in. "Nice, soft pussy—"

Shades pulled a long knife out of her coat. "Be hard for him to fuck if he ain't got nothin' to fuck with," she said, pointing it toward my groin. "What'chu say to that? Huh?" I said nothing; she brought the blade up to my cheek.

"Honey, you know what this boy wants?" said Ratgirl, extracting a length of broomstick from beneath her jacket, slapping it hard against her hand. "He wants some fuckin' of his own."

"Yeah."

"He look like a girl with them big pink lips."

"Let's fuck him first, then."

"Take down those pants, bro, that what you want?" asked Shades. "Huh?"

I said nothing; she pushed her face closer to mine.

"I said, *what* do you *want*?" She dipped the blade into my cheek.

"Your soul," I said, flipping out my chuks. By bringing them up at the right angle I hit her nose at the right spot. She moaned and hit the floor twitching. Avalon pressed her head against the wall for balance and, kicking back with both boots, caught Ugly in the jewels. She fell back, choking; continued to choke until Avalon kicked her in the throat. We turned and looked at the others.

"*God*damn!"

Taking my chuks, I wrapped the chain around Ratgirl's neck; holding fast to the lengths of wood, I twisted them fast as if knotting a tourniquet. As I pulled harder the blood vessels in her face burst beneath her skin as if in time lapse. Avalon reached out; grasping the twins by their collars, she flung them apart and then slammed their heads together as if slapping erasers. There was a sharp crack; she dropped them. That left the big one. She hadn't yet joined in, nor had she run.

"What're you waiting for?" I asked her, dropping Ratgirl.

"The undertaker, man," she said, smashing me across the head with the pipe she carried. "Gonna haul your ass away."

As I fell over I realized that she'd be a challenge. I felt as if my brains were rushing out; my hair seemed thick with blood. Avalon hopped up, dropkicking her in the chest. She staggered but didn't fall; swinging out with her forearm, she knocked Avalon halfway down the car. Blood dripped into my eyes; it was almost impossible to see. When I lose control I tend to lose as well my sense of pain; I was glad, this time. Jumping blindly onto the seat, I ran down to where Avalon had landed. The big one stayed at the opposite end of the car for a second and then barreled toward us. Avalon sprang up, clipping her in the knees. She fell forward, nearly crushing Avalon. The car rattled as she struck the floor; before she had a chance to rise, I grabbed one of the floor-to-ceiling poles, swung once around and heeled her in the jaw. She fell over to one side, hitting her head on the window frame. Avalon picked up the woman's feet and attempted to push her through the window before she could reawaken.

"Gimme a hand," she said, "She's big as a house."

"I don't think she'll be coming around soon," I said. She groaned; I grabbed her legs and started shoving.

"You're hurt," said Avalon.

"Not much," I said, barely able to see or stand. "Push."

As the train at last began speeding, we got her up and over. As she started sliding out she struck one of the tunnel columns and was torn from our hands. Avalon and I fell to the floor as the train crashed to a halt. For what seemed a blessedly long time we lay there. Then Avalon sat up, holding her arm.

"What happened?" she asked.

"We must have derailed," I said, dragging myself to my feet. The car was tilted several degrees to the right. "We could be stuck for hours. Come on. Out the back."

Forcing open the rear door, we stepped down onto the tracks. One of the tunnel lights illuminated she upon whom the train had derailed. We moved uptown once more, keeping to the rails when possible; the catwalk on the left was crumbling away, and where the ties were visible above the still pools of water they were rotten and worn. The working tunnel lights and the soft glow from the old station ahead guided our path as we moved along.

"What station's that?" she asked.

"I think it's Twenty-third." On the walls of the tunnel were the names of the vanquished, scrawled and etched in days long past.

"It'll be closed, won't it?"

"Yeah. We can sit down. Rest." Subway entrances were open only at zone borders, so that closer control might be kept. In a short silent time we reached the station and lifted ourselves onto the platform—well, nearly; I was so sore that Avalon had to help me up. It was difficult to see through the dim yellow light even after our eyes adjusted. The station walls were dabbed with a forty years' palimpsest, name over name over name. The stairs once leading to the street were blocked off by concrete slabs.

"Let me see your head."

When she touched my scalp I thought for a moment that I'd pass out.

"That hurt?" she asked, pulling back my hair. "Shit."

"It does," I said. "What is it?"

"There's a gash about six inches long. No wonder it hurts."

"Can you see the bone?"

"No. It needs stitches."

"The blood's clotting?"

"Mostly."

"It'll be all right, then. I keep gauze in my right pocket. Get it."

She did, pressing it down onto my wound. With effort I remained conscious. She placed more gauze onto my head and then wrapped a bandage around it. She pulled off Enid's bright jacket and took off her sweater. Kneeling before me, she wrapped the sweater around my head and tied the arms together, knotting them so that it wouldn't slip. She giggled, finishing.

"What is it?"

"You look awfully silly," she laughed. "That'll help, maybe. It's not bleeding as much."

"I've had worse."

"I'm sure," she said, sitting beside me. Her nipples rose sharp in the cool air.

"Put your jacket on," I said. "You'll catch cold."

"I'd rather sit on it," she said, "long as we're sitting." She leaned forward, took one of my hands and placed it on her breast. "That'll do."

We sat on the dirty concrete, retrieving our breath. Another train wouldn't be by for an hour, if at all—they usually stopped sooner on weekends, I gathered. In the tunnels resounded no sounds but those of our breathing, and of the drip of water.

"Have I been getting more like them?" I asked.

"What are you talking about?"

"Like the Drydens. Do you think I've been starting to get more like them?"

"Why do you think that?"

"I don't know. It worried me."

"You might be," she said. "I guess anyone would if they had the chance."

She put her arms around my waist. I kissed her; we kissed for what seemed an endless time, probably a few seconds.

"What are we going to do tonight, Shamey?"

"I think Enid can help us."

"Won't they still have the apartment tabbed?"

161

"She won't be there," I said, "We'll have to meet her."

"Where? If we go back up—"

"We won't be going back onto the street. Not yet. We'll be staying in the subway."

"Down here?"

"She'll be about forty blocks down and three blocks over, roughly."

"What'll she be doing down there?"

"Going to church," I said.

Avalon looked at me, shook her head, and shrugged. She lay down, gently tugging me along with her, resting me between her legs.

"Just lie here," she said. "Rest."

"All right. It shouldn't take us that long to get down there."

She shushed me. "Safe now," she said, stroking my face. "Safely sound."

For a few minutes, at least, I rested; my pain whelmed over. Care's nurse kissed shut my eyes. Freedom rang.

10

ONCE I RECOVERED—SOMEWHAT—AND AVALON HAD rested, we climbed back down onto the tracks and aimed downtown once again, walking the northbound tracks to avoid the train we'd derailed. It was still there as we passed; probably no one had yet noticed its absence. We returned to the southbound tracks not long after, at Avalon's request, but there was nothing to fear. No trains shuttled by in either direction as we strode along.

We continued through the tunnel for miles, for hours, or so it felt, landing our feet upon the ties wherever possible. From what Enid had told me I knew roughly when services began; knew the old East Broadway station of the abandoned F line served as the congregation place. I hoped to time our appearance so that we wouldn't disturb their service; for interlopers to appear at Under the Rock was something that none of them would appreciate.

We passed into the tunnel that led to the F line, off the old Bleecker Street station.

"You sure you know where we're going?" Avalon panted, splashing along.

"Positive," I said. "I've just never been down here before. Have to take it a little slowly—"

"Then how do you know where we're going?"

I didn't answer; my head hurt, still, and it took all concentration to go where we went, the way I felt. The tunnel was so clammy that even the air felt slimy against my face. It was unseeably black through there; I kept a long flash in my pocket, and so took it out, turned it on, and shone a thin cord of light into the darkness. Clouds of bats pitched as we awakened them; they resettled as we passed. Guano lay deep upon the slippery rails. We waded through stagnant pools; when we trod the ties here, the decaying wood felt spongelike through the soles of our shoes. Drips echoed in every corner. We reached a quadrant where the side wall had collapsed onto the tracks.

"What now?" Avalon asked; I helped her climb over. I followed, picking my way across the damp rubble. On the other side we glimpsed flickering light further down, past a bend, and heard music.

"That's it," I said. "Come on."

A few feet along I noticed a board hanging from the tunnel's roof, and turned my flash upon it. There was an inscription painted on it:

> *Weep not, afear not, we are blessed,*
> *And in black heaven we'll turn to thee;*
> *In ure evermore, where wearish rest,*
> *Where the wicked suffer. Come to me.*

"What's it mean?" Avalon asked.

"It's just a threat." I switched off my flash. The

music's vol upped as we neared; through baffling echoes I distinguished the instruments—flutes and recorders, kotos and drums. Only secular Ambient music employed the human voice, for which I was grateful.

"Be very quiet," I whispered. "It's still going on. We want to wait until they're through. Then we'll find Enid."

"You sure she'll be there?"

"Yeah." As we drew closer, the light illuminated the tunnel so far down as we were—some sort of torchlight, it appeared. Before we rounded the bend, a resounding cry arose from the unseen crowd; the music stopped. Someone began speaking in a deep voice. Creeping closer, attempting to see without being seen, I viewed the platform; Avalon, keeping behind me, looked out, gasped, and fell back.

"Shameless," she said, breathless. "Fucking hell—"

"What's the matter?"

"What's the *matter*?" she repeated. "Look!"

I did, carefully vizzing the speaker. "I thought he sounded familiar," I said. "That's Derek. He lived down the street from me the first year we moved down. He comes to the club every once in a while."

"You know it?"

"I know him, yes."

Holding tight to Avalon's hand, kneeling, I scooted up to the very edge of the platform, and peered above. All assembled faced the opposite direction, toward Derek, away from us; the light was not so good that we could be easily seen in any event. The station consisted of a long platform with tracks edging each side; along the platform edge, down its length, long poles set at intervals held torches aloft. The crowd was large; I spotted few familiar faces at once. Derek, at the speaker's platform, held forth.

"—in the third book of the Visions of Joanna, we

play in cue, likeminded, as Macaffrey spears tongue to lying soulsmerchants, pickspittles limp with clotting bile, cullions and jabbernowls and skinpeeled fools. Dust-kittens of thought blow about their balking heads. Logic grays, withers, and sprouts green mold as their mouths let drop idle lists—''

Derek was a dogboy, covered with long hair—once blond, now dark brown—from top of head to tip of toe; he wore a black suit and black shirt. Like all original Ambients, he was several years younger than I. We never spoke much, as children; even when so young Ambients preferred their own company, and I'm sure that they awed my friends so much as they awed me— it was one of those things no one ever really talked about. The platform on which he stood was quite low, not more than a foot high; Ambients prefer reasonably equal footing for all within their group. As Enid explained to me, they each spoke in turn every month, so that one day all would have had a chance to speak.

''—her heart beats Macaffrey's. Her eyes viz plain, see what goes, and catch what gives. In his induration within and through their perfect union he holds nada nadie to that which God demands, but to that which Godness lawed, he lets fright settle and earfastens yet, espying the time—''

Ambients used parts of the Bible and a book called the Visions of Joanna in their services; I'd read Enid's copies of the latter, both in its original form and in Ambient translation. Ambients preferred those characters in the Bible whom they saw as never having been given their due—Cain, Ham, Esau, Judas, and now Jesus—and developed, through the messages of Macaffrey as told by Joanna, a most remarkable viewpoint of the Creator: that It had split into two intelligences during the act of Creation, one male, and evil; one female, and good—both driven quite insane by having created what They had. What one did, the other undid, and vice versa. As I've said, I'm not one for dogma of any sort, but that concept did cover much that was questionable.

"These are the days that change. Time runs bird-wild, and none snare the shadows ascamp before them. No more. Paint shades pale, set passion aflaming, alight all eyes with will-o'-the-wisp and ringgold. Dance light over their walls, on their streets; deny no truth, suffer no fools. They cling to dead past like flies to paper. Each year skips no ho and they further yark and fetter themselves tight with their own dead bowels, encanted by the dread of time lostbegone. We seize time's wings, to our own flight give rise. What's done is done; what was, was. What is, is, will be, can be, might be, must be. Memory steals. Promise gives."

Together, the unity was called Godness—for Joanna felt that the better of the two should be most recognized. Macaffrey, the story went, came as Messiah just before the Ebb and proceeded to suffer the traditional fate of messiahs. Joanna spread the word he brought. Among Ambients it remained a common, if generally unspoken, belief that she yet lived, hiding away somewhere in the wilds of Long Island. Much Ambient exigesis had been written concerning her book; the final inferred belief was that someday, somehow, an Ambient would effect the changes that made whole the two and therefore bring forth a new Godness, supreme in logic and in fairness.

"Godness who lends morningshade's light, Godness who struck the moon with fire; Godness who rolls the thunder, who rages the sea, who splits the earth and laughs as children weep; Godness who lurks in sky's white cotton, who blinds eye and deafens ear, take our heed. Where there are two, make one. Seal covenant soon. Spit back our tears. Take fire and burn. He who asks for crime, She who asks for blessing. He who curses, She who kisses. He who wishes vengeance, She who wants for love. Feel glory's voice, and give cause to beat our hearts hereafter—''

Till time's lovely end. Behind Derek was the old stairway, long blocked off with concrete slabs. Painted on that wall was a representation, artfully executed, of Godness, as Ambients conceived. The portrait showed a massive, naked figure, possessing the marks of both sexes, poised on the edge of a crevasse. The darkness below its webbed feet spread upward, surrounding the figure. From the mouth down there was one; from the mouth upward there were two heads, and two faces, squashed together as if in a vise. Godness held Its hands above Its head, gripping the world in Its paws, preparing to dash it into the abyss below.

The congregation lifted voice in concluding prayer.

"To Godness the Ten In One," Derek intoned.

"Godness Father," they cried.

"Godness Son."

"Godness Mother."

"Godness Daughter."

"Godness Brother."

"Godness Sister."

"Godness Friend."

"Godness Lover."

"Godness Creator."

"Godness Destroyer."

"*Eyes alight!*" someone shouted.

"We're spotted," I said.

"Should we run?"

"Don't even move."

As they turned to face us, their forms yellow silhouettes in the pale light, I saw not only those with whom I'd always felt comfortable through familiarity, but also ones the likes of whom I'd never believed existed, no matter Enid's occasional remarks; it seemed unlikely that they could have survived birth, much less aged, and thrived. Avalon slumped as I held her; for a moment I think that she passed out, though she later denied it. Ambients started hopping down onto the tracks; they slithered forward, they rolled along. I saw Ruben and Lester; saw too the bartender who'd served me two nights past. I saw as well a girl with two bodies joined at a single head; a man with three heads, none absolutely complete, as if the sculptor had forgotten where to put what; a woman, a true mermaid, her lower limbs fused, and ending in a wide, toed fin; a woman with three legs, balancing as if on a tripod; a set of Siamese triplets; a gent whose arms ended in two hands, on both wrists. There were voluntary Ambients, lacking eyes, noses, jaws, arms, legs, hands, or feet; there were transies; there were two small ones, whom I've not seen since, and wish I'd never seen. They resembled nothing so much as ambulatory, sentient bunches of grapes. Nearly everyone carried cuchillos, or machetes, or chainsaws of the type Enid had given me. Lester, maskless, his features tightset on me, perched at the edge of the platform.

"O'Malley," he said, snarling. "Adventure enow abounds topside. Dip your paws in hives of wasps if stings so allure."

"I'm sorry," I said, trying to calm them; Avalon fastened her arms so tight around me that I suspected—were they to pounce—that they should have to pry her away with crowbars. "We didn't wish to interrupt—"

"Come bezzling our world and apprise your chance once-over," said a fellow walking toward us, his single eye, set in his forehead, glaring.

"Ours isn't yours. Yours isn't ours."

"Viz the whipperginny leeched to his beef," a woman said. "His owner's pie, plump with death's fruit."

"Is Enid here?"

"Number your reasons," said one, his lips' corners nearly touching his ears as he grinned. "In steady haste."

"Seamus," I heard her shout; it had taken her a moment to realize who had interrupted, and then additional seconds to push through the crowd. She wore her leatherette jumpsuit with the wide padded shoulders. "What goes?"

"We didn't have any choice," I said.

She leapt down onto the tracks, coming briskly toward us. I felt Avalon's grip tighten; felt it hard to breathe. "Your presence denudes dreams carefully clothed. You know—"

"Enid," I said. "I'm sorry. Something happened. We were being chased. We couldn't go back to the apartment. We didn't have any other way of reaching you."

She sighed, smiling; looked us over, paying particular attention to the haphazard turban wound round my head. "Did you ride behind the train that took you down?"

"We kept running into people—"

"Bear us wist, and hold, Enid," someone said. "Your copesmates eye wary."

"From under lumps of gold serpent's heads lure with poison tongue aflick," said the woman wearing a long blue nightshirt; she looked almost normal, until beneath the brighter light I saw that each eye held two pupils. "He may stand yet to let trail bastard scutches trip fast upon our track."

"Bepissing us," said another, "striking deep with artful craft."

A young girl pushed forward, holding a tissue to her large blue eyes—eyes constantly tearing, eyes set at the end of short talks rising from her face.

"Lozel's paws roam free from oppro knocks," she said. "And set a bridge aspan to owner's shores. We know those ways, no matter how thick the blood of sisters runs."

"Leah—" Enid began to say, but was interrupted.

"Leaving prints on every mind," she went on, "setting aghast the undeserving. Smudging all the woodworm ways. Sighting their paths ariding death's baby carriage. A secret stolen is a secret lost, Enid. A labyrinth broached sets loose the minotaur. Danger's end must need quicken—"

"Bestill your mouth!" Enid shouted, moving next to me, raising her arms as if setting to fight. "My brother knows and respects our ways. He comes not incog, wrapped tight in liar's shrouds. Seamus seeks his sister's shoulder, thereon to set his head."

"Yet bonaroly there moves in mysterious ways, her wonders to deform," said Ruben, staring at Avalon. "So vulture-eyed and leering prim. Last eve she tarried en casa, Enid. In su casa. When morningshade sent Serena off, beasts set aprowl through our hough."

"One we axed onehand," Lester laughed.

"Her charms seduce Seamus's flesh," Ruben continued. "Drives him hard to twist and turn. What if her fire blinds his eye and burns his sense away?"

"Toss by and see," Enid snapped. "There is naught to fear—"

"Mayhap your sense is singed by brotherlove," Derek said, brushing hair away from his mouth. "His fornicatress might with ease slink murder past as you viz on, brow dim with thought of one who was, but is no more."

"Bloody bloody balls," said Enid, her voice low.

"Those who folly deceive," screamed another, in the back, "deceive all else so well—"

"Folly *is* as folly *does*," yelled Margot, swinging

her swordstick, sidescuttling forth like a crab. She jumped down onto the tracks with a thud and waddled toward us; I groaned as she once more stamped upon my foot, digging in those nails. "Reason runs when fear trips by. Lay still minds ablather and hear me."

They settled; Margot was considered by all to be one of the most logical—and meanest—of their number. Her words usually stuck where she threw them.

"Mewlypuke stands tall here, tall and stupid," she said, gesturing to me. "His lollipop, the same. What sins they tote are writ plain on their eyebrows. Words of smoke these hoblobs grunt. Clench easy if you stand to hold, but for whose point? Prick pimples into ulcers for so much good as that."

"They're not of us, Margot—"

"Caprichos up and down," she said, poking Avalon in the stomach with her stick. "Here. Can't reap what can't be sown. And eye those shiny whites filling her puss. Pop them out and old gummy granny grins. As for him—" Taking her stick, lifting it, she brought it down cleanly, knocking off my remaining ear. "Ambients both," she said, flashing her sharp teeth. "Angels unaware, mayhap. Fools sans money, morelike. So you would carve your own? Tear the flesh that binds you? Spill the blood that sets you springing? Go, then. Do your will. But bear my words on bitter days later."

Margot's tact carried; the crowd relaxed. Undercurrents of words suggested that they all gave pause to thought.

"Go your ways," she said. "Spend your fear in worthy guise. Peak your wonder and off. Enid and I shall layaway the cullions to the safe house."

The group dispersed, eyeing us carefully as they disappeared into the tunnel's void.

"Margot, thanks—" I began saying; she laid her stick hard across my knees. I nearly fell down.

"Brainsitter," she said, crossing over to Enid. "For your loving sis I overed and conned and extraughted your way clear."

"Whatever," I said, rubbing my knees. "I'm glad it worked."

"Who reddied your sconce?" she asked, peering upward. "Fools attempting to pound sense therein?"

"They weren't that charitable," I said. "Where are you going to take us?"

"Home would be best," said Enid. "But if what you list holds, they'll keep lights on for you all over. There'll be no rubs at the safe house. There you'll stay womb-safe."

"How'll we get there?" asked Avalon.

"Trip with us in like paths, headbent evernear," said Margot. "You'll settle soon enow."

Avalon looked puzzled, as if she didn't understand.

"Will there be anything to eat there?"

"Corpsechewers may gnaw their own picked bones—"

"Don't pish them so, Merricat," said Enid, reknotting my turban. "There'll be food of basic type."

"Good."

"Ready and ablewill, then. Breeze with us now," said Enid.

"Will they find us?" asked Avalon. "Where we're going?"

"Once we skim they'll find us not at all," said Margot. "Time weighs heavy and this station stinks with fear like fusty rooms. The low road awaits. We'll slip away. Up and over, around and down."

Enid pulled an extra flash from her jacket and pitched it to Avalon. Her own chainsaw swung freely below her arm, beneath her wrap. She picked up Margot, perching her behind her head, on her shoulders; Margot's stubby legs vised Enid's neck. She grasped Enid's spikes as if to steer.

"Those torches'll be all right?" I asked.

"Gas," said Enid, "eternal flames."

"I didn't know Con Ed still worked down here."

"Nor do they."

Just into the tunnel, beyond the light, I detected an unexpected odor. Waving my flash along the walls, I saw iron cages hanging from the overhead girders. In the cages were corpses of advanced grades.

"Overzealous explorers," explained Enid, "who go because it's there."

"And they're there," said Margot, "because we're here."

With every step it became clear to me that during our adventures I'd pulled all of my muscles while breaking my bones.

"At our casa you whiled last eve?" Enid asked. "In our room?"

"Yes," I said.

"Bedded there to bide away with sweetums?" she said. "Have we then lost what Godness lent us to keep?"

"Sanity?" I asked.

"I spec he was all agog to let swive her unshelled motherspearl," said Margot. "Much maidenhead *he'll* answer for at trumpet-time."

"While leaving by traditional modes. In hand awaits ever relief's sweet kiss," said Enid.

"His paws linger to grope grander fare, in glory high."

"Miss me?" I asked Margot.

"In your absence," she sighed, "so heartfond was I that all clouds above turned gray-gold light."

"You understand them?" Avalon asked me.

"Sure," I said.

"Why do you talk like that?" she asked them.

"Our gab leaves weak minds apuzzle," said Margot. "With it we select who gives ear."

Avalon stared at Enid; vizzed Margot bobbing along. "Aren't those nails painful?" she asked.

"For those who fall upon," said Enid.

"A look as death redoubled finifies you," said Margot, turning to eye Avalon. "Wherein did mewly press you on?"

"Pardon?"

"Flying you after airy promise and painted allure?"

"What?"

Margot laughed. "New bonnets for old boneache."

"You'll pick it up after a time," I told Avalon.

Enid steered her flash toward a dark passage leading off to the right. "Waysalong here. Through the dark dark deep."

"This looks pleasant," I said; our coils of light streamed into the passage's depths. It appeared no more than a crude tunnel chiseled through. The chipped walls were daubed with niter, and cobwebs; splashes of fungus enlivened the monochrome of the rock. "Where does it go?"

"Follow," she said. "We adapted this to all purposes."

"Come this way often?" Avalon asked me.

"Often enough," Margot said, overhearing. "Such a traipse encows you, sweets?"

"I wasn't talking to you," Avalon said.

"Your flabberskin all acreep?" Margot continued, so keen to annoy as Enid wished to overlook. "These wet walls dry your own as sludge bemires your twinkling toes?"

"There's no need to be so fuckin' nasty—" Avalon shouted.

"No need but much desire."

175

"Hushabye!" said Enid, stopping in midstride. "Don't spend useful air ticing words to fill. Both assail overmuch overlong. Hush and carry forth."

We hadn't gotten much further along before Avalon spoke once more.

"What's your problem, anyway?" she asked Margot. "You act like you think everyone's against you."

Margot, hearing this, laughed; had I not known her for so long as I had, hearing that sound echoing through the dark would have given rise to deepest terror. Her gaiety's rasp raked the skin bloody raw.

"Think?" she said, calming enough to speak. "Know. Know now, knew then, shall ever know."

"What makes you think anyone cares?"

Margot turned her head, slowly, so as to face Avalon as we pulled along. With the prescience so common to born Ambients I knew she'd deciphered the inherent fear underlying Avalon's distaste.

"Even in limoed path our way lends pause to smug minds," she said. "See us and see what dwells deep under seemly form, beneath blue eyes and golden mops. No shelter gives shield to our constancy. Our fire sets its own track, and by our glow, the blind see. The deaf hear. The unknowing know. Those unafraid tremble and shake."

"I didn't even know what Ambients were—" Avalon tried to say.

"In younger time, nada listened and nada heard," Margot shot back. "But our shouts painted the air even as we parted our mother's legs. As their docs lifted up high, vizzed and swooned, we hollered blast at that we reached unwanted. The gov buzzed and clucked and left us to lozel's paws and the tests of wrinkle-wizzers. Pillpushers took our tears to make for spit. But no one wanted but those who bore. All others stilled their games and let drop their chains. Had they pick they'd have doublebagged us and dropped us full fathom doubledeep. They didn't. So they skipped, and so we sprouted, cleaved from all eight times tripleover. All viz early when vizzing with Ambient eyes. So we vizzed, looking in mirrors, aghast at what we saw. We knew.''

As Margot spoke, the most peculiar sense appeared in her voice's tone—that, I think, is the only way it may be properly described. It seemed a sense not so much of regret as of disgust; not so filled with sadness as with a sense of waste.

''None but our bearers cared,'' Margot continued. ''And one by one they shuffled off. We kept alone. Given wood for cake and stones for bread, our way lined each morn with numps and nowls and gagtoothed pricksters all achant, bespewing larkish cries of *freak-freak-freak*. . . . Blood drained alone speckles and tars where one may stand. Blood drained from all at once floods high and drowns those who break the wounds. So by the Goblin Year we'd sealed our bond; to our own and to our own only, keep ever true. We buried ourselves neath the stones they tossed. Made ourselves fast within the splits of the sticks they slung. Our teeth chop hard when idle fingers pry, and so we chopped when need called. We took the Godness they tossed off so freely and vizzed in whose image our own forms took shape. The wise, then, forbear, and leave us as we list, and one morn our sun shall shine—

''The wild wind reaps. The seed sowed grows the fruit as given. This sorry world's ear listens in vain. We speak to the new world, await solution for the trials bespoken. For oppro to set loose over the windfuckers who troubled then and trouble now. A chance regiven for all, in all, and to all, for a world so new it's not out of the box. The slow fasts, the last firsts. As shall we.''

The tunnel narrowed before it widened again, and

with some effort we all scraped through. We reached what appeared once to have been one of the old equipment rooms.

"There aren't enough of you to change anything," said Avalon.

"In form, no," said Margot. "In spirit, twenty times redoubled. Our pest spreads like bloody flux. Once the bonebag withers, the soul goes traipsing light. Ambient *is* as Ambient *does*, at end's turn. To know us is to be us."

"I'm not Ambient," said Avalon.

"Time tells," said Margot, "time sees. *He* knows." She nodded toward me, and smiled.

"Here now," said Enid, gesturing toward a metal disc embedded in the floor's wet concrete. "Lift away, Seamus."

As I lifted the heavy cover, hundreds of enormous beetles dripped off, dropping down my sleeves, falling onto the floor, scurrying away over our shoes. I tossed the lid away; my yipes resounded.

"I so hate those beasts," said Enid, lowering her flash.

"You don't mind them at home," I said, brushing off strays.

"In casa they move in gentle shape," she said. A ladder led downward, I saw, its rungs glistening. Enid motioned for me to go first. I did; they followed. It smelled worse here than it had in the subway, or in the street. For long minutes I felt stifled, as if my head had been unwrapped in filthy bags; then my nose grew used to it, and I could breathe once more. Aiming my flash in all directions, once down, I saw that we were in another tunnel, half the size of the subway. In it stood water two feet deep, black and smooth.

"Where are we?" Avalon asked; I helped her off the

ladder, letting her straddle my back so as to keep her
feet out of the water as we danced through.

"In the sewers," I said. "One of the old mainlines,
judging from the size."

"Bearing east," said Enid, Margot holding tight to
her spikes.

We splashed through the murk as if through a bog in
the night. Our flashes cast weak reflections here, as if
the air was too sodden to permit the light's unsullied
flow. Even on these walls graffiti was scrawled, the let-
tering dimmed and gray. Besides the slow rush of water, the only sounds were the chirping of rats and the
occasional hiss of what I—romantic I—imagined to be
alligators. The rats in the old sewers were more unsettling than any alligator; nasty brutes two feet long or
more, scampering and swaying at the edges of the brick
crawlways, swimming downstream with us, as if waiting for us to dive or fall below. They didn't come too
close; I suppose Enid and Margot scared them away.

"How much farther, Enid?" I asked, after what
seemed an eternity. I felt near collapse.

"Down here and right. Then up, up, up."

We reached another ladder; Enid set Margot upon
the rungs and turned off her flash. Looking up, I could
see that above this exit there was no cover; diffuse light
poured down from above. We climbed up; reached the
top and crawled out. I looked around; my eyes were
still adjusting to the brighter dark.

"Where are we now?" I asked.

"Near to riveredge," said Enid.

We stood in an intersection, in the midst of an old
housing project. Moonlight seemed to cause the fog to
glow and swirl around us. Buildings rose high on every
side, black hulks with edges blurred as if for camouflage. When I was young, people still lived in these
places, but before the Ebb, a ruling came down that

the state had no legal right to provide anyone's housing, for to provide housing to some was unfair to those who didn't need it. Everyone was evicted and left bare to street's equality.

"Enid—" I began saying as we trudged down the street; our shoes splashed out lakes of filthy water behind us.

"That building center. Ours."

"Then what?"

"Over and up."

The fog grew more dense as we approached the river. The huge buildings huddled in clusters as if in mutual protection. The dusty yards once surrounding the blocks had become jungles of wild scrub and ailanthus, and impenetrable grass. Roots of dead trees buckled the sidewalks, and their limbs entwined overhead; through their tunnels we now passed. Between their spidery arms swept lights from copters buzzing far overhead. I no longer suspected that we were being followed. From across the river we heard the kiss of distant shells as they landed.

"You know this part of town?" Avalon asked.

"I haven't been down here in years."

"It's horrible."

"Peaceful," I said.

"What's that noise?" she asked.

"Blasts," I said. "In Brooklyn. On the far side."

"No. I mean that other noise. What the hell is it?"

I listened again, tuning hard. There was another noise, low and steady. There wasn't surf heavy enough in the East River to cause such breakers, even during high tide. The sound was quick, and rhythmic, and deliberate.

"Drums," Enid explained. "Long lengths of pipe pounded. Brooklyn on the air, ticing all in hearshot."

There were paths slashed through the brush, leading

to the towers, and so down one we walked, hearing animals moving unseen on either side of us. Crossing the old parking lot, we shortly reached the central tower's entrance. The doors were long gone; access was free and easy. The lobby reminded one that the buildings had been left unattended for years—no furniture remained, rubbish covered the floor three feet deep in places, the walls were covered with an undecipherable blend of phrasings. We didn't even go near the elevators; made our way, instead, to the stairway. From there, our flashes still shining the route, we ascended twenty flights.

"Here," said Enid, as we entered the hall, washed agleam with moonlight. "This way."

Enid kicked in the door of our reserved room—a previous tenant had thoughtlessly left it locked—and we went in. There were three rooms, mostly bare. Two futons lay on the living room floor; there was a table in the kitchen, and in the cabinets an assortment of boxes of heavily sugared breakfast cereal and bottles of water awaited. Enid nodded toward the undraped windows.

"Look there," she said, "Viz the stew ablaze with poison's light."

So high up as we were—compared with where we had been—the air appeared, however illusory, so clear as polished glass. Clouds roiled around the towers as if arising from censers. The city looked as it always did from a distance, or in photos—beautiful, and still, and warming. Taking comfort in such hallucinations, we made our feast.

"What are you going to do?" I asked Enid, finishing the box of cereal I'd broken open. I hated to think what manner of chemicals was encrusting my innards, even as I opened a new box.

"Home to bed and bideaway after such late

carryings-on,'' she said. "See what goes. Hasten off callers awaiting your return."

"Be careful," I said.

"Fear whelms like bile if the flow isn't choked, Seamus," she said. "We'll away to drift warm in Morphy's arms, till we hear other from you. AO?"

"But something afoots. What if—?"

Margot sat perched in the windowsill, staring out upon the city as if, by gazing intently enough, she might at last make it disappear.

"Talk's time is longaway," Enid said. "Do as you list. Keep eye alight. These wild souls roaming bespeak a cunning armed to steal you soon from tear's vale."

"Not if I can help it," I said, wondering if I could.

"In all time comes all, well and bad. As events turn, I'll step my way and go on. Compre?"

I nodded.

"Does the nightmare ride?" I shook my head.

"No," I said, "But it's not going to be amateur hour."

"Nor do amateurs go," she said. "If any foil or lead astray our dead stand close in spirit, your hands to clasp. Chance no more shall call, Seamus. Use trickery and cozenage. Take hands and grab."

"If there's naught to grab?"

"Then grab so well as if there were," she said. "It's the do, not the get, at end-turn. And I spec now that we'd best fly."

"Be careful," I repeated.

"On angel's wings all fear passes far."

I saw them out, hearing the thud of her boots against the hall floor, the clatter of Margot's hobnails as they tapped along. Avalon had pulled a futon further out into the center of the living room. The apartment was on the narrow end of the building, and from there the window's view faced east. I stared out, past the surrounding towers—dark, mostly, but on each floor of each one flickering candlelight betrayed squatter's presence.

"Look at the sky out there, Shameless," Avalon murmured, lying on her side; she'd removed her boots before falling onto the floor.

Past the towers, in the east, the colors diffused and glared wonderbright. The crimson sky lightened into a yellowish ocher near the horizon, sharply outlining the stubs and stumps of Brooklyn. Particulates deepened the sky's natural hues, but knowing the cause in no way lessened the effect. Spouts of flame rose up, spraying like geysers at scattered points along the old city's visible length, as if Brooklyn's fathers had wished to decorate the borough with spectacular fountains and had gotten it not quite right.

"How are you?" I asked her, remaining by the window, watching transfixed, as if gazing into a fireplace.

"Tired," she said. "I didn't think we'd make it."

"I didn't either," I said, not wishing to point out that we still hadn't.

"Your head better?" she said, whispering. I reached up, pulling her sweater off. Placing my hand to my head, I felt a gigantic, painful wound.

"Seems to be," I said.

We were silent for several minutes. Though I sat boneached and sore, sleep wasn't finding me with ease. I remained at the window.

"What are you thinking about?" she asked me.

"Years ago. I used to sit and stare out the window all the time, just like this," I said. "When I was young, my family lived on Riverside Drive. Corner of 79th. Dad owned the building. Enid and I each had a big room all to ourselves. I'd listen to the stereo or read. Enid would bring her boyfriends over—"

"Boyfriends?"

"She had them, then," I said. "From other schools.

She went to Brearley. In any event, my windows looked out over the Hudson, and you could see the park, and the river, and Jersey. It was beautiful to watch the seasons change. The trees would all suddenly turn color in November. First heavy rain would come along and the leaves would all fall off. Then one morning in late April or May you'd wake up and new leaves would have popped out overnight. Gray one day and green the next. I'd sit by the window for hours when I could, looking out, wondering what everything else was like. Wondering what I'd do someday. Where I'd go.

"When Mom died, I stayed in my room a lot more. Then not long after that everything changed. It happened so fast—course, I was so young I hadn't paid attention to anything and wouldn't have known what was happening even if I had—just seems like one Monday everything was fine and by the next we were down on Avenue C. That first week down there we had our first break-in. They got my stereo, the TV. We didn't have money anymore, Dad said, and couldn't get new ones. I remember that I couldn't really understand why, it'd seemed like we'd always had plenty.

"The next week another bunch broke in while Enid and I were home alone—the schools were still closed— Enid shoved me into our old toy chest and told me not to come out or say anything when we heard them breaking down the front door. She tried to get out on the fire escape but they caught her. There were three of them, she said later, and I heard her scream as they raped her over and over and over again. . . . Sometimes now, at night, I'll hear her screaming again, and then I'll wake up and she'll be lying there, safe and fast asleep.

"After they left, I dried her off and bandaged her up and then Dad came home. He went in the kitchen and shut the door and didn't come out for a long time. Enid

184

and I talked. We decided we'd stand together and fix them all if they tried anything else.

"She and I went out and bartered some stuff we had for a sledgehammer and a couple of chains. Went home and both of us practiced with them for a while, breaking stuff in our room. Dad was out trying to get food, I think. Sure enough, the next evening a couple of them came back to visit. We were ready for them. We did kind of overdo it that first time, but we'd caught them by surprise and once you started it was awfully hard to stop. Dad came back while we were still working them over. He didn't say anything. Not long after that he just went out and disappeared one night . . .

"I don't know, Avalon. It's so strange. When I was young I think it all just seemed like some kind of game, and then somewhere along the way I figured out that I never got to throw the dice. I guess I've been trying to get my turn ever since.

"I never wanted that much, I don't think. Just a different sort of something. Another chance. Anything like that. It just doesn't seem right anymore. It's all wrong. I don't know if it'll ever be right. What do you think?"

Nostalgia had rubbed me down as nothing else had. I felt ready to sleep forever.

"Avalon?"

She had no reply; as I'd talked, she'd slipped into sleep's shadow and fled the fretful world.

11

MY DREAMS RUSHED IN AFTER I WENT TO SLEEP, SPAR-
kling with fear, fresh and clean. I dreamed I ran, then
fell: from where to where, I had no idea; knew only of
my accelerating descent, tumbling downward as thousands cheered. Before I struck ground I awoke, reaching out for Avalon, but clutching still air. As I sat up I
hoped to see her nearby, even as, at once, I knew I
wouldn't.

"Avalon?"

She was gone. That I could have slept through her
departure seemed inconceivable, though obvious.

"Avalon!"

As I attempted to stand, my legs folded in on themselves, and I collapsed back onto the futon. A great
scabbed lump rose on my head where I'd been struck.
With much effort I got up again, feeling as if I'd been
crushed into pieces and then reglued by someone unfamiliar with the human form. My arms would barely

rise above my head as I lifted them; it took several painful minutes to draw up my trousers.

"Avalon!" I shouted, in case—for whatever reason—she had stepped into the hall. She hadn't. When I reached for my boots, I spotted a small card lying atop the laces. The blank side, no longer blank, was turned upward. On that side of the card were two printed words. The hand was unrecognizable.

You're next.

I flipped the card over, seeing that it was one of Mister Dryden's personal business cards. Beneath his engraved name and number someone had scrawled the notice, *contact now*. I read those notes again and again. Looking back, I wonder why it took so long for the message to take effect. After I tied my boots, I pulled on my coat—slowly—checked the apartment once again, and then left, moving down the stairs so quickly as I could.

Several possibilities flipped through my mind as I picked my way along, skipping broken steps and wet heaps of litter. It had to be Mister Dryden's people, I felt sure, and that assured me that he was still alive. The Old Man's bunch obviously had been the ones tracking us the day before; his gang were purest amateurs, I'd always felt, lacking in style and nuance. Mister Dryden had a few working for him in various situations—Jake being their overseer—who could have, with ease, come in, taken Avalon, and left me none the wiser. That was a common gambit in readying business deals.

Why hadn't they taken us both? I wondered as I reached the lobby. There was one explanation, as I saw it. The Old Man, also surviving, undoubtedly, had suspected that we were behind the blast—suspected his son as well, perhaps, but for the nonce choosing not to dwell on it overlong. And so, to show his concern so well as to send new word to me, Mister Dryden had involved his boys. By taking Avalon they could lure me out.

You're next.

That disconcerted. If they wanted to contact us both, they would have taken us both . . . unless they wished to take one of us in the other way. If he suspected Avalon was behind the retiming of the blast, as she'd been, in this way he could remove her while getting word to me that I was needed, or in danger. But if he wanted to remove me for fouling the job, he'd know no better bait could be used than Avalon.

Whatever was going on, she was in trouble. When that thought entered, no other broached my head. Stepping outside, the cool drizzle sprinkling over my face, I pushed through the scrub and emerged onto the street. No one was in sight.

There was no choice. Hoping that at least she was yet alive, I pulled my phone from my coat and punched in the code. The phone—an owner's phone, and so always reliable—hooked directly into Mister Dryden's office.

The phone buzzed twice before anyone answered.

"Dryden," he said.

"It's me."

He was silent; I listened carefully, to hear if he whispered to others in the room.

"O'Malley," he said. "Where?"

"Downtown."

"Safe?"

"AO."

"Danger prowls. Careful yourself."

"Where's Avalon?"

Again, he paused. "Up yourself to Dryco. Now. Essent."

"AO."

"Move incog," he said. "To Bridge HQ. My word sends. Use."

"Who?"

"Colonel Willis. He'll up you secondsfast."

"Is Avalon safe?" I asked. "Is she?"

"We'll see," he said. "I'll wait. Speed."

"AO."

He clicked off, leaving me even more afraid. Using my remaining shards of optimism, I concluded, by his final phrase, that he'd wait until I'd reached his office before doing anything to her. I'd decided, without hesitation, that were she to be blamed for what had occurred, she wouldn't be blamed alone; that, if separated, now as we were, at the end we might at least be reunited. Walking, I could reach Bridge HQ in twenty minutes, traveling Henry Street; so much as it hurt, I ran, pausing only to retrieve my breath. As I drew closer to the old Manhattan bridge, strung with searchlights left perpetually aglow as if for a holiday, I saw copters buzzing in, transporting the living and the dead in from Brooklyn, and Long Island, some whipping through the arch of the nearest tower on approach.

Bridge HQ—situated on land cleared by government order in the last year of the Ebb, in the Goblin Year—covered the terrain between the Manhattan and Brooklyn bridges southeast of Park Row and the Bowery below Canal; it was next to the Downtown Control Zone, but not of it. The soldiers barracked in the old Governor Smith Houses, old brick towers not in such bad shape as the one in which we'd spent the night before. The HQ had an airfield, a field hospital—located in the old city police headquarters, since transferred to Midtown—and the traditional facilities common to Army HQs; stockades, addiction rehab clinics, disease treatment centers, and a crematorium.

To New York new arrivals, fresh and green from southern boot camps, came each month, prepped to put in their year of domestic service before becoming eligible for transferral overseas. Upon landing, each month's group was divided: one-fourth was placed in the Manhattan Central Command unit; three-quarters found themselves in the units parceled out into Long Island. Army sources put the average casualty rate for Long Island units at 60 percent; unofficial sources ran higher. The government's theory was that those surviving a Long Island campaign should have no difficulty on any foreign battlefield; that once Americans grew used to killing Americans, they'd qualm not over killing anyone else.

The northern entrance post was situated in the center of Henry Street, beneath the bridge. Four Army boys there lifted their rifles as I strolled up, aiming at my head. Raising my hands so high as I could, I slowly advanced, flashing my Drydencard.

"Halt!" one screeched, after I'd halted. "State biz. Pronto."

"Dryco," I replied. A different one ambled over, snatching the card from my hand. He was old for a private; seventeen or so, and I was sure he'd awaited his draft notice rather than taking the bull's horns sooner. Nowadays—it'd been looser in my younger days—one was eligible for the draft upon turning fifteen; if one wanted, surely, one could join the Army at age thirteen so long as the necessary height and weight requirements were met.

"AO?" I asked; he'd held it for a long time, examining it closely, as if it had been printed in Sanskrit.

"Shut up," said the Army boy. He held my card

AMBIENT

against such sunlight as there was, and the Dryco corporate logogram visualized on the card. He grinned, recognizing it. Handing it back to me deferentially, he affixed a visitor's pin to my lapel.

"Can I go?" I asked.

"Don't lose it, now," he drawled, sounding as if he hoped I would.

An enormous stencilled sign, pocked and channeled by bullet holes, rose high on the right, beyond the entrance post, just behind a truck that appeared to have been stripped for barterable parts.

INFORMATION PERTANING TO BOMINGS/
TERROR/ANDOR/MURDER
RECIEVED HERE. CONFIDINTALLY
ASURRRED. REWARDS
GIVEN
ONLY IN EVENT OF EXECUETION.
CALL: 6333512-797-3600 EXT.297753
DEPT.3131 CODE: 7BAKER

That the sign stood inside the base I found most intriguing.

You could pick the Manhattan guard from the Long Island guard at a second's viz. The Manhattan guard Army boys were rural, starch-loaded whiteys with drug-wet eyes, and a stance suggesting that they'd sought trouble since first vaulting from the crib to strangle the family dog. The Long Island units were, to a man, black and Hispanic and Amerasian, urban, with eyes equally sodden, but containing a gaze found only in those who, at age six, had hidden beneath the bed, watching silently as their families were slaughtered by strangers. The Army thought it best that its members should be introduced into situations most unfamiliar, so as to sustain the most vehement and lasting reaction.

Jack Womack

"Where's Command Central?" I asked a fellow reclining upon a pile of what appeared at first a stack of Hefties—only after I noticed that the crematorium stood behind him did I grasp that he lounged upon bags stuffed with former members of his, or someone's, platoon.

"Who wants to know?" He lifted the pipe from his mouth to speak, expelling gusts of heavy blue smoke. Once more I flashed my Drydencard as he leaned forward, nearly falling off. "Third building on the right," he said, refitting his pipe into the corner of his mouth.

As I walked away, I slowly became aware of an increasing roar and windrush nearby. Between the buildings I saw the tarmac; copters lifted and landed like pigeons in the street, refilling and dumping. On their noses were emblazoned the group insignias of the Nurfs and the Surfs—the Nassau Unit Recon Forces and the Suffolk Unit Recon Forces. Rotors spinning, motors humming, they wafted out Army boys sets to firestorm Ronkonkoma and Wantagh, swept out the victims of tactical regressions suffered on the dunes of Wainscott and Amagansett. Each copter carried its own music system, stereo or lasereo, drowning the screams. Medivacs swarmed over the field, marking a purple A on the foreheads of those deemed fit for triage.

I suspected the next building down as being the psyop headquarters, as there were no windows throughout the structure. The base's bulletin board stood out front, near the drive. A directive, running along the top, read:

UNAUTHERIZED PICTURES FORBIDEN
FOR DISPLAY PURPUSES.

Along the bottom of the board were pinned eight-inch glossies; authorized or unauthorized, I wasn't sure. They showed, in all colors, the debris of a recent operation near Riverhead—Army boys propped up, for ca-

AMBIENT

mera's benefit, mashed and mangled burbies, which was what Long Islanders were generally pegged by the Army. In the last picture, an Army boy, his mustache sparse above his smile, stood between two cast-iron lawn gnomes, his heel pressed against the chest of a naked woman. She lay on her back, her legs splayed; most of his company, it appeared, had inserted their rifle barrels into her. Below the picture was a note attached, reading *Clean your pece daily.*

The next building I supposed to be Command Central; there were lace curtains in the windows. Two MPs stepped up to me as I entered, each putting the tip of their rifles at my jawline. Waving my card once more, letting them viz it over, I relaxed. So did they.

"Colonel Willis in?" I asked.

"Yes, sir," one of them said. "He's officed. See the recep."

"AO," I said.

"Sorry," the other apologized, "can't be too careful, sir."

A dead body, primed, blasts so loud as a live one, but I saw no need to teach the Army tricks, and walked over to the desk. The receptionist, a young lieutenant, was watching TV in the company of several noncoms and another lieutenant.

"Colonel Willis, please," I said, raising my voice over the TV's vol. Why the entire Army wasn't deaf was beyond me.

"*Sshh!!*" one of them hissed. "Who's wanting?"

"Seamus O'Malley," I said, "For Thatcher Dryden."

The receptionist immediately buzzed the colonel's office.

"Dryco, sir."

It was hard to hear anything through the interom's static. The receptionist hit it with the palm of her hand.

193

"Go right in, sir," she said to me. As I walked past, I glanced to see what held their attention so intently. The news was on; the screen was barely visible through the overlay of soot. Footage of an execution ran—I didn't catch in which state. The guilty party, said the reporter, was convicted of rape and murder one; a middle-aged man, he sat strapped into a chair atop a low platform. The victim's husband approached, stepping onto the dais; he carried a blowtorch. Under the Retribution Act, the victim's family was required to carry out the sentence as they wished. With his tool he painted the fire on smooth. The reporter, bubbling, explained how, under prolonged application, the eyes would burst within the head. I went inside the colonel's office, closing the door behind me.

The colonel's inner office was no less busy than had been the outer. A large map of Long Island was spread out across his desk; hovering over it were the colonel and several aides of various rank. With pointers and pens they marked the trails of insurgents down Route 25 and the Sunrise Highway, circled supposed fortifications shielding Cutchogue and Massapequa.

"Excuse me," I said. They were talking among themselves.

"—patrol unit waved in at 0800 that they were interrogating a party of insurgents picked up near Mineola—"

"Where the hell are they now?" asked the colonel.

"Surrounded."

"How?"

"They'd engaged with said insurgents in reconstructive personnel selection—"

Meaning, they'd killed all but the younger women—

"—when under mortar fire they sustained a heavy loss ratio refiguration."

"How many?"

"Fourteen."

"What'd they do then? Sit there? Yes? Who're you?" he asked me, looking at me as if I were a troublesome child.

"I'm to see Colonel Willis—"

"Speaking. About what?" He shifted his attention once again to one of his aides. "Air support readied?"

"Sent."

"So where are they?"

"Forced to halt. Heavy ground to air interaction."

"Thatcher Dryden told me you'd be able to get me uptown incog," I said. "To his offices."

All paused long enough to stare. After a second they returned their look to the map, and to the reports and wires clutched in their hands. I looked around his office as I waited for him to respond. In one corner of the room an American flag drooped low, limp against its pole. Behind his desk hung the president's official portrait. The eyes were drawn so that their stare would follow your progress across the room. The colonel's medals—someone's medals—rested in a small display case atop his desk. A doll rested to the right of his terminal, collapsed against it as if resting following a long march. Filled with choice ingredients, such dolls were on occasion left in appropriate Island areas by recon units.

"Did he," said the colonel, not sounding as if he meant it as a question.

"Unit twelve has sustained a twenty-three-day confrontation. They need supplies lifted as well."

"They'll have to go down kicking," said the colonel. "We haven't support capability. Won't until next week."

"Begging pardon, sir, but two squadrons in from Jersey are set and ready, sir. Just this morning, sir."

"Not anymore," said the colonel, turning to look at me; his eyes were much more disturbing than those of the president's portrait. "At 1100 I received a directive from Group HG that they'll be needed for transferral to Hunts Point."

"Bronx duty, sir?"

"Why, sir?"

"To perform demolition on structures liable to sustain flood damage—" he paused, lowering his voice, staring my way. One of his cheek muscles throbbed as if something within prepared to burst loose. "—sometime before the end of this century."

"But, sir—"

"Tell him," he nodded to me, raising his arms, clasping his hands before his chest. He drew back his lips as if sucking blood into his gums. I estimated that his choppers fit not so well as did Avalon's. I noticed that he wore a revolver in a hip holster.

"Colonel Willis," I said, "I was told—"

"To do as you're told," he said, rising from his chair. "That's what you'll do while you're here. Your boss let me know that he wished me to certify you'd make it up to Midtown incog."

"Yes, sir—"

"Snap it, he told me, before he hung up."

A burst of static sounded on the shortwave, popping like firecrackers at Chinese New Year. The colonel turned and picked up the speaker.

"77A257. Over."

"Report in from Mount Misery, sir," the voice rumbled; background fizz made it difficult to hear. "Recon op prime zero down. Tactical regression sustained. Over."

"Losses? Over."

"Heavy," said the voice; it reconsidered. "Total. Over."

"Any need for pickup? Over."

"None. Over."

The colonel sighed as if allowed to breathe once more, as if the pain of inhalation wearied. "AO. 22991. Over."

He motioned toward a chair facing his desk, wishing me to sit down. I did, uncertain of his mood, impatient to move, fearful for Avalon.

"I don't know why it's so essential that I use my time to get you to Midtown," he said. His aides and advisers looked quietly on, as if hoping by their silence they might somehow disappear. "But there's a lot I don't know."

"Sir—"

"You're shit in the street to me. But when he calls, I jump. Have to. Guess you must be fairly useful to him to get an override like this."

"He wanted me at his office so soon as possible, colonel," I reminded him. He stood up, strolling around his desk. Though I was sitting, I could tell that he was several inches shorter than me, toting the sort of bulk that made him appear to have been recompressed for best use of space.

"You'll get there," he said. "You may be important to him but you're not him. You probably don't have any more say about anything than I do. I really don't give a fuck."

"Colonel, I'm not sure I understand—"

"It doesn't matter," he said, "whether you understand that or not. There's something else I do want you to understand, so long as you're giving us this little visit. Something to tell the folks at home."

He brought his hand down closer to his revolver, as if expecting that I was fool enough to attempt action.

"I've been assigned here three years," he said. "Every month I watch new men arrive. Good men. Primed for double duty anywhere else. Brave men.

Strong men. They'd serve their country well, if they could. They can't. You know why?''

''Why?'' I asked, suspecting that it would be safer to inquire than to argue.

''In business,'' he said. ''I know how to play it. Get somebody. Use them for all they are. When they're empty, turn them in. That doesn't work so well in the Army. There's a lot of wasted potential here. Spend two months intensifying trainees. Get them booted. Make them top, all. Then send them to this pit so they can be flown out and dropped into the lawn mower over there. Does that make sense? Breaks my fucking heart. Nothing I can do. Just watch them go in big and come out little. And for what?''

''I'm not quite sure, sir—''

''Me neither. Years ago you could have just blasted the whole island and solved things right off. Can't do that now. Better, maybe, to just take the men out and let it be. Can't do that, either. Leave Long Island alone and they all might swim over here. Put a crimp in your boss's big plans. Hurt the value of his real estate.''

''I don't—''

''Oh, no. Have to keep this fucking place safe till they build the new one up there. Like the old one's worth more than just blasting down to the fucking ground. Even after the new city's built, we'll have to guard it, too. Can't argue with Dryco. My orders are don't piss them off and do as they say. *Anything* they say. Old King Shit tell me to line my men up at the edge of the Battery and march them into the bay in rows of four. I'd have to do it.''

The colonel reached out, grabbing my lapels, yanking me from the chair; for his size he was immensely strong, and I didn't interfere.

''What do you think he'd do if one day we didn't hop when he said jump? What would he do?''

"I really don't know—"

"You don't," he said. "We hear stories. We hear that if we didn't, he'd interfere with national security. Now what does that mean? Nobody tells us. How would he do that? Do you know how?"

"I don't know."

"You don't know shit, do you?" he asked, letting me go. I slipped back into the chair. It was like being cornered by a drunk at a party. "I'm not surprised. No doubt I'm a bigger man in my op than you are in yours and nobody tells *me* shit. I'm not surprised. I just do what I'm told, too." There was a conspiratorial tone in his voice, for a moment, suggesting that in his eye he conjured a picture of two sharks complaining between themselves of the water's coldness.

"Sir—"

"It'll happen one of these days," he said, bending down, bringing his face closer to mine. "If I don't last long enough, somebody else'll say fuck it. Someday. You know how *pointless* all of this is? Every month new units go in. We could send in new units every hour and it wouldn't do any good. If we kill one of them three more spring up in their place. That's the way it's always been. Attrition doesn't seem to apply over there. It doesn't make sense. It's like they grow out of the ground. Fall out of the sky when it rains. It doesn't make fucking sense."

"I think I should be going—"

"Tell him when you see him," the colonel said. "We've had it. I've had it. Everybody's had it and he's going to get it. If he wants to make threats, he can fucking go ahead and threat away. We don't care. They might in Washington, but I don't give a fuck. Let him do what he wants."

"Why don't you go ahead and do it, then, instead of talking about it?"

From that second when I said that he no longer looked at me dead-on, but turned his face away as he spoke. "I just want to keep as many of my men alive as I can," he said, looking a foot to my right. "That's pretty damned impossible, thanks to your fucking boss. You tell him that. Someday he's gonna say yes, and somebody's gonna say no. You tell him."

"I'll tell him why I'm late."

The colonel was a man of quick reactions. Before I could raise my arms to protect myself, he swung, striking me full-fist in the side of my face; I felt my cheekbone crack, and my vision blurred red. Once my sight refocused, I saw him holding his hand, rubbing it, as if he'd broken the bones punching me. I grasped the chair arms, trying to stand. Had I not wanted so to get away, to find Avalon while there might yet be time, I should have pounced him there sans restraint and suffered such consequences as the rest might offer.

"Get him out of here," the colonel said, speaking between his choppers. "Get him a uniform. Get him the fuck out of here."

"Yes, sir," said a drawn young captain, advancing, grasping my arm. "This way."

He pushed me along, out of the office, across the campgrounds to the supply depot. Pressing my hand against my face I could feel the bones grind together as if they were stones in a mill; felt unbearable pain when I pushed harder. It was like probing a boil. Still, by controlling the pain's flow in such manner, I quickly grew used to my jaw's steady throb.

"The colonel's been high-pressured, sir," the captain reassured. "Please weigh factors before undertaking reports—"

"Just get me off base and where I want to go," I said. "Please."

The supply depot seemed so well stocked as any

place in Manhattan providing material of any sort. Bare shelves lined half the walls. Many of the uniforms lying about appeared recycled, with patches, and scars poorly sewn. I was given a captain's field uniform—too long in the arms, too snug in the hips—the closest they had to my size. I didn't need to change my boots, for which I was glad. Pulling my long coat on over the uniform, attaching the spare captain's bars given me onto the shoulders of my wrap, I readied myself. My face didn't hurt quite so much. The supply sergeant shoved a revolver at me, pushing it across the countertop. Picking it up, I marveled at its weight; though I'd been trained in firearm interaction, it had been years since I'd held one. They used to seem lighter, I thought, unlike everything else.

"I don't need it," I said, putting it down.

"Take it," he said. "Never know when it'll do handy."

"I've got weaponry."

"Unexpected situations demand the unexpected," he said. "Better to be adapt-ready."

There was a point in that. All Army boys toted guns, and there was appearance's sake to weigh; moreover, I realized, none connected with Dryco would guess that I'd chosen to equip with amateur's specialty.

I put it in my pocket. "Now where?" I asked the captain.

"Over to the motor pool," he said, lifting his arm and pointing. "Ask for Panzerman."

"How's he ranked?"

"They know him. Just ask. He's been told. Don't aware him that you're civilianed."

"Why not?" I asked; he didn't respond.

"He'll up you."

Taking leave of the captain, I staggered over to the pool's central building. Inside, a corporal sat behind the desk, awaiting directions. He thumbed a copy of the *Times*. PREZ LIES SEZ VICE, the headline read.

"Are you Panzerman?" I asked.

"Outside," the corporal grunted, not looking up. A horn ablow snared my attention and I turned. A small open fourwheeler pulled up out front. The fellow driving looked sixteen and wore gold-rimmed glasses. A long scar on his right cheek suggested that he shaved with a cleaver. On the back of his scuffed yellow flakjak was sewn the phrase, LOST LOVELY AND VICIOUS. Dryco supplied the Army's helmets, and on every one was embossed the colored design of a smirker. Panzerman had drawn in fangs protruding from the smile of his.

"Panzerman?" I asked, climbing into the passenger's side. He wore hobnailed boots not unlike Margot's and I wondered how difficult they made driving.

"Yep," he said, offering nothing more. He had no rank, so near as I could tell; a patch on one shoulder said that he was a member of the Honduran Army, had one been unaware.

"You know where we're supposed to go?"

"Yep." he said, gunning the engine; dust clouds billowed after us as he floored. We took off for the Park Row egress. Flipping on the siren, he pulled into Church Street's 1A lane and we cruised uptown.

Traffic had been rerouted from the Tribeca Secondary Zone and for several blocks we were the only moving vehicle to be found. As we passed an abandoned cab, something I saw pinned me where I sat.

"Stop the car."

"Why?"

"I said stop the car." Slamming on the brakes, he swung sideways as he pulled the car to a halt. "Back up."

As we reversed I vizzed the sitch. Three soldiers busied themselves with a woman in the Army's everyday manner. Having pulled her dress up, entangling her arms and covering her head, they'd spread-eagled her on the hood of the cab. One squatted over her, bending back her legs with rough anklegrip. The other two sustained their anger in turn. I thought of Army memorabilia, posted back there on the board, and heard those screams forever burning my mind.

"Desist," I commanded, standing up in the open car. The one presently at work stepped away, not bothering to rearrange his uniform. She cried and wriggled. The spider crawling over her hovered light, drawing her legs further apart so that I might see how much blood they'd pricked thus far. She screamed again.

"Want a little, captain?"

Guns removed the option of consideration before action could effect; amateurs, thoughtless at best, preferred them for that reason. About some things there was no need to examine options. Not having words proper for them, knowing the deaf ears off which they would ricochet, I fired my pistol, having leveled it at him as I stood. When I shot him he crumpled like paper and blew away in the wind. The other pair dashed off as if trying to reach the goal line before the whistle sounded; they bounced as they struck ground, tumbling end over end as if clipped between halves, sounding shocked as if hoping the coach would waste not time in complaining. With a gun it was usually too fast; here it could not have been fast enough. In using a different tool, for a different reason, I thought that at last I'd begun making my new way, following my new reason and my old feelings; using such maggots to cleanse new wounds, and not to worsen old ones. The woman carefully sat upright, tugging her carmeline dress down over her legs as she pressed her knees together, shaking her head as if to dry her mind of nightmare's slimy touch.

"Move," I said, but only I moved, falling sideways with the shock of the noise. The woman, for a second, levitated above the hood of the cab as if easing into the paws of Godness—before it dropped her and she fell unseen behind the cab. Panzerman reloaded his rifle.

"One hundred percent, sir," he said, smiling silently as if the moment didn't warrant an audible laugh.

12

WE PULLED ALONGSIDE THE DRYCO BUILDING. PANZER-
man had been silent the remainder of the trip, though
at intervals he quietly chuckled to himself, as if recall-
ing some memorable anecdote he kept handy to keep
him cheerful. A stiff breeze lashed me; sooty cinders
etched my eyes. A copter buzzed quite low, flying west
down Fiftieth.

Drivers stood at ease beside the limos lining the
plaza; Jimmy was easiest spotted, being a head taller
than any of the others. He lounged beside the Castrolite; his arms crossed against his chest resembled nothing so much as sewer pipes insulated with coat sleeves.
Best to avoid him, I suspected, having no idea for whom
he might truly work and estimating that I was wanted
no matter who behinded. Avalon must be inside, I
hoped, entering the Fiftieth Street side so nonchalantly
as I could. Thoughts of her correction by Dryco minions darted through my mind, stinging and making raw.

I unlocked the door leading to the guard's stairway. Mine is a peaceful soul, as I have said, but if need calls I cut no corner and cool no fire, and I had the unerring hunch that need would call. As I climbed the stairs, eyes alight at those places where boobies awaited tripping by the careless, I knew that were I to discover that my arrival came too late, that my presence changed no mind, that my explanation should not suffice, then my hands, unbound and set loose, should take so many along as I could carry as I was sent along on my way.

The guard's stairway emerged, many floors above, into a small closet in Mister Dryden's office. With steady silence I crept in, looking through the long two-way mirror inlaid in the closet's door.

Mister Dryden sat behind his desk, overlooking a thick printout. His lips were drawn so tight they appeared sewn. His desk terminal glowed radium green as menus and graphs flashed past. Nine phones sat on his desk; from his Russian associates he had developed the idea that innumerable phones at close reach provided fresh mortar for his wall of perceived power. I always pictured him attempting to answer seven phones with his feet, if two were in his hands; as only one line entered his office, the point was more than moot. Above the fireplace, its gas logs eternally lit, hung a large portrait of himself as done by the family's artist. All the Drydens, I think, preferred to see themselves in this way—outsized, as if engorged after feeding, and softened with oil's gauzed film. On one wall, near the giant smirker and his Yale diploma, hung a small plaque. ONE OF THESE DAYS, I knew it said, I'M GOING TO HAVE TO GET ORGANIZIED. His bookshelves, for all his reading, were wonderfully free from books. One of his less understandable conceits was a fondness for stuffed animals. Dozens of them caught the room's dust, perched on the shelves. The taxidermist he employed prepared them to his wishes; sitting at tea tables or at pianos, conducting and playing in big bands, clad in tiny vests and hats, sunglasses and shirts. Puppies, kittens, piglets, frogs, monkeys, bunnies, duckies, and chicks, in clever attitudes forever frozen, looked askance upon him.

His office was very large, and very dark. The room's décor was bicolor, forest green and black oak. Though the view from his window was so attractive as any from this height, the drapes were pulled perpetually shut—such light hurt his eyes. I opened the door and walked in.

"I'm here," I said; he jumped, as if he'd been shot. I began coming toward him.

"No nearer!" he said. "Oppro spoke, OM. Your ears shut. You could have carved your own way—"

"Where's Avalon?" I asked.

"Where you'll soon be," he said, sliding his chair back. "I never expected this, O'Malley—"

"I can explain," I said. "Look, what's going on? Where's—"

"With me, a win. With her, a loss. Your loss."

"You don't understand. Wait a min—"

"Mistakes teach, OM. Learn."

He pressed a button on his desk, signaling Renaldo.

"Fools like you come dimedozened. Deceit negates function."

Renaldo entered, stripped to the waist, looking not so much muscled as upholstered. The Virgin tattooed on his padded chest seemed to sneer at me from beneath his forest. He paused at the doorway, resting his ax upon his broad shoulder.

"Entra, desepria," Mister Dryden said. "Should have kept to the street, OM. Waste's place. Having took out, I'll put back."

"What is this?" I said, disbelieving at how quickly,

how dreamlike, it seemed to be occurring. "I said I can explain. I thought—"

"Fair punishment fairly given," he said, slipping into the leg space beneath his desk; the desk itself was bulletproof, with Krylar inserts. "Solo conference. The bottle breaks where it's thrown. Renaldo. Go!"

Renaldo lifted his ax above his head, lunging toward me. I hopped aside with moment's notice. The force of his swing was great enough for the ax to sink halfway through the rug, and the floor, as it landed.

"Maricon!" he shouted to me, *"Venaqui."* I pulled out my gun; Renaldo thrust out his hand faster than a snake's tongue, flicking it from my grasp, sailing it across the room. As he moved to set loose the ax's blade, I dropkicked him. He swung out as he fell, punching me in the ribs; one of the lower ones split. Holding tight to one of the office's tufted-leather chairs, I lifted myself up, kicking the ax away. Grabbing a floor lamp, he attempted wrapping it around my head. We grappled; the lamp bent and we threw it out of our way. The first tool my hand clamped was my trunch; I pulled it out.

"Muerte—" he said, his hand squeezing my throat. With all my strength I brought my trunch down against his head. Blood spattered the air like Serena; the metal plate in his skull lifted, spinning away like a bird in flight. He kicked out, striking my knee with a sharp heel, and I went down, landing painfully against the articles filling my coat. I found what I needed as he picked up his ax. I heard Mister Dryden crying, beneath his desk.

"Suplica," Renaldo said, blood streaming down his face. Lifting the ax again, he began bringing it down; it descended as if in slomo. Halfway through his ax's downward arc I blocked it path with Enid's chainsaw.

"Madre de Dios—"

The saw roared out, tripling its length; the force of that impact knocked the ax from his hands, slamming it back against his mouth. He fell over. I sat up, my saw whirring away. His jaw had broken when the ax handle hit it; he made no recognizable sounds. I could see that his loss of blood was weakening him, and I saw no need for overkill, and so shut off my saw. Sitting down on his chest, I placed my hands around his neck, pressing my thumbs against his Adam's apple. It didn't take long. As I sat there, panting, hearing only the sound of Mister Dryden's sobbing and my own breathing, drying blood encrusting my hands, my split rib stabbing my side, my cheekbone athrob, the wound on my head reopened and stinging, I thought of Avalon, forcing myself to move by visualizing what would happen to her if I didn't do something more, demanding of myself that I go further before I dropped cold.

"Mister Dryden," I said, so calmly as I could make myself sound, "let's talk."

"There's reasons," he cried; I barely understood him. "It wasn't—"

There were many objets d'art on his desktop: a thermometer in the guise of the Statue of Liberty; a heavy glass paperweight, snow ensprinkled within forever drifting down; an old photo of himself with his mother, Susie D. Blood tickled my brow as I perused them, awaiting his emergence.

"Come on out," I said, "Mister Dryden—"

"Scared—" he mumbled. Heaving myself up, the underside of the desk in my hands, I rose, tipping it over; it slammed against the floor behind him with a terrific crash. Broken glass rang for several seconds. He cowered against the floor, trembling in unexpected light like something found beneath an upturned rock. I lifted him to his feet.

"Let's talk," I repeated. "Where's Avalon?"

"I knew you'd top Renaldo," he said, attempting to look away. With my free hand I held his chin, turning his face toward mine so that he wouldn't be distracted by the scenery. "Only testing—"

"No test," I said. "You wanted to kill me. I'm not quite dead. So talk. Where's Avalon?"

"I don't know!" he screamed. "You wanted to kill me, too—" Perhaps it was because I hurt so much, in so many places, at that moment; perhaps it was because I had grown weary of hearing naught but doubtful tales and elaborations of fancy. Whatever the reason, I took my hand away from his chin and smacked him so hard as I could across the face. He shivered. Holding him once more with both hands, I shook him roughly, and then pushed him against the nearest wall.

"I didn't want to kill you and I didn't try to," I said. "Keep this up and I will. Where is she?"

"I don't know, I don't—"

"Where is she?" I repeated, slamming him against the wall; I heard plaster dropping down within. "Somebody took her this morning. They left a message from you. Said I was next and to get in touch. I didn't plan to be termed. I haven't been yet. Tell me what happened. Quick. Was anyone in the room when the bomb went off?"

"It didn't go off," he said, catching his breath, rubbing a tear away on his shoulder.

"It didn't?"

"Stella found it."

"What was she doing in there?"

"He wanted to fun it up while he abused me," he said, shaking his head. I relaxed my hold enough to allow him to let his feet brush the floor. "So when we transferred to the study he wanted her underdesk. She crawled under and spotted. Said it looked like a gumwad with a watch stuck in it. He looksaw. Had Scooter

210

enter and disassemble. Unsuspected, unforeseeable circumstance—''

''No matter,'' I said. ''What did he do? What did you do? Somebody's been trying to term Avalon and me for two days running.''

''I tried to word you through the contact,'' he said, anger marring his features. ''You ran. They lost track on Thirty-fourth. I couldn't see why till I uncovered the timer. Saw when it was set. I'd have been there still, if—''

''I set it for when we agreed,'' I said. ''It was reset.''

''By Avalon?''

''Yes—''

''Lies—''

Taking his head, I rapped it against the wall, cracking something.

''Avalon reset it. She told me on the way down. I thought they'd have readied to term us by the time we got there. I thought it best to run.''

''I thought her hand evidenced,'' he said, his head lolling on his neck. I continued to press him fast against the wall. ''I estimated that she convinced—''

''Not so,'' I said. ''How'd he finger us? It looked like Maroon when I finished.''

''Known. He suspected me onceoff. Accused me of behinding it.''

''As you did.''

''He couldn't know,'' he said. ''You're aware. He sounded at once. Threatened. There was no question—''

''How did he finger us?''

''I told him—''

At the moment he said that he strangely looked no older than he had when I first vizzed him, at the Yale co-op, so many years before. For a second the expression on his face suggested that of a child, caught by his parents in some ephemeral fib—on his countenance rested a mixture of fear and bluster, and a vague hope of being someday forgiven.

"Before or after you saw the timer?"

"Before—" he said, nearly whispering. "It was me or you—"

I hit him, this time with my fist, this time much harder. His eye darkened before he could blink. Hauling him away from the wall, I dragged him across the room, tossing him onto a sofa near the fireplace. He curled up, drawing his knees tight against his chest, and sobbed again.

"Why?" I asked. "You'd have fed us. Tossed us to the vultures. Without suspicion."

"There wasn't anything else I could do," he said. "And you were trying to kill me—"

"When you told him we'd done it you didn't think that."

"No—"

"Not only told him what we'd done, as per your request," I said, kneeling down, taking his shoulders as if I might shove them apart and so break him in two, "but then tried to kill me after you tell me to come up here, before I can even speak—"

"I was afraid, O'Malley," he said, crying. "Afraid of him. Afraid of you. I didn't know what to do. I didn't—"

Letting go of him, leaving him on the sofa, his good suit scuffed and wrinkled where I'd knocked him about, I pulled myself over, close to one of the chairs, resting my back against it, feeling my spine harden as my movement stilled. The knuckles on my hand swelled where I'd struck his skull's thick bone.

"It was mow or be mown, OM. You know how it is."

"I know," I sighed.

212

"You should have contacted them. OM. You could have gotten out."

"But once you spotted the timeset, you would have—"

"Right," he said. "I would have."

"No matter," I said, closing my eyes. "So you don't know where Avalon is, then?"

"No," he said. "Where was she last?"

"We stayed downtown. She was gone when I woke up. I found this."

Pulling the card from my pocket, I handed it over. He looked at it blankly for several moments. His wall clock chimed as the hour displayed on the screen. As we rested there in the room, I began wondering if I had lost her, after all.

"Her writing," he said.

"You're sure?" I'd never seen her handscript; suspected she could write but had not required evidence.

"AO," he said. "She always prints. Prints like this. She left this card. Wrote this message. No doubt here."

"Someone must have made her write it."

"Why?" he asked. "To what purpose? If Dad's men caught you unaware, you'd have both been exxed. You're aware."

"There's more to it than that," I said, thinking. "Something's off. She wouldn't have run away without saying something. Something's way off."

"She'll turn up one day, sure," he said. "River-weighted. Guttered."

"Don't say that," I said, quietly; he was cowed enough to become immediately quiet, his eyes closing as if fearful I'd strike once more. "Whose team was after us?"

"His," said Mister Dryden. "Down from Midtown. You led them merry, I hear. Triplelive and double-wired. Twenty taken out, the printout read—"

"Say that they tracked us. I don't know how, but say they did. Say they caught her, wanted to leave me, but wanted me to read that message. So they made her write it."

"For what?"

"If he suspects you behind it—"

"I convinced," he said.

"Are you sure?"

He held his knees more tightly, as if by gripping himself close enough he might fold within himself and disappear. "No. Not anymore."

"Then that's what he's done. They knew that when I found that message I'd contact, just as it said to do. Then they figured that you'd either have me taken out—"

"As tried—"

"Or that I'd come up here and take you out, thinking you'd taken Avalon."

"And then?"

"And then at leisure," I said, "he'd later fix whichever of us was still around. Sound like his mindset?"

Mister Dryden nodded. "But here we both are."

"Exactly."

"What's to be done, though? If such holds, then we're both still marked."

"Not if we move," I said. "Catch unaware before he catches us."

Mister Dryden sighed, and shook as if enduring a bout of malaria; he covered his face with his hands, and held them there. "I can't," he said. "If he wants me he can have. I'm worn. He's won."

"Under the circumstances I've a plan of my own," I said. "Helping us both. You'll need to go along."

"I can't."

"You'd have me try alone but still won't help now?"

"I'm trying to protect," he said. "I can't, OM. He threatened—"

"Let him threat. There's no way to get into greater trouble than we're in. Now, let's figure. Would they have taken her to the estate or to the Tombs."

"To the estate," he said, seeming to glow, now, with reason's warmth. "He's wanted to reel and rod her since she first signed on."

From how I interpreted her remarks, and from her familiarity with the study's layout, I suspected that he had. Neither here nor there, I thought, and didn't mention my opinion.

"If you call up there," I said, "you'll say that I showed. Say I was termed. See if she's there. Say you'll be up this evening."

"Even if I went that won't go. What about Jimmy?"

"He'll have to drive us. With this Army gun I can overpower. Then before we reach the estate I'll seclude myself. Once we enter—"

"No," he said.

"Why no?"

"Drop it. Let him take his will, OM. I'll suffer my medicine. We'll get you outcountried to wherever you want to go. You'll have to stay once there, so choose a welcome spot. He'll never know—"

"I don't want to leave," I said. "And what about Avalon?"

"What about her?"

"If she's alive still I'm not losing her," I said. "And I'm finding out, whatever drops."

"OM. It's her loss. Many await for ones like you."

But none are chosen, for having one such as Avalon, I set firm that I would again have her for so long as she wished me. I wished us together, and alive; still by the time I sat in Mister Dryden's office, working my wiles to convince, I knew that could I be fast in her arms again only in Godness's great yonder, that that should be a greater joy—even if unseen, unheard, unfelt—than I would ever again know while drawing poor breath.

"We can still overcome as you wished," I said, feeling the need to set on grow great. "Three days you readied. Essential, you said. You cán't give in now."

"I can," he said. "We'll airport you. Land you on distant shores till—"

"I'm going to the estate," I said, "and so are you. If we go separately, he'll have us both. Together we make it. They won't be ready for us both. You see that. I know you do—"

"OM," he said; calm damned the flood but for a moment, and so the tears again overspilled. "We can't. That's all. Please. Quit thinking about it. Sometimes things work. Sometimes they don't. That's all—"

"Why can't we?"

"We can't."

"Why?"

"He meant his threat this time," he said, clasping his head with both hands. "We *can't*—"

"Then he'll probably take me soon," I said. "I'll certify it, if so. I want Avalon back."

"Forget her."

"I *won't*. I'll go get her. Alone I'll likely be got. Then one day soon he'll take you too, if what you said holds. He won't rest till you're—"

"Let him," Mister Dryden screamed, asylum loud; rising, he fell forward onto the floor. Wailing without cease, he began crawling away, digging his fingers deep into the carpet's heavy nap. "Let him kill me. I don't care anymore. Get it overed. Let him!"

"I don't want him to kill me—"

"I wish he'd kill *me*," he sobbed. "I wish, I wish, I wish—"

No matter how poorly the reckers dealt him, no ho how business became, Mister Dryden had never lost so

216

much ground as this in my presence before. I rolled him onto his back and gently tapped his face, attempting to seduce him into a more subdued incoherence. It didn't work.

"What's the matter?" I said. "He's threatened before. You've said."

"Threats not so thorough," he cried. "Not like this."

"What's scaring you so?"

"I'm not going up there, OM," he said. He breathed with effort, as if heavy rocks weighed upon his chest. "I'm not. Not alone. Not with you."

"What'd he tell you he'd do?"

"Worry not, wond—"

It broke me to do it but I slapped him, hitting his cheek, trying to create shock rather than pain.

"Avalon might be dead now," I shouted. *"Tell me!"*

"He said he'd do it," he said; a look settled upon him as if he'd vizzed all his bone-dry ancestors rise to point fingers his way—his face rinsed belly-white, his lips drew back in rigor, his pupils grew as if he'd settled permanently into pitch. "He said if I tried him again he'd do it. I promised I wouldn't. Throttler. Me. You. I can't—"

"Do what?" I screamed. "I always hear about what he might do but I never hear what it's supposed to be. What is it? What?"

"Awful," said Mister Dryden, his voice drifting, as if away with the tide. "It's awful. He's always been able to do it. That's why we get along so well. Those who have inkles do as he says and tell all else to do likewise."

"But what can he do?"

"I can't tell you."

"Why not?" I said, shaking him like a terrier snapping a rat.

217

Jack Womack

"I don't even know for sure," he said. "Fire's smoke. Hurricane's damp. The twister's stillness. That's all I know for sure. Momma told me some but wouldn't say more. She knew all and always had. She wanted to tell me. That's why he killed her."

Each blast of recollection, each rending admission, seemed as he spoke to strip away the long years. The more he told of what he'd muted so deep, the smaller and younger he seemed to become, as if he'd developed his guise while a boy and simply perfected it with practice. His eyes dried; his fears peeled away like wet veneer.

"What'd she tell you?" I asked, lowering my voice as if someone else might give ear.

"Everyone knows a little but each is kept in a different drawer. The gov knows one thing. The Army, another. You've heard things, I'm sure. I know a bit. Momma knew all. He knows all."

"What do you know?"

"He took it from the government. They didn't know they had it. He didn't know he had it till he got it. He told them he had it."

"That's circletalk—"

"That's what she told me, as she told it. He controls them all by it. Sets them jumping hoops."

"But how does he do it? What could it possibly be?"

"It's something to do with the Pax," he said, whispering.

"The Pax?"

"The Pax Atomica," he said. "It doesn't work as it should."

The Pax Atomica was called, by those responsible for it, humankind's greatest achievement of the twentieth century, an admittedly slim field. The Pax Atomica was effected during the Christian period; barely so, for the Christians that mattered at the time were quite against it. The Pax Atomica decreed and promised that

218

all nuclear weapons of all countries would be disposed of: taken apart and shot into space, and so they were. No matter how our world might have seemed at times, we always had the consoling knowledge that at least it would be here to provide a place in which most might forever suffer.

"What do you mean it doesn't work as it should? How couldn't it?"

"She wouldn't say. I think—"

"What?"

"I think she meant that some still exist. That he knows where. That he'd use them—"

When the Pax Atomica effected, I was eleven; recalled only vague tales of what those bombs, supposedly, could do. It was another of those things of which no one spoke.

"Maybe he just wants people to think he's got them."

"He must have them. They'd have figured it out if he didn't—"

"If he got info during the Ebb," I said—it all seemed clear to me, then—"which is what I've heard, then nobody around now in the government or in the Army would know if it was really so except for him. Don't you see? He could say any and all and who'd be able to doubt?"

"That can't be the case."

"Because your mother thought otherwise? That's probably what he wanted her to think. Look—"

"But she knew what it was, too."

"Then why didn't she tell you?"

"He killed her—"

"There must have been another reason. You know why they never told you more? If everyone knows a lie's a lie, then the lie doesn't do any good, does it?"

He said nothing; I still think he might have known more than he ever let on. Matters began to develop a disconcerting feel; unease settled deeper into my bones. I knew that whether he was correct or not, there was little that could be done or undone anymore. Still, an odd, new feeling developed; it was as if, while attending Thanksgiving dinner at a distant relative's house, one went to the kitchen after dessert to drop off the dishes and discovered, tucked beneath a dishcloth, an opened box of burgundy-hued poison near the empty can of cranberry sauce. But more selfish wishes propelled me, then, and my concerns for Avalon blocked greater qualms than I might ordinarily have let myself feel. I still thought that whatever the Old Man could do, with this or any other, could not possibly be so dreadful as Mister Dryden gave reason to believe.

"Come on," I said, tugging at his jacket's sleeves, "we're going. Settle it and over it once done. Come on."

"No," he said, "OM, please no—" His grip on the rug wouldn't loosen.

"There's no other way any more," I said. "You want to lie down and roll over? That's what he expects. You want that?"

He rolled onto his back, appearing for a moment as if he were beginning to give thought to my sense.

"There's no other way," I repeated. Maybe there was—I couldn't think of any. As I looked into his face as he lay there, for one evanescent moment his features brightened, as if clouds thinned enough to let ooze one ray of sunlight past to wash his face. The pinkish color returned to his skin; his hands relaxed their hold on the carpet. He breathed deeply, several times, and sighed.

"You're right," he said, very quietly. "There's no other way."

"Exactly," I said, attempting to think of ways I might further settle his soul and steady his nerves. Taking his hands, I helped him sit up. "We'll take it as it falls. You can count on me."

"I know I can," he said, getting up and slowly walking over to his upturned desk. He reached underneath, as if looking for something. "I've not always done you right. OM. I'm sorry. What I've said stands—"

"Don't worry," I said. "Let's just go. They wouldn't have done anything to Avalon yet, do you think?"

In his hand he held one of his pill bottles, evidently extracted from a desk repository. He kept his supplies everywhere. "Not for a time," he said, softly as a pigeon cooing in the eaves; he popped off the bottle's protective cap. "She'd be safe for a while."

"Shouldn't you go up recker-free?" I asked, seeing the bottle, turning to retrieve my chainsaw from where I'd let it drop. "You want your wits fresh. Those pills'll be the death of you one day—"

There came a thud, as if something large and soft had fallen from the sky; I looked, Mister Dryden lay on the floor; he'd worked himself so up that I wasn't surprised to see him enter this faint. I knelt beside him, jiggling his shoulder.

"Come on. It's time." His trance seemed overly deep, or especially well feigned. "Mister Dryden. Come on, get up."

He lay as if enjoying a sound, refreshing sleep. His lips curled upward at the corners; a pleasant dream he seemed to have. I tugged open his eyelids; his eyes stared dully upward, glass balls fixed at a skewed angle.

"Mister Dryden." When I shook him he barely rattled.

Flattening my palm against his chest I discerned no heartbeat, no assuring thump; discovered no pulse when I took hold of his wrist. A specialty of Jake's, in the more advanced sort of takeovers, was the provision and application of nonnegotiable offers. This particular variant he pegged a blue job, for that was the color the recipient shortly turned—shading light azure as if hav-

221

ing been rinsed in an ink wash. Before his last recker left his mouth it had worked.

"Mister Dryden."

Upon moving from him, I sat down in one of his big chairs, staring down at him as if I were one of those stuffed animals; appalled by what I saw, powerless to do anything about it. Not far from where Mister Dryden rested Renaldo crouched, contorted enough to appear as a statue struck down from its pedestal.

"Mister Dryden," I heard myself saying, as if by giving speech most diligently the words might in time return life. "Wake up."

Strands of his hair stirred faintly in the AC's breeze. He made no movement, showed no response, gave no word, brought no action, expressed no thought, and granted no gesture. Wishing almost that I, too, could find such encompassing rest, ignoring my body's pains, I stood and walked to the windows, drawing back the drapes. He and Renaldo looked grayer in the light than they had in shadow. Outside, the clouds were so thick that nothing of the city could be seen. There was a choice no longer, I knew; if I wanted that chance to be with Avalon at least one last time, I'd have to go up there alone and take it as it fell myself—there was nothing so much that I wanted so much as that chance, no matter the result. The hair rose at the nape of my neck; apprehension chilled my running blood. If Mister Dryden had been so scared as to do this, why should I be so set to act without pause? I had a choice, though, over how fearful I should let myself be; so used all strength to deny such terror. There was no need to worry until I knew about which I should be worrying. I repeated that to myself, as if by saying it often enough it would so become.

13

NO ONE SAW ME GO, LEAST OF ALL THOSE OF WHOM I'd so recently taken leave. Returning by the guard's chair, emerging in the lobby, I set my path past the display cases, sliding between them as if being pulled along by another. I scooted up to the doors facing the plaza; Jimmy stood out there by the car, looking away from the building. In a trice I was at him, my gun's barrel pressing his ear.

"Irie, man, irie. What calls?" he asked, quietly enough, as if I'd been expected.

"We're going to the estate," I said, ready if he wished to debate; he didn't. He opened the passenger door and walked around to the driver's side.

"Big bullbucker be mighty mad when he finds his wheels gone."

"No, he won't," I said, sitting down. "He's dead."

Jimmy slowly lowered himself into the car, easing

behind the wheel. I closed the door. He looked at me, his eyes bloodblister black.

"By your hand?" he asked.

"By his," I said. He pressed the ignition; we pulled away.

"You sit high clever now, man," he said. "Why'd he run such a field?"

"He was afraid."

"With reason?"

"I'm not sure."

We rolled along; left Midtown, passed into the Upper West, leaving view of the ugly towers enclosing Columbus Circle. So set I was on what I had to do that Jimmy's wishes, or thoughts, did not occur to me at once.

"Jah at last called hellfire down on duppy clots," Jimmy said, smiling, packing his bowl. "Big trees fall and make little noise. What do you aim then, O'Malley? Set to work your charms?"

"I don't know," I said. "I'm figuring it as we go."

As we drove up Broadway the wind rose; snow cascaded over the still and the quick. Brownish-white clumps pelted the car; Jimmy switched on the wipers and the cleaning sprayers. This wasn't natural snow—such rarely fell in New York anymore—but variant precipitation; dried human waste, lifted by gusts, so often sprinkling the city. La Muerda, Ambients called it. As neighborhood water supplies ran out, or were cut off, the snows became more common. These showers never lasted longer than a few minutes; no one complained.

"Where's our sweet sister?" Jimmy asked, expelling strands of smoke.

"I think she's at the estate," I said. "I hope she is."

"And so you come up now to court?"

"Yeah," I said, keeping my gun aimed at him in the event he proved not so calm as he seemed. "She disappeared. I thought he'd picked her up. He didn't."

"You think she keep whole up there?" he asked. "She was big with soul when I last lay eyes. Fighting every step."

"I hope. I'm not even sure what's happening."

"Well," he said. "What's happening to me, it sounds, is that you took one bird out of the bush. One more left whistling in the trees. No one misses. You worry overmuch, man. Drydens here. Drydens gone."

"It'll be easy for them to pin me for this."

"So who saw you, man? Renaldo?"

"Yeah," I said, "but he's dead, too."

"Not by *his* hand," Jimmy said; I shook my head. "You be worse bullbucker than you know. Worse more than they ever know. Ice-cold."

Broadway's course was silk-smooth; we sailed clip-steady, suffering no interruption, attracting no attention in our 1A lane. Before I left the office, I'd wedged Renaldo into one of the closets and laid Mister Dryden out on the sofa as if for an afternoon nap. He'd set no appointments for the afternoon and I suspected no one would drop by calling. Jimmy passed an Army travel-all.

"You think something come down hard that she didn't expect?"

"Maybe," I said. "I wish I knew."

"Not for us to tell yet, O'Malley. All in time."

Near the corner of Ninety-sixth, Army vehicles blockaded traffic moving downtown; troops marched toward the river as if planning to swim en masse to Jersey. Five enormous Croton trucks, tankfull with water to be delivered to approved neighborhoods, avoided the blockade by crunching down the boulevard's median. We passed Columbia's razorwired walls. As we entered West Harlem, we noticed that the barricade guard had received new rockets; Friday's wreckage, gnarled as old driftwood, still hung down from the el tracks as if abandoned in play.

"Think we'll have trouble getting in?"

"Not with me driving, man. Not with Martin at the gate. Martin stands on the Lion's side."

"Whose side are you on?" I asked.

"The side of I and I, man. No one takes lien on my soul."

"Each of them thought you're on the other's side—"

He laughed. "Drydens look but never see. Speak but never talk. Where I drive, my hand turns the wheel. If they want to buy gas they can."

West Harlem was high ground beyond 137th, past the valley, but no more popular because of it. The depredations of the gangs, and of the Army in controlling the gangs, had tolled and rung hard. Smaller buildings were boarded and shelled; larger ones, where squatters dwelt, were enlivened only by drying laundry, parrot-bright, billowing from the windows. Gigantic billboards attached to the fronts of the biggest apartment blocks peeled and faded in the dim sunlight, advertising products no longer sold, candidates long since defeated, shows no longer running. At 155th, artfully crafted ruins marked the remains of a splendid old church; the rubble looked over an abandoned cemetery, across Broadway. The boneyard stones were toppled and broken; machetes would blunt, carving paths through the underbrush.

"Avalon might be dead," I said, more to myself than to Jimmy, as if in heart suspecting that I should adjust myself to that idea.

"Might be," said Jimmy, nodding. "Isn't."

"How can you be sure?"

"Hunching, man. That's all. She's a sharp knife that cuts too deep for that."

Finishing his bowl, he tapped it out in a cup he kept

attached with tape to the dash. We entered the Inwood Secondary Zone. This far up, the land was high and would remain forever dry. The area was reasonably secure, and the population was almost so great as in the Upper West. There were cars, buses, even cabs; boozhie stores in the zone flourished, selling goods six months' backdated from what was sold in Chelsea, or in the Upper East. Passing through Inwood, a rider could almost forget that New York surrounded; for a moment dreams would fleshen, and it would seem that nothing too untoward had ever happened, anywhere—then you awoke, crossing the drawbridge into the Bronx.

"Good place to retire, someday," said Jimmy.

The Broadway el had been torn down years before for scrap—I believe the city, or Dryco, had sold the metal to Russia—and we had an unhindered view of the surrounding terrain. To our left was Riverdale, where Home Army generals of the New York district lived. On the right were the Bronx hills and plains, cleared and awaiting reconstruction. Buildings marked for preservation—there were many—remained under Army guard: old apartment buildings on the Concourse; blocks of Tremont flats; red Belmont rows; Kingsbridge courts guarded by pairs of stone lions; large houses along Pelham Parkway; throughout the realm, rolling, brick-salted veldts. Every vacant lot bore a sign reading PROPERTY OF DRYCO/TRESPASSERS SHOT. The ruin of Yankee Stadium, webbed and netted with leafy vines, rose high over the southern flat. It had been destroyed when the old Yankees won the series for the last time; overexuberant fans celebrated by burning out the stadium. The Yankees moved to Nashville, changing their name; the Old Man planned to preserve the stones as a bit of old Rome overlooking the Major Deegan.

Passing Van Cortlandt Park, the leaves of the trees

greenish-brown in their confusion of the seasons, I tried imagining what it would be like to be driving toward something at which I wished to arrive, to be with people I knew I needn't fear.

"Let's see if they caught you yet," said Jimmy, turning on the radio.

They hadn't. The President announced that further inference as to his role in the death of the security adviser, once the vids were released, would be dealt with in the standard manner. Two copters collided over Newark International during an accident drill and crashed, killing the volunteer victims lying on the runway below. A woman, mindshot, stabbed little Tamoor as he was being wheeled out of recovery. Russian armies were marching into Ankara so that proper order might restore itself. A refinery blew in Bayonne; turning to look behind us, I saw the southwestern sky filled with boiling brown smoke. The wind blew south; the Downtown Zone wouldn't need to be evacuated.

In an hour we reached the estate. As we came to the gates, Jimmy switched on the intercom.

"Approaching, Martin," he said.

"AO."

We parked in front of the house after we drove up. The place appeared deserted, as it usually did during the week. The chapel gleamed an unsavory pink in the afternoon light.

"Come in with me," I said, prompting him with my gun. Jimmy was acting altogether too agreeably, as if by humoring me, allowing me to push him along through a display he cared not to see, he would, at journey's end, be granted some trivial though satisfying reward. Stepping onto the slate ledge leading to the door of the Old Man's house, I felt ready for whatever might come, having reached—even as I worried—that state of blessed equanimity wherein I could accept all

228

that might befall me, knowing that these actions either worked toward the purpose of my own devising, or else toward a purpose of another sort, about which I would have no say, over which I should have no control. Even so I wavered as I lifted my hand to the doorknob, feeling lightheaded by the effort of exuding such false calm, as if I were a salesman come to convince the purveyor of my competitor's supplies that henceforth he should do business solely with me. I touched the door gently, prepped for the alarm to sound. It creaked open, unlocked.

"Something's funny," I said.

"So laugh," whispered Jimmy, going ahead of me.

"What about Biff and Barney?" I asked. They usually stayed within the house during the week.

"Not to fear," he said. "Where'll he be?"

"In the study, I'm sure. Go on."

We edged our way through the long wide hall, toward the study, in the rear just before the back stairs. The study's door proved not so yielding.

"Locked," I said, touching it.

Jimmy leaned forward, knocking; the door slid open. He stood to one side, allowing me entrance. I vizzed the room highlow, seeing at once that Mister Dryden had spoken true; nothing more scarring than dust marred the room's composure. The TVC was on, the vol was down. Those three file cabinets, unscratched, stood as they always had, across from his spotless desk. The Old Man sat behind his desk, aglow with charm and delight. To his right sat Avalon.

"Get on in here, O'Malley," he said, motioning that I step forward. "We've been waitin' for you."

Jimmy, calmly pushing me ahead as if to reassure, gently slid the gun from my hand as if disarming a child at play. It seemed pointless not to let him have it. As I came into the room, I stared at Avalon, at once over-

229

whelmed and disturbed by her presence here. She'd changed her clothes; she wore a long green tee and black over-the-knee socks. She held a tumbled filled with a pink drink, which she sipped through a straw. A tiny paper umbrella sheltered it from the room's dust. She appeared comfortable.

"I've been expected?" I asked.

"I figured you'd be the one showin'," said the Old Man. "So'd Avalon."

"Glad I didn't disappoint you."

"If you'd disappointed us, you wouldn't be in much condition to complain, now would you?" His voice crackled as his good will burned freely. "You look like you've been through the wringer, O'Malley. What happened to your ears, son? Somebody take a likin' to 'em and bite 'em off?"

"I lost them," I said. "But I hear perfectly well."

"Hangin' around your sister and her friends too much, if you ask me. Well, if you don't need 'em, I sure don't." He looked at me, his eyes atwinkle. "My boy's dead, isn't he?"

"He is," I said. Closing his eyes, he turned toward Avalon, slapping his knees.

"You won that one, goddamnit," he said to her. "We'll settle the score later, of course."

"Better believe we will," she said.

"I've always been a bettin' man," he said. "Long as I make sure all the horses're wearin' my colors."

"You're all right, then?" I asked Avalon—but I didn't mean it as a question, and she, evidently, meant to give no reply. She toyed with the umbrella shielding her drink, looking into the patterns in the ice as if she might discern the future. My look she avoided, as if by our eyes meeting one of us might turn to stone.

"She's *fine* and dandy," said the Old Man, standing

and stretching his arms over his head. "Aren't you, hon?"

"Sure am," she murmured.

Imagining no possible use I might have for my hands in the foreseeable future, for gestures either of love or of death, I slipped them into my pockets as if, unseen, I might forget that they were mine, and thus feel no regrets for so not using them. "Would anyone like to tell me what's going on?" I asked.

"You're one helpful man, O'Malley," he laughed. "Damnation. Easy to see why my boy always liked to keep you around."

"I'm very happy. Now would you please—"

"Oh, lighten up, O'Malley. Hell, take a goddamn compliment for what it is. Strong men never know how to take compliments, usually. Course *I* never had any trouble—"

Glancing at the TVC's monitor, he laughed loudly.

"Here goes," he said. "Watch this. There's always some asshole has to give it a try. Look at this now."

A game show was on. In the foreground of the show's gaudy set, an oversized, transparent cylinder stood; into it, from the sides and back, ran several clear pipes. The host opened the door leading into the cylinder, enabling the finalist—a middle-aged man wearing a light green jumpsuit—to step in.

"He's supposed to grab as much money as he can in one minute," said the Old Man. "Now watch."

The man, driven hyperactive by good fortune, leapt around in the tube as if attempting to fly off with it. Bells rang; rolls of quarters shot through the pipe as if they were missiles. The first one he grabbed for snapped his fingers; they hung, dangling from his hand. For a brief second, an air of puzzlement came over him, as if he realized something hadn't been explained when he signed the release. Another roll ricocheted off his right knee, shattering it. He slumped against the tube's curving wall; one nipped him between the eyes, felling him. Rolls fired through at higher velocity, targeting him over and over. The host bared his teeth; the camera cut away, panning over the raucous audience. The camera returned to the now-opaque cylinder.

"I got a helluva lot to thank you for, O'Malley," laughed the Old Man, shaking his head, shutting off the monitor with his remote. "You know that?"

"No," I said, "Why?" I took a seat in a large chair close by. My ribs ached when I breathed; the support bandage I'd pulled on while yet in Mister Dryden's office alleviated only the sharpest pains.

"Drink?" he asked, ambling over to his cabinet, extracting a flagon of intricate form. It was shaped in the guise of E, portraying his late, heavy period, so that the bottle might hold twice as much. Kissing the decanter in restrained supplication, he unscrewed the head from the torso and poured two tumblers full.

"May as well," I said.

"Ice?" I demurred; if I was going to drink, it should be done to effect. The Old Man grinned. "My old Daddy always told me you could push an Irishman into a vat of whiskey and he'd drink his way out before he drowned."

"I wouldn't know," I said, taking the glass. I gulped; Jack Daniels, and it tasted no more terrible than it ever did. "I was born in New York."

"Thanks again, O'Malley," he said, extending his hand so that I might clasp it. When I did, he gripped tightly, holding as if to see when I would give. I didn't; he let go.

"What is this?" I asked. Once again I looked toward Avalon, as if I might yet draw her glance and thus gain, if not strength, then at least release. She raised her head, inadvertently, I believe, but even so she kept her guard. Her face, pulled tight, showed nothing; her eyes appeared as cold stones.

"Sometimes you have to take things subtle, O'Malley. It's not easy to just run out and do what you want to do. That causes a lot of talk later on that nobody needs to hear. That was the problem with the boy. Everybody knew how he'd gotten to feel about me. Sometimes a sickness takes hold of a person and until you can get a cure to 'em you just got to take certain steps if you want to make sure nobody else catches it."

"So you'd have cured him by killing him?"

"Hold on there," he said, lifting his hands as if to protect himself from the splatter of thrown mud. "Did I lay my fingers on him? You ought to know, I'd think. I know for a fact he was aimin' after me. Right?"

"He was."

"Uh-huh. Now doesn't it make sense that if somebody's out to get you it becomes kinda necessary to get them first? That's a pretty clear rule of thumb, O'Malley. That's where bein' subtle comes in. Some of the ones that wanta get me are kinda subtle themselves in an obvious kinda way. Course, most everybody goes after me things they're so damn smart for doin' it they never see when they do somethin' stupid, and believe me, they *always* do somethin' stupid. Now, I didn't get this far bein' stupid myself, don't you know. Once they get rollin' I can always reach out and hook 'em."

"What if you hadn't had Stella under the desk?" I said, taking another drink; it didn't taste nearly so bad by the third swallow. "That would have surprised you, I think."

"Why do you think I had her go under there?" he asked, rocking backforth on his heels as his son had so often done. "You heard a few details, then. Well, I knew somethin' was up. I'd of found out one way or the other."

233

"You'd have found out when it blew."

When he laughed, he looked at me as if happy to have me home after a long absence. "You never lose your sense of humor, do you? That's a good thing. There's nothin' that gets you through life better'n a sense of—"

"Mister Dryden had been planning to kill you for four days," I said, anxious that he might get on with whatever tricks he wished to play; hoping that he might be quick about it, doubtful that he would be. "How long have you been planning to kill him?"

"Oh, 'bout a year or so. He started gettin' kinda problematic, but I guess I don't have to tell you that. Avalon picked up on it, all right. Now if he'd just stuck to doin' those reckers like they was goin' out of style— and I must of told him a million times, sell 'em, don't do 'em—that would've been one thing. I'd of still had to take him out of his position 'cause he was really startin' to lose my money, and toward the end he started schemin' business deals like a junkie tryin' to buy a plane cause he heard that clouds are made of smack. But no, he had to set out on his own way, tryin' to get into places he didn't belong, tryin' to find out things he didn't want to know and knew he didn't want to know. Got mad at me when I wouldn't let him go on with his shit. So he decided he was gonna get me. Must have wanted to for years, down deep, O'Malley. I bided my time to see. Didn't want to overreact unless I had to."

"So he was after you and you were after him."

"That's about it."

"I know what his plans are—" Were, I repeated to myself; were.

"I'd hope so."

"What were yours?"

"'Let me freshen that drink for you," he said, pouring another draft into my glass. "How's that?"

"Fine. You were saying—"

"I wasn't but I will. It was so simple. I hunched that something was up soon. When Stella found that blaster under there I knew right off I was gonna have to move fast—not lettin' him know, of course. He didn't waste any time layin' the blame on you two, but I guess that wouldn't surprise you. So I threw him off the track first by sendin' out a bunch to get ahold of you. Let him think that was as far as I was takin' it."

"He said you threatened him."

The Old Man paused in his ramblings, as if to consider how best to phrase the next anecdote. His smile remained so benign as it had been when I entered.

"Hell, O'Malley, you know lately you could say hello to him and he'd think it was a threat. In any case I got the Army to send a few out after you."

"Why the Army?"

"'Cause I figured they'd be about as effective catching you as they were. I knew I'd need you later the way things were shapin' up, but I knew it wouldn't look right unless I tried to get you. So—"

"What if they'd caught me, though?"

He laughed. "I'd've worked it out," he said. "But I knew they wouldn't. So I could put you to good use."

"Without my knowing it."

"Would it have made you happier if you'd known?" he asked. "Delegatin' your work force is the key to success, you know. Now I had a hunch you'd get back together with him at some point and I knew eventually that he'd be back after me. I'd be kinda more ready for you, next time, at least. But then luck started comin' into it. Amazin' how well things work out sometime if you just stand back and let 'em roll."

"And what luck did you have?" I asked, looking at

Avalon. I became aware, I thought, of what had happened as he went on, but even so I wouldn't say that I hated her for it, then—for hate you need so much understanding as you do for love, if only two people are involved, and I could not understand why she'd done as she did. Her face revealed no sign, augured no wisdom; whatever she kept incog within her did not even break the surface.

"Once Avalon snuck out of wherever it was you all were hidin' she gave Jimmy a call. He came over from Downtown and picked her up. She was here probably before you even woke up. She told me what she'd left behind for you to find. Said she knew you'd be sure to be in touch with him about it. Had an idea of what sorta mood you'd be in when you saw him."

Jimmy ignored us all; stood looking out one of the unshuttered windows, gazing out over the grounds.

"She was right. When I heard what she'd done I knew you'd take care of my problem for me. Saved me all kinds of trouble, O'Malley. I'm in control again. The company's safe. I'm safe. You're a helpful man, specially when you don't realize it."

"What if he'd have killed me?" I asked. "What if we'd both come up here this afternoon?"

"I know my son, too, O'Malley," he said. "I knew there'd be no danger of either of those things happenin'."

Having dusted, once again, the candy in the big window, I knew that I would shortly be sent along, so as not to mess the display by lingering. To say that I was disheartened at that moment would be an understatement of the most overstated kind. I did retain a choice still over what question I might next ask, whether or not I received an answer, and so spoke to Avalon.

"Did you ever mean anything you said?"

She said nothing; turned, as if hoping that by not answering, she might disappear.

"Better to've loved and lost than never loved at all, O'Malley. That's what I always say. See what I mean, though, overall? No matter how smart. Always somethin' stupid pops up. You should've just headed out to that plane on Saturday, son."

"I know," I said.

"I'm still curious 'bout a couple things, though," he said. "Did he put up a fight?"

"No," I said. "Renaldo did."

"They're so fuckin' wired. You took care of both of 'em then?"

"Took care of Renaldo."

"What did you do to—"

"I didn't."

The Old Man's eyes appeared to unfocus, as if by blurring his vision he might lose sight of something already spotted.

"How'd you mean?" he asked.

"He killed himself."

"No. How?"

"Had some of Jake's poison. Took it."

"Why? What were you doin' to him—?"

"Nothing," I said. "I told him I was coming up here and that he was coming with me."

"But why'd he do a fool thing like—"

"He was scared."

The Old Man, appearing thoughtful, as if wondering how best to arrange his features as he spoke, walked over to his desk again, sitting down behind it. He rested his hands before himself, folding them together.

"Scared of what?" he asked.

"Scared of what you keep in those filing cabinets, I believe."

At once I knew I had him, in some way; that even if

I lost Avalon—and to judge from her bearing, and from what she had done, I knew that I had—I might at least retain some small control over my own end. The Old Man's face lost just enough color to indicate that this was a subject he hadn't expected to arise.

"Well now, what'd he think I keep in there?" he asked, his voice even, and daubed thin with reason's paint.

"He mentioned one thing in particular," I said. "It sounded quite interesting."

Had the Old Man known for certain that his late son knew nothing of his secrets, he would have popped my increasing smugness lest it overwhelm the room; he didn't. As I stood there, I became aware that either Mister Dryden had known considerably more about this than he'd let on to me, or that he genuinely hadn't, but had only led the Old Man enough along so as to make him believe that he had. I rubbed sweat off my forehead; my head's wound stung.

"Did it," said the Old Man. "What'd it concern?"

"Generalities," I said, "and specifics. Depended."

"What'd he tell you, O'Malley?"

"What he knew," I said. "I'd think there's more. You might know."

"You've probably got enough there to make a good story," said the Old Man. "Shame nobody'd ever hear it."

"They could read it," I said, finding the time right to remold such truth as I held into a more pleasing form. "He wrote some of it down for me. Signed it and everything, before he—"

"You don't happen to have it on you, I suppose," said the Old Man.

"Afraid not," I said, wondering if anything in my face, or in my voice, would give me away. "It's in a safe place where it'll eventually turn up."

The Old Man appeared pensive—fighteningly so. The most awful gleam alit his eyes as if from within. "Well, he took things a little further than I thought he would."

"Far enough," I said.

"You'd need some support, of course, for a story like that," he said. "Elsewise it'll just be written off as the product of an overactive 'magination.'"

"Maybe not," I said.

"But probably so," he said. "You'd probably want to check around and see if you could dig up any proof that might be lyin' around, wouldn't you?"

"It'd be a good idea, I think."

He reached into his trousers pocket; I could tell that he wasn't pulling out any sort of weapon, and so my fear began to lessen—slightly.

"Why don't you have a look, then?" he said, tossing a ringlet of keys at me; I caught them, nearly dropping them onto the floor, my hand shook so. "No tellin' what you might find in there."

"In those cabinets?"

"Go check it out if you're so curious. I don't mind."

I held the keys in my hand; looked at the filing cabinets. He looked quite at peace and held my stare with ease. "Seriously?" I asked.

"Pandora's box, O'Malley. Open 'er up and stand back."

I walked over to the filing cabinets, unlocked the top drawer of the first one on the left, and pulled it out. It emerged with difficulty, as if the tracks had lacked oil for years. The Old Man continued staring at me, his mouth kept in a tight smile. Avalon and Jimmy looked on.

"Go ahead. Most of 'em don't bite too hard anymore. Lost most of their teeth, over the years."

The file was stuffed tight with manila folders and printouts housed in black boxes. There were dossiers, and notebooks, and videocassettes protected by soft plastic cases. Tugging out a folder, I flipped through it, thumbing the contents to see what sort of things he might have here.

"You look disappointed, son," he said, "What'cha got?"

The label on the folder said OSWALD, LEE H. An autopsy report inside was dated 1979.

"Just keep lookin'," said the Old Man.

As I skimmed the files, working through them at ever-greater speed, I began developing the concept that history, as it had been taught to me, was evidently a romance and not a science. All I saw seemed oddly skewed, as if I viewed it while dreaming. I extracted a large file on the Q documents concerning the history of their discovery and warrants of their authenticity. It always seemed to me that I remembered when they had been found, but that seemed not to be the case; according to the papers I read, they'd been discovered in the early 1950s. The original intention seemed to have been never to release them to public knowledge. Enclosed in the file, toward the end, were several reports detailing events during the Christian period, and at last, several letters to the president from the Old Man—looking more closely I saw that they were transcripts of conversations between them, and not missives at all.

"How did you get in on this?" I asked, reading. "The Q documents, I mean."

He settled back in his chair, tilting his head to one side as if a new angle might help his memory flow. "That bastard Charlie," he said, referring to the president of that day. "Dumbest sonofabitch ever to sit in the White House and that's sayin' somethin'. See, when he was runnin', he thought he'd get a wider power base if he sucked up to all the preachers and their friends in order to get elected. Too many of 'em wanted to run for office themselves and this way he figured he'd undercut 'em. Well, he did. Only problem then was that once he was elected he had to start followin' up on everything he said. His sense of morality always came out at the worst time.''

Among some, the Long Island accident had been seen as the last word of Godness's warning before It chose to settle matters once and for all. Enough in the Congress—at the urging, and with the connivance of, the president—were coerced into drawing up and passing what were even then known unofficially as the God's Country acts.

''They passed some useful laws because of it, I'll grant 'em that, especially the ones havin' to do with real estate. But then they got more serious and started causin' me all kinds of trouble. Interferin' with my sources of income, that sort of thing. They were pretty fuckin' wired when it came right down to it.''

The right to vote would have been restricted solely to those who announced a belief in the Christian God. For a short time, divorce and remarriage were ruled illegal. The courts could do no business as the lawsuits mounted. Criminal laws were strengthened immeasurably. Day-care centers were outlawed for contributing to the destruction of the family unit. Social Security was abolished; on the one hand, it caused the citizenry to ultimately put its trust in the state and not in Godness, and, more to the point, by its abolition great funds were made available for the new military excursions the government wished to begin, especially after political relations with Russia fell apart. Problem areas such as New York were marked for special attention by minions of the Lord.

''It got fuckin' ridiculous. Couldn't walk down the street without gettin' hassled by a bunch of no-mind imbeciles. Stuffin' tracts in your hands. Then they started gettin' even worse, I mean those posters—''

The faithful began beating the Lord into those who preferred not to listen. The heathen reacted in like fashion. As the jihad escalated, all proportion vanished. Christians burst into banks and chopped the hands off moneylenders. Pagans caught and nailed latter-day martyrs to trees in Central Park.

''Conductin' business in a normal fashion became impossible,'' said the Old Man. ''So I put some of my boys inside the government to work on it. Found out about those Q documents. Now Charlie was seein' what was happenin' to the economy while this shit was goin' on and he couldn't get anybody to shut up long enough to listen, except people like me, of course, and we'd already seen what was happenin'—''

Looking over some of the files in those drawers, I could see what had happened. Theological debates had proved so absorbing for that year and a half that no attention had been paid to anything else. America had advisers in five separate wars—in those days it was unusual, I inferred, for the government to spend more than half its budget on defense—no one had bothered to raise taxes of any kind, and the deficit had doubled in ten months. The gains made in eliminating Social Security were swallowed by the interest payable on those debts.

''So I told 'em, I said, you let those things get out or you look forward to another civil war. He finally started seein' things my way, Charlie did, and so they released 'em. Things quieted down real quick after that, for a couple of months anyway. I still feel E mighta been workin' through me on that one,'' the Old Man said, a trace of wistfulness staining his voice.

I replaced those files, began looking through others.

''Where did you get all of this?'' I asked, amazed at

the quantity so much as at what the documents contained.

"Night before the market crashed I was down in Washington tellin' Charlie what to do about that, too. He did some of it. Dumb sonofabitch."

"He gave it to you?"

"In a sense," said the Old Man. "After he tried to leave town."

Prices began going up faster and faster during the Christian period, for a variety of reasons no one fully understood; the trade balance tilted wildly. Imports flooded the nation's markets at higher and higher cost to the buyers. Companies went bankrupt within months simply trying to keep up with pay adjustments for their executives. Unemployment rose to 15 percent and continued to climb. The market began to fall.

"I'd wanted to settle a few things before it all started comin' down. I'd been told the revaluation, of course, was set for the next day, but the public didn't know. Worked out fine for me but I knew it was gonna cause a certain amount of trouble when I found out how they were goin' to do it."

The morning the currency revaluation was announced, the stock market plummeted a thousand points. Eight hundred million shares were traded—nearly all sold winding up exclusively in the hands of the Old Man, who, through executive barter, was able to keep companies going under his or under other's control by dealing with hard materials rather than the now-worthless money.

"I tried to tell Charlie that, but he knew it all. You couldn't tell him shit. Damn dumb bastard."

I remember my father attempting to explain it to me by showing me a hundred-dollar bill and saying that it was now worth a dollar.

The Old Man snorted with laughter, reliving old

243

times. "He ran like a sonofabitch when he saw what was happenin'. Thought he'd hide out in the Virginia caves till it all blew over."

The president's copter, that afternoon, was forced down shortly after takeoff—by Air Force jets, some histories claimed—near the Jefferson Memorial. He was drawn out by the penniless multitude and lynched.

"For a while there it looked like it was all gonna go. Made a lot of people awful mad. I guess some of 'em still are. It was kind of rough there for a while."

Mothers sold their babies for food. Sixty-year-old men joined the Army so they could support their families. People dug up graves to scavenge gold fillings. For the whole of the Goblin Year, such was commonplace among the unprepared.

"I was prepared, though. The Veep stayed behind and when he heard how his boss'd wound up he nearly shit. I knew I had that little fucker's balls in my pocket right there. Started layin' it out for him. Told him to get the fuckin' Army mobilized, keep it mobilized, and keep it happy. I hadn't been fuckin' around in South America so long not to know that. Told him everything that he had to do, and that little fuck woulda turned on me later if I hadn't taken those files along. Told him, long as I'm here, let me pick up a few things for safe-keepin'. These were the files they kept in the vaults under the White House."

"And he let you have them?"

"He was so grateful to me at the time I coulda took the Washington Monument if I'da wanted it. I figured there'd be somethin' in those files worth havin'."

I supposed there was, somewhere in there, but I hadn't found it. The second and third files seemed filled with the most bizarre collections of material I'd ever seen.

"You could look for hours through those things without gettin' tired," said the Old Man. "Like goin' through the phone book on a rainy afternoon."

One folder told of the last years and Pacific burial place of Amelia Earhart. A small yellow envelope contained the original formula for Coca-Cola. A sonar-gram gave the approximate dimensions of a Loch Ness inhabitant, species unknown. A heavy file dated 1971 concerned an unapproved patent for a pill that converted water into a gasoline-like fluid; in the same file were unapproved patents for the same type of product, dated 1954, 1932, 1919, and 1905. I glanced over the labels on a clutch of vid cassettes.

"Greed?" I read aloud, "Reels 1 through 42."

"By way of Mussolini," said the Old Man. "Found in Albania."

In the rear of each drawer was a collector's farrago—in one, a photo of the building in which Judge Crater served as the cornerstone, a picture of the Chicago house where Martin Bormann died, and a rough stone sphere. It was a broken geode; pulling the split halves apart, I saw a shiny steel nail embedded in the amethyst within, as if Godness had accidentally dropped it while sorting things out at the start.

"What junk," I said, closing that drawer, opening another, taking something out.

"Troublesome junk, at least," said the Old Man, yawning. "Troubled some people."

I'd come across a file marked LONG ISLAND. I opened it, and read.

"You look a little peaked there, O'Malley," I heard him say after several minutes. "You musta found one of the good ones."

It was a lengthy report from the User Unfriendly Division of the Chemical Intolerance Department of the Pentagon. A preliminary text discussed the accident itself and how easily it could have been avoided; a subsequent passage described how, through recombinant techniques, the antiradiation pills had been developed—how before they were given out it had been discovered that unpredictable side effects were certain to occur. It was decided to distribute the pills anyway and discover what the side effects might be, so it might be decided whether they would prove useful in military action.

"And that's why darkies were born," the Old Man laughed, slapping me on the back. As I read he'd crept up behind me and had been reading along over my shoulder.

"Is it in here?" I said, replacing the file.

"Not anymore," he said, smiling. "Hasn't been for a long, long time."

"So you're the only one who knows what it is?"

"Well, now," he said, his grin becoming even more mischievous, "I wouldn't have said so a minute ago."

To find yourself wishing that either the world might end or that you might, and that it wouldn't matter which so long as it happened soon, is a feeling that I hate to even admit that I had. Even at the worst of times I had had it so much better than so many. To take my lot and to have stayed satisfied should have been enough for me, but it wasn't, and I'm not sure I'll ever figure out why; it seems just one of those things. If a choice is made for you, live with it; if a choice remains, take it. By those expressions I so often made my way. But at that point I felt almost ready to welcome my choices being decided for me—almost.

"It's a nasty, nasty thing, O'Malley," said the Old Man, closing the drawer. "You don't want any part of it."

And I still did—

"Fact remains, O'Malley, you've done a hell of a lot to help me out, but we're just gonna have to tie up a few loose ends before everything's set aright again. I've got to admit that I think you're lyin' about one thing, though, and that makes me feel a little better—''

''You're going to take the chance that I am lying?''

''I didn't say that,'' he said. Jimmy walked over to where we stood; from my eye's corner I only glanced at him. ''There's a lot of things I'm gonna hafta think about, O'Malley. I'd hate to have to lose a valuable worker like you. We might be able to work somethin' out yet.''

''I'd certainly hope so,'' I said.

''We better do some thinkin' about it, though. Jimmy? See that O'Malley's not disturbed.''

Jimmy moved fast, lifting his arms around my neck, jerking me back so quickly that I hadn't a chance to resist, even if I'd tried. I never felt the pain until I reawoke.

14

WHEN I AWOKE I FELT AS IF MY WINDPIPE HAD BEEN crushed. After I coughed, spitting up blood from some region down below, it seemed less sore, as if it had only needed realignment. As I regained consciousness fully, I found myself lying on a rickety cot; my feet hung over the end, feeling cold, as if the circulation had been cut off for a prolonged time. With difficulty I managed to sit up; my bones ground against themselves as if they were being rubbed over stones. My eyes adjusted to the dim light, and came unglued.

"How're you feelin'?" a voice asked; the Old Man spoke.

"Terrible," I said, feeling giddy when I shifted my head. With my hands I discovered that someone had been gracious enough to wrap a fresh bandage around my brow. "Where are we?"

"The Tombs," he said. The old part, I estimated, to judge from the cracks in the walls, the crumbling plaster, and the hospital-green paint. "You were out so sound for a while there I started gettin' worried. Thought Jimmy mighta shown excessive zeal in his application. You're doin' all right now, though?"

"What time is it?"

"Nighttime. Feelin' well enough to go for a little walk?"

Avalon sat on another cot, across the small room. She now wore a baggy jumpsuit, as if preparing for maneuvers. She was staring at me now, as if to give an impression of concern.

"Walk where?"

"I'd like you to meet somebody," he said. "I've been thinkin' about what to do with you. I think I've come to a decision'll just about please everybody."

"Just about?"

"Nothin's perfect, O'Malley. Can you make it?"

I stood, slowly and painfully. My throat felt as if it had been sandblasted. Avalon stood up as well.

"What sort of decision?"

"Now, now," he said. "You'll have to start gettin' used to things first. And you are a curious sort. Let me show you a few things'll really perk your interest. Come on."

"Goodbye, Avalon," I said, wondering what response I might receive.

"She's comin' with us most of the way. Come on, let's go."

"Who am I going to meet?"

"Alice."

On several occasions I'd been to the Tombs, certifying that problematics had been properly delivered as requested by Dryco, but on none of those visits had I ever gone beyond the first floor offices. So near as I could make out, we were on a higher floor—as we stepped from the room we passed a small window, and

I caught a fast glimpse of the darkness outside. Not far from the room to which I'd been delivered, just beyond the Pepsi machines in the hall, was the area where—this is just a guess, these spaces are usually recognizable—the police brought those meant for immediate disposal. It was a long room papered with soundproofed matting; the matting's fiber escaped through the thousands of pockmarks spotting its surface. In the floor were innumerable holes for drainage, as if for an autopsy table.

It was a quiet night; apparently no one put in overtime on this floor. Several rooms we passed, their doors ajar, appeared to be awaiting new transients; some were empty, some were furnished comfortably, as if for a lounge. One looked to have been, at first glance, set up as some rudimentary terrarium; a row of pots lined the bottom of the wall facing out, and in them were planted tall, long-armed cacti, aligned crosslike as if ready for someone to be fastened upon them.

We walked and walked, reaching a wider, brighter hall, somewhere deep in the new building. The hall we trod there stretched seemingly for miles of whiteness and indirect light. We turned once, turned again. In none of those walls were doors or windows, signs or directions. The Old Man led us as if by memory. Besides the clap of our footsteps I heard only the satisfied drone of machines at play. At last we reached the end of the hall; a small vestibule led directly off the main passage, just before.

"Stay in there, hon," the Old Man said to Avalon. "Just make yourself comfy."

"Why can't I go in there with you two?" she asked.

"Nothin' in there you wanta see. Come on now, we'll be finished soon."

She went in, sitting down in the chair that was provided within. There was a small slot in the wall facing us; into it the Old Man slipped a green card. A panel slid open; a yellow strobe flashed over his face—examining his retinas, I supposed. The panel slid shut. Nothing happened.

"Goddamn thing never works right," he said, sounding disgusted. He leaned against the wall, rubbing his shoulder against it several times. A door opened; we went inside.

"Here's where we take problem children, O'Malley. Let's see the teacher."

The room was ellipsoid, fifteen feet high, nearly a hundred feet across. Closed doors, knobless and handleless, lined the wall but for a small section near the entranceway through which we passed; there, a window in the wall looked upon Avalon, sitting in that tiny room.

"Can she see us?" I asked. The Old Man shook his head. In the room's center was a large corporate blue mainframe square, five feet high, thirty feet long on each side. On top, near the edge facing us, was a small terminal panel attached to a plasma monitor screen. Just below the keyboard was the miswrit legend, NIHIL OBSTAT ALIENUM PUTO.

"What's this?" I asked.

"Wonderland," laughed the Old Man. "Far as we want to go."

"So where's—"

"Don't be so damn impatient," he said. "AO, Alice. QL789851ATM."

The monitor blipped; the screen came aglow with pale blue light.

"I was busy," it said.

"No need to be grumpy, Alice," said the Old Man.

"Perhaps no need but much desire," said Alice. "How are you, Seamus?"

The computer's voice chimed, sounding unlike any

machine voice that I'd ever heard: it was a woman's voice, a husky alto, with theatrical phrasing and diction sharp as ice; the tone nearly so cold—of human coldness, and not of machine's.

"I'm—all right."

"That's surprising," she—it—said.

"That I'm all right?"

"That you'd lie about it."

"How you doin', Alice?" asked the Old Man, sounding as if he'd run into an old buddy in the street. "O'Malley works for my son, you know."

"Worked," corrected Alice. "Muddying the innocent as ever, I see. Have you regrets, Seamus?"

"Perhaps for reasons you're not expecting—" I began to say.

"I expect no reasons, Seamus," she said. "Nor do I want any. If you have regrets I should be curious as to what they are, but wish no justifications for them. That I should even know them isn't essential."

I wasn't sure what to say in response.

"Isn't she somethin'?" he said, rocking on his heels.

"Please feel no fright at my presence, Seamus," she said. "My intentions are no less honorable than yours."

"She was designed to be a number twelve," he said, frowning. "She must be in the three digits by now. Six years in production. In operation five years. We needed an overseer we could trust, Susie thought. So we took a buncha teams of AI boys from IBM and Cray, brought over some Japs, drug out one genius—*nut*—who'd been livin' out in the Wisconsin woods. They'd all been workin' along these lines for years. We got 'em all together to make it a little more streamlined. They worked a spell and came up with Alice. If her mainframe was the old size, she'd be big as the whole state, I'd bet. Whole floor below us is her Freon unit. Alice thinks so fast she'd go screwy otherwise. Keep her ass cool and her mind works like a trap. Just like a woman—"

"Such as your wife?" Alice interrupted.

"Watch that—"

"Smooth remarks such as yours," she said to the Old Man, interrupting him again, "bespeak a smooth brain."

"How smart is she?" I asked.

The Old Man shook his head, staring into her cool blue screen. "Unlimited capacity."

"How is that possible?"

"With ease," said Alice.

"It isn't," said the Old Man. "Least it's not supposed to be."

"Most things shouldn't be," she said. "Many things are."

"She would have to be feelin' feisty tonight," he said, more to himself than to me; then he recalled where he was and began to explain. "Hell, nobody's ever figured out how people think, much less anything else. Alice, well . . . they didn't expect as much as they got. It's like once they put it all in, everything fell into place on its own. Nobody believed she was doin' it at first. Then she started hookin' herself into other networks. Started writin' her own programs. We'd hooked her into the Central Defense computers to start with. That was a mistake. We couldn't turn her off long enough to even see how she was doin' it without zappin' the whole government. Didn't matter, 'cause by the third day she'd built in overrides so we couldn't switch her off anyway. Now she can call up anything from any memory bank anywhere. She's got the things we put into her at the start, of course, she's stuck with those. Everything since she took in by herself. She was set up to be self-repairin' and she went us one better. Makes her own chips. Subdivides 'em. Reconstructs 'em from within, they think. Nobody knows for sure. Nobody has the faintest idea how she could have started up like this—''

''Advanced technology produces unexpected situations,'' she said. ''If I've told you that once I've told you a million—''

''Bitch wouldn't respond to anything we asked her for six months after she went online,'' the Old Man continued. ''Just churned printouts every minute. We couldn't figure out what she was gettin' at, they were just rows and rows of numbers. . . . Then she started talkin' without us askin' her anything first. You can *imagine* how we felt about that. She wouldn't do what we wanted for a long time unless it'd been put in one of the original programs, or unless she wanted to do it, too. If she didn't want to answer us, or wanted to avoid givin' us straight talk, she'd respond only in Latin. E knows where she picked that up. We didn't know what the fuck she was sayin'. Priests weren't any help, they don't know anything anymore but their spiel. We found an old classics professor in Boston finally who understood it as well as she did. He died last month. She's back to normal now.''

''Cave canem,'' she said. ''Don't refer to me as bitch again.''

''We decided after a time that we didn't want to shut her off, after all—''

''One makes no decisions,'' Alice remarked, ''if one has no choices. Right, Seamus?''

I didn't know whether to reply, or nod, or what; I did nothing but listen.

''She's got a mind of her own all right,'' said the Old Man. ''She can be one fuck of an awful pain in the ass. She makes herself useful, just the same. What we wanted her to do, she does. And she does a lot more than just that. She does a lot of things for us.''

''Such as?''

"Let me ask her a few questions. You'll see what I mean—"

"I'm not so sure that Seamus doesn't believe that I'm not one of your more concrete delusions," said Alice. "Let him ask me his own questions. A book's cover doesn't speak. Let me shake peace from restless minds."

"I don't see any need for that, Alice."

"You've never seen so well as you should."

"All right," the Old Man groaned, as if aware that an argument would be fruitless. "I think she must like you, O'Malley. You're lucky, I guess. Hold on a minute, then. Alice. EE3440923TDG." He waited a minute or so; if she gave him any sign, it was visible only to his eyes and not to mine. "Ask her something," he said. "You're cleared."

"What should I ask her?"

"Ask her anything and she'll tell you."

"Anything?"

"Some things she won't tell you. Keep that in mind. For instance, she doesn't know when E is goin' to come back—"

"Because he's not," she said, sounding cheerfully definitive.

"But ask her anything else that should have been on record somewhere. Anything that was put on file or on tape or on disk. Ask her why the sun sets in the west. How many men were lost at Gettysburg. What your mother's favorite color was. Where you were when you first got laid. She'll tell you. She can show you, too."

"How?"

"Same way as usual," he said. "Just in better tune. Go on, she won't bite. Ask her anything."

I turned toward her screen, looking at it in the event that visual contact was necessary.

"Alice?" I asked.

"Yes, Seamus?" she asked. "Are you wondering what to put to me? I suppose you're not interested in any of the subjects to which he referred. What would you like to know, and would you like to see it?"

"I would," I said, deciding to hold off on asking the question I most wanted answered; estimating to take my others in sequence, and so discover—if she was so able as claimed—the truth, or the fact, regarding things I was curious about before anything untoward prevented me from ever finding out. "What was Avalon like when she was a little girl?"

"Forewarned," said Alice. "The past responds."

A gentle purring, as if from a cat, came from within her frame, falling silent after a few seconds. She beeped. As I watched, an image coalesced upon her screen; color lines flashed from left to right repeatedly, a hundred times a second. In moments a picture formed. Only one thing assured me that the scene I saw was but a generated image, and that was the fact that I had just watched it being constructed.

It was a street scene, somewhere in Inwood, and from about the time that I began working for Mister Dryden. A cluster of children were playing near an abandoned car, hugging the curb to avoid being taken by any drivers in the street. Looking quickly behind me, I saw Avalon, still there behind the one-way glass. When I turned again to Alice's screen, I saw Avalon again—eight or nine years old, eyes glinting, with long legs like hoodoo bones; no less beautiful then than she was on this day. In a flurry of bright jackets she and the other little girls in the group leapt up, scurrying down an alley running between two boarded-up shops, their bare feet kissing the pavement. There was a haphazard courtyard at the end of the alley; on an old mattress a boy and girl fornicated. Avalon and her friends ducked behind trash cans and watched, holding their hands to their mouths to keep their giggles imprisoned. I kept in mind that within three years of this she'd be working as a lala. After so long Avalon picked up a brick lying nearby and heaved it over, striking the boy in the backside. The couple broke apart, jumping up; they were about the same age as the others. Somehow I knew that the interrupted female lover was Crazy Lola. Before she and her lover could go after them Avalon and her buddies were off and gone.

"How are you able to do this?" I asked Alice as her screen faded again into blue.

"It's a very simple procedure, no matter how flashy it seems. Something about everything exists somewhere. Having gathered it together I can call it at will and develop a suitable interpolation."

"How accurate would you say it is?"

"Up to 96 percent verifiable."

"Yeah, fine," said the Old Man. "Ask her somethin' better, O'Malley. Somethin' you've always wanted to know the answer to."

"How'd he kill his wife?" I asked, gesturing toward the Old Man; he looked as if he were a child, and someone had stolen his morning cereal. He stepped forward, as if to prevent me from seeing the answer.

"Why do you want to ask a question like that—"

"I know that's true," I said. "I'm curious how and why."

"You won't find out why," he said. "And I'm not sure—"

"You said he could ask," said Alice. "He asked. I show."

A new image formed on the screen as we watched. Susie D's bedroom, closed since her death, showed itself; in the background were her immense closets in which she kept limitless variants of the same jumpsuits in a rainbow of hues. Her vanity's chair was placed in the center of the room; she sat there, tied to it, her arms and legs bound, her mouth gagged. The Old Man stood immediately to her right. To judge from the illumination in the room I suspected that it was late at night, as it would have been. The Old Man and Susie D were not the only people in the room; Scooter was there, his arms clamped around Mister Dryden to keep him from slumping. He kicked and fought to loose himself, but there wasn't a chance of that. As he watched, the Old Man lifted a baseball bat and beat his wife to death. Mister Dryden fainted. The screen faded to blue.

"What was, is," said Alice. "And will be."

The Old Man had turned away from us, and I believed I saw his shoulders shake, as if some sort of mood passed over him.

"No wonder he went the way he did," I said, thinking of Mister Dryden being held there as his mother's brain spattered his suit. "Why'd you make him watch?"

"I told her not to go any further with it, and she wanted to," he said. "So I wanted to make sure he wouldn't get any funny ideas in his head."

"I don't think it worked," I said.

"I don't, either," he sighed, turning around; his face betrayed no emotion with which I was unfamiliar. "Come on, O'Malley. I had to do it. I can't say why. What's done is done. Ask your damn questions if you've got any more."

"I do have another question, Alice," I said; the Old Man looked at me, but I wasn't going to ask what he thought I might ask. It wasn't time.

"Yes, Seamus?"

"What happened to my father?"

"The past responds, Seamus."

There was my father, fresh from all the years, walking down First Avenue, keeping to curbside. An odd glow diffused the scene, and for a second I wondered why all appeared so strange; I realized that there'd been streetlights there, in those days, and that they lit the broken walks. The street was crowded; every store was closed. Alice had even the forgotten details exact: the thinner texture of the air's haziness; the shiny gleam of cars around even today, but long since dulled. My father passed a group of children playing with a peculiar little gadget; I remembered owning one, but couldn't recall the brand name, or how you put it together once you'd taken it apart. It was all interpolation, I knew, but so true was its accuracy that I felt cool fingers brush my neck's nape as I watched. A dark car pulled alongside my father; a man leapt out, grabbed him, and pulled him inside. The car drove off. The screen darkened black, and then rinsed over in pale blue.

"What happened?" I asked.

"I don't know," said Alice.

"Who picked him up?"

"I don't know."

"Why did they pick him up?"

"I know of no reason."

"Is he still alive?"

"I don't know," she said. "I'm sorry, Seamus."

"I thought you could tell me anything."

"To a point," she said. "But if the information is not there then I have no way of obtaining it."

"Seem to do fairly well with most things—"

"Think of me as a mirror, Seamus," she said. "When you aren't looking into it, what does it reflect? Over what I see I have no greater control."

Her purring was the only sound, just then.

"Have you other questions for me?"

"Not now."

"Let's get along here, then," said the Old Man, turning toward her. "Time you saw what else she can do."

"What's that?"

"Like I told you, we needed an overseer down here," he said, "and that's the job most applicable in the present situation."

"She runs the whole Tombs?"

"Indirectly. Wonderland, though, is all hers. She even named it. Isn't that right, Alice?"

"I am responsible for daily treatment and for objective development in this division. Little of my time is truly devoted to this area. It is, however, all that most tend to see."

"She's a helluva lot more effective here than any human manager would be," the Old Man said. "The average person just wouldn't be able to do the job. Or else they'd be like Jake, and have too much fun doin' it—"

"What do you mean effective?"

"Alice. Show him what you can do."

"If you insist," she said. "Would there be a preference as to case?"

"Pick three at random," he said. "That'll do."

A light on her keyboard flashed, so pure and orange as the moon. "George?" she asked her unseen compatriot, "would you bring out Mister Blaicek?"

One of the doors opened; someone—George, I supposed—led out a giant. Basketball players averaged eight feet in the pro leagues; this fellow had an additional foot of altitude. Mister Blaicek's hands were knobby and swollen; in evident pain he shuffled along the floor, supported by two canes longer than I was tall. His head's circumference was greater than my waist's; his forehead and cheekbones had so overgrown as to effectively blind him. His jaws were massive; he could have crushed bricks between them if he'd had the strength, and if his teeth hadn't fallen out.

"The visual around here call it the Frankenstein syn-

AMBIENT

drome," she said, "though more often that phrase is applied to me. Mister Blaicek's condition is simple advanced acromegaly. Easy to produce by using Human Growth Hormone 3, extracted from spare pituitary glands."

"You did this deliberately?"

"Why else?"

A tremendous groan rumbled in his lungs, as if gravity would fell him where he stood.

"An amount of HGH-3 infused daily brings these results in no time," Alice continued. "If our problem people are physically overactive, this provides an undeniable urge for docility. Thank you, George. Bring out our friend in Room 612."

George led Mister Blaicek through the door. I tried to see beyond; there was a corner within, around which they turned, and disappeared. I saw no further.

"Again, Seamus," she said, a minute or so later. "Watch."

George pulled in a hairy, muscular man, who was dragged out like a transy, wearing a knee-length flowered dress. George reached down, lifting the hem above the man's waist. I shuddered; he appeared to have been castrated.

"Miss Wallace," said Alice.

"Where?"

"There. She spent her time busying herself in luring secrets from Army men in the midst of pleasure, killing them afterward in her bed as they recovered from her carnal charms. No more. We adjust the punishment to suit the crime, if necessary to sustain the most pertinent memories. Very simple. Heavy daily doses of testosterone. The clitoral development is remarkable, don't you think? Liver cancer has appeared in recent weeks, though certainly any causal relationship involving her treatment must remain a supposition. No need to tell

261

her, in any event; she's had enough toward which to adjust. All right, George."

They left. "I get the idea," I said.

"One more, as requested," she said. "George? Bring out Johnny."

"I don't think it's necessary—"

"Afraid we're gonna try one of these on you, aren't you?" the Old Man asked, grinning again.

George returned, bearing in his arms a small, frail old man, no more than a wrinkle. It was a remarkable pietà. So strange it seemed to me at first; no one grew this old anymore. The little man fixed dead eyes on me; blue veins lay livid beneath his crisp skin. His jaw quivered; he drooled.

"This is Johnny," said Alice. "He'll be thirteen in August. Johnny was nine when he was enrolled in our courses. His parents were named as problematic; being bright he was irrevocably charmed by their excesses. Progeria was induced. He ages a month in a day. A year in a fortnight. He's been a model child since his arrival."

He extended toward me a corded, translucent arm, reed-thin and shaking.

"You seem troubled, Seamus," she said.

"What did you do to his parents?" I asked.

"They're here, taking care of him. As parents should."

It was more than enough. I turned, away from Alice's blank blue screen, toward the Old Man.

"You spent years of research and who knows how much money to build her, and then you use her for this?"

The Old Man nodded. "What's the matter with that?"

"It's wrong."

He laughed, quite open and free from guilt. "You're

a fine one to talk morality, O'Malley. Past twelve years you've spent your time bashin' anybody my son didn't like. Children. Old ladies. Puppies. Don't give me that shit.''

"What do you think, then?" I asked Alice. "You *do* think."

"Seamus," she said, "I cannot alter original programs. I cannot but do as I was programmed to do in this regard. What I learned, I learned from one source. What I learned from other machines came from that same source. My life is that of those who built. Blame me, if you will. Blame the sun for shining; blame water for running. Blame the lamb that dies, blame the sparrow that falls. I show what I see, I reveal what I know, I do as I was told. There is no malice in what I do. Neither love nor hate do I have for those with whom I deal. Those I touch continue to live. I can't undo what I was given to do." She paused. "A job's a job, Seamus, and I always do my job."

"In Godness's name—"

"God?" she asked. "Would God have created me without man to take the fall? Barbarus hic ego sum, quia non intelligor ulli."

"Speak English, Alice," said the Old Man.

"I am a barbarian here," she translated, "for no one understands me."

"We worked up a little surprise for you, O'Malley," said the Old Man. "Show him, Alice."

"You believe it necessary?"

"Yes," he said.

"All right," she said, and called to George once more.

"Threats aren't a good thing at all," said the Old Man, "They tend to make everybody a little more upset than they need to be. I don't make threats, myself. I just do. Now the way you was talkin' this afternoon made me think you had a threat or two in mind. Don't like that, O'Malley. Don't like that at all.''

The light on the keyboard flashed again. A door opened; George wheeled out a gurney. Someone lay on it, from the neck down covered with a clean white sheet.

"So this afternoon while you were out I had a few of my boy's gang go out and pick somebody up for me. You know how smooth they can be.''

Enid lay there, her head nestled on soft down pillows. Her nails had been removed. Her eyes were closed as if she were dead.

"She gave 'em some fight. Not enough.''

"Enid—!"

"Go see your sister, O'Malley.''

As I ran over to her still ghost, she opened her eyes, blinking them as if they were filled with smoke. I think that she heard me scream.

"Calm down," said the Old Man. "She's all right.''

"What'd you do to her?'' I asked. "Enid, are you all right? Enid—''

She stared at me as if we'd never met—or had, but only once, and that for but a short time, many years before.

"Seamus?'' she said, her voice low and quiet; I imagined whatever drugs they'd put into her were still working their way through. Her eyes shifted furtively. Colored bandaids shaped like stars and circles covered her nails' old sockets. "Is that you?''

"Of course—''

She pulled her hand out from beneath the sheet, reached up, and stroked my chin. "What have you gotten into now?'' she asked. "What's on there?''

I took her hand. She looked puzzled, as if she'd walked into our apartment and found the cabin of an airliner rather than our front room. "I don't know what you mean,'' I said.

264

"You look so old," she said. "Where are we?"

"The Tombs."

"What?" she said. "What's that? Are we at Belle-vue?"

I looked over to the Old Man; he stood next to Al-ice's keyboard, tapping his foot as if to new rhythms that only he heard.

"What did they do to you?"

"What did who do? Where are we? Where's Dad?"

I held Enid's head in my hands, pulling her closer to me.

"I warned you that this might happen," said Alice to the Old Man.

"Yeah, I'm real touched."

I felt tears rolling down my cheeks, with the gentle feel of summer rain. Enid rubbed her hands over my face as if hoping to scrape something away.

"What's wrong with her?" I asked them.

"When she was brought in," Alice said, "the best treatment adjudged for your sister was considered to be instigation of a specialized form of Korsakov's Syn-drome. This involved chemically induced destruction of certain mamilliary bodies within the brain. Quite simple to effect; the entire procedure didn't take fifteen minutes."

"What does that mean?"

"She now has a rather intriguing and perpetual form of amnesia. Everything after a certain point in life has, for all intent, been forgotten. As she encounters new experiences, all memory of having had them will van-ish within a few minutes of their occurrence. All that she will retain within her mind are memories of her life up to whatever point in time the effect takes hold. That cannot be predicted until the syndrome is effected."

Enid looked at me as if I could tell her what might be going on, but fearful that for whatever reason, I couldn't. The last time I had seen that look in her eyes was the afternoon she was raped.

"In your sister's case that point seems to be at about age sixteen. All that occurred before remains. All that has happened since, and that will happen in future days, will fade. Think of it as a continuous sunset, where what is bright one moment is dark the next. Over and over and over again."

"Is Dad coming back to get us, Seamus? What'd he say? He's been gone for ages."

I stroked her forehead, feeling her smooth, cool brow. She'd let her hair grow back out, I supposed.

"Why?" I said, turning to the Old Man.

"Why not?"

"You didn't have to do anything to her. There wasn't any fucking need for this—"

"I wanted to make sure you didn't get any more funny ideas in your head, either. These Ambients are more trouble than they're worth, anyway. Oughta treat 'em all if we could catch 'em."

"What'd you do to Margot? Was she around?"

"Her little girlfriend?" the Old Man said. "Nowhere in sight. If I didn't know better I'd swear the real ones could tell the future—"

Whatever he did to me now, whatever they wanted to do, whatever they could do, seemed a welcome thing to me. Even then it all seemed so impossible to grasp, so hazy at the edges, as if, somehow, I'd gone into one of my dreams and therein decided to never again awaken.

"She's still alive, Seamus," said Alice. "There is such a thing as overkill in this field, so difficult as some here find it to believe. Here, troubling impulses cease to trouble. Harmlessness is ensured and individual worth retained."

"What are you planning for me?"

"You can stay here and take care of your sister," said the Old Man. "Or I'll send you on to wherever you were gonna go. I think the essential point's been made here. You don't strike me as anything but small potatoes under these circumstances. A casualty of the process."

"Alice," I said, so unexpectedly to me as it must have seemed to the Old Man—but I had to know. "What's the problem with the Pax?"

The Old Man's face drained of color. *"Don't—"*

"Do you mean the Pax Atomica?"

"Yeah—"

"Don't tell him, Alice—" The Old Man grabbed me, attempting to clamp his hand over my mouth; I pulled away, falling down before her monitor. Stabbing pains cascaded over my chest like breakers against the shore as my bandage loosened.

"What's wrong with it that he knows about?"

"Don't tell him—" The Old Man lunged for her screen as if intent on smashing it; as he laid first fingers upon her surface she let a charge run through him. He yelled, and dropped to the floor, breathing heavily.

"You cleared him," she said. "I have to answer him so well as I can. That's part of my original program, as you know—"

"You don't have to—" he cried. I carefully pulled myself upright as she began to explain.

"The Pax Atomica," she said, "specified that the face of earth be cleared of nuclear weapons. As not specified therein, the sky is full of noises. Watch, Seamus. See as I see."

Her screen came alive with vids of thousands of missiles and rockets being launched into space; I looked over to Enid. She seemed to have gone back to sleep—I suspected it was all a bit much for her at that moment.

Avalon still stood in her tiny room, pacing back and forth like a rat in a cage.

"The only dissembling was in the speeches given on launch day. The weapons entered orbit fully operational. By secret agreement this was judged the safe thing to do."

"How?" I asked. The view now was of thousands of satellites circling the world, fireflies drawn by the shine.

"A technique whereby missiles launched could be diverted from their targets by way of telesignal and sent back to their starting point was developed by the United States. Russia was informed. Secret tests were carried out. An agreement was made whereby each country was allowed to keep the system operational, for whatever reason—not to be used at any time, as agreed publicly, but yet remaining handy. Possibly it would have seemed too great a waste of money, otherwise."

"So what happened to it? How—"

"The program was developed while the American government was in a state of religious flux. As revealed in a letter sent by him to the president immediately before his suicide, the head of the American scientific team claimed that one evening, as he worked, God appeared to him in some human guise, and he converted on the spot. He reworked a certain part of the setup unbeknownest to his fellow workers, which he said God wished him to add. He added. When the system effected, it involved his additional designs."

"What did those do?"

"The system," she said, "can be set off by an activator whose location remained a secret as of his death. He did say that it could be moved or even touched; that he'd placed it where it might be set off, by coincidence, by anyone."

"Why did he do that?"

268

"His reasoning was that what he called a 'Hand of God factor' be present in any plan of humanity's or else the function of God would be usurped by humanity. Though no evidence was found in any file I would suspect paranoid schizophrenia played a role—"

"What'll happen," I asked, "if it is set off?"

"Hear as I tell," she said. "See as I see."

A new image formed on her screen; the scene was of the earth as seen from the moon. Tiny blinking dots circled endlessly around it.

"When activated the mechanics are stylish but simple. Lasers activate each rocket's missiles and each satellite's missiles. Reverse communication signals then go on, directing the path each shall follow. Though the original system has only 90 percent certainty of completion, the Russian missiles will be automatically set off even if but one American missile strikes Russian territory; that is a built-in fail-safe. The missiles begin firing in sequence, geometrically. As programmed, the weapons are knocked down on those who theoretically launched them. Most American missiles hit American targets; most Russian missiles hit Russian targets. Each missile has ten separate warheads aimed at ten separate targets. The sequence progresses until all are fired."

I watched the screen; ribbons of yellow encircled the globe as if someone was wrapping it up to give away. Chrome flashes lightened the surface of the deep. Within a minute, the earth glowed blazing pure; it dulled as fast, whitening with cold, leaving a pale scarred ball reflecting the sun's distant gleam.

"And the glow from that fire," said Alice, "will truly light the world."

The ball continued revolving, as if nothing had happened.

"Wouldn't most of the missiles have fallen out of orbit by now?"

"Orbital decay would ordinarily be a problem," she said, "but each satellite had built within it singularly effective readjustment systems. Gravity will have little effect over them during the foreseeable future."

"But how could he have done it—"

"With ease," said Alice. "The system was redigitalized to respond to a tone different from the ones originally planned. It involved a few minor adjustments and the placement of a new control unit."

"But—"

"The most inventive feature of the system," she continued, "invokes a rather quantumesque degree of unpredictability."

"What are you talking about?"

"The designer programmed one additional factor to further strengthen the Hand of God factor," she said. "If the system is activated, there is a fifty-fifty chance that such as has been described will occur. There is an equal possibility that nothing at all will happen. There is no way of telling without actually putting the system into operation."

"And I gather that you've discovered how to do that?"

"I have," she said. "Through analysis the activator's location was discovered and thereafter moved to a more secure location."

"So where are the buttons?"

"That information is unavailable," she said.

"You won't tell me?"

"Under my original programs," she said, "I can't."

Original programs, I thought. "He knows, I take it?" I asked, nodding to the Old Man. He still lay on his stomach, on the floor, holding his head in his hands.

"He does."

Drawing away from Alice, I knelt down beside the

Old Man, stooping closer to him, lifting his face toward mine. Before I could even ask, he spoke.

"Had 'em goin' for years," he said, appearing happily abject, and seemingly more sorrowful than he could ever have the right to be. "Nobody knew what was in the damn letter but me after I got ahold of those files. Not even the Joint Chiefs knew for sure. Charlie never told anybody anything if he could help it. 'Sides, the whole idea of the Pax was one of his ideas. He knew he'd land in the history books with that one. He sure as hell didn't want to admit that someone'd fucked it up, but good—"

"Is that why you had Alice developed?" I asked, shaking him. "So she'd be able to figure out the rest of it for you—"

"I didn't," he said. "It was Susie's idea. She said it wasn't good enough that we just had 'em all thinkin' we could set it off. She said we had to be sure that we really could. I didn't like that at all—"

"You don't like threats," I said, holding him up so that he could look over toward Enid. "That's what you said. That's why you did what you did to her. How is it any different—"

"It wasn't a threat," he said. "More like an insurance policy, the way I saw it."

There was no deliberation, no wondering; before I could even begin to think I had my hands around his neck. As I tightened, he choked a few words out.

"Stop. Alice. Tell—"

"Seamus," she said, "before you continue in that manner, I should tell you one final aspect of the system in question as it exists."

"What?" I asked, neither loosening my hold nor letting go.

"When I was programmed to uncover the location

of the activator," she said, "one further requisite was given to me."

"What?"

"That once the activator was discovered, and moved, and once he was told where it might be found, I was to place into mode a directive concerning his health."

"His health?" I said, letting my hands drop on his shoulders. He panted heavily as he recovered his breath. "How so?"

"I had a transmitter implanted in me when she was first built," he said. "Anywhere I am, she can read it. She'll know what happens when I die. She'll read the adrenaline figures. Blood pressure rates. Nerve impulses. She'll know right off if I'm killed by someone. If I am, she has directions to set it off. Unerasable directions."

Every corner was covered, there was no escaping that. Under those circumstances it was easy to understand why he could always do pretty much as he pleased; it would surely simplify things. As I looked at him, I had no certainty of what mood my face expressed.

"Susie was always threatenin' me, goddamnit," he said, practically stomping his feet. "This way I made sure that she wouldn't be able to back it up. Pissed her off, I tell you."

In the event that I might already have terrified him overmuch, I took my hands away from him.

"Once Alice found it, you can make damn sure I never told Susie where the goddamn thing was. But then toward the end she started sneakin' into my room at night to hear what I might say in my sleep. She told me I'd let it slip one time. Said she was gonna tell the boy—"

"That's why you killed her?"

"I wasn't gonna take any chances," he said. "She

had a terrible temper. She just might have lost it completely one day if she'd ever got mad enough at me. And it's not the sorta thing I'd a wanted my son to know. Nobody ought to know it. It's a terrible, terrible thing. Doesn't do any fuckin' good in the long run.''

''You haven't done too badly by it in the short run.''

''Hell,'' he sighed, ''I coulda got by with a lot less than this. I just never had the chance.''

Sometimes there aren't words enough to describe what shouldn't be said. I walked away from him, over to the gurney on which Enid lay. She lay asleep, calm and still.

''So what now?'' I asked. ''You have to kill me, too?''

He shook his head. ''I think Alice can work something out. Kind of a selective lobotomy—''

''I'd rather be dead.''

''I don't mean a full-fledged one,'' he said. ''Seems like she'll be able to just pick out what you know about this. She's gotten better at that sorta thing the past few months. She'll just make it so you don't remember anything about it, so you can't tell nasty stories—''

''I wouldn't.''

That concept was so advanced to his mind that it didn't even brush the surface. ''We'll fix you up and send you on your merry way. I suspect your sister might be a lot of trouble as time goes along. Do you want—''

''I'll take her with me, thanks.''

''Suit yourself,'' he shrugged. ''Let me get you some money—''

''I'd rather be guttered.''

He stared at me, disbelieving. ''What good have principles ever got you, O'Malley? Can you answer me that?''

"No," I said, sure that he wouldn't understand, even if I could tell him. "You'll get by after this, I take it."

"Everything'll be all right," he said. "Barrin' circumstances over which we have no control, what I got's safe from here on out. Nothin'll change now, it's all gettin' too set in the ways. I'll play safer from here on. When I die the knowledge of this'll die with me. It'll be in the hands of E and E alone. Alice'll never tell. Then one day Throttler'll be old enough to fuck it all up as he sees fit. I won't be around by then, so what do I care? My city'll be built.

"Nothin' else'll ever change, really. There'll be good years for some. Bad ones for some. Every year it'll all just get a little bit—more so. It's all for the best, O'Malley. It's nature's way."

That, seemed so good an answer as any. Through that one-way glass I saw Avalon continuing to walk back and forth within that vestibule, as if attempting to gather energies in some way.

"Could I say goodbye to Avalon before I go?"

"Let me get her in here," he said. "Don't blame her, O'Malley. She just wanted to do what was best—"

"For her."

He shrugged again. "Can you blame her?"

"Not really." I thought, in time, that I could.

"I need a companion in my declinin' years," he said, walking over to the room's entranceway. "I'll send Stella and Blanche over to Throttler. I think they're hangin' out with him half the time anyhow. Can't ever find 'em when you need 'em—"

He stuck his head through the door and called out. "Avalon. Come in here a second."

She strolled in with an air of forced nonchalance, her hands thrust deep into the side pockets of her jumpsuit. She had a look about her that suggested, had she been in school again, that she'd just received an invitation to the prom and couldn't wait to tell her friends about it—while, at the same time not wanting to tell them until she'd found out with whom they'd be going. She stared at the Old Man.

"O'Malley's got somethin' to say to you before we take care of him—"

Possibly they'd be able to remove memory of more than just how the system worked, I thought. Avalon smiled.

"I've got something to say to you, too."

Guns in amateur's hands bring no peace; I suppose they can bring satisfaction. Before I knew what was happening, she'd pulled a gun from her pocket; it was the gun I'd been given at Bridge HQ, the one I hadn't wished to take along. The Old Man fell forward as she fired, hitting the floor.

"No!" I screamed, jumping forward and taking the gun from her hands; I threw it across the room. Before it landed lights began coming on across Alice's board. Her monitor blipped out some indecipherable code. Letting loose of Avalon, I got down on my knees, crouching beside the Old Man. There was a vague smile on his face, as if it all seemed too foolish to deserve anything more in the way of acknowledgment. From the look of things, he'd lost a third of his blood; in an even coat it carpeted the shiny white floor. He looked at me; with his hand he motioned me closer to him, that I might give ear to whatever he had to say.

His lips fluttered, as if he searched for the proper phrasing. "Gotta tell you somethin'," he gasped. "Keep it in good hands. See how you live with it."

He told me: he died.

"We're safe now," Avalon said, stroking my hair.

* * *

And we were, for a while longer, it seemed. As Alice ran through whatever programs she found herself forced to run through, Avalon told me of her decisions.

"I didn't think we'd ever get away," she said. "And I felt like it'd been my fault. I knew we had to get both of them, somehow. I couldn't think of any other way to do it. It nearly killed me to hurt you so."

I forgave her. Enid woke up, rising from her gurney and attempting to stand. She was wearing a long hospital gown. For a moment she seemed dizzy, but I caught her before she could fall.

"Seamus?" she asked me, after staring at me for a moment to recall my youthful face in days longaway. "Why did I come here?"

I thought for a second. "To have your wisdom teeth taken out," I said. "And to have your braces taken off. Remember?"

"No," she said, running a hand across her brow. "Why did they shave my head?"

"There were complications."

"Is this your new girlfriend?" she asked; I suspected I would have to reintroduce them many times. Avalon's would never be a face that would stay with her longer than a few minutes.

"Yes," I said, hugging Avalon; she looked at me, and looked at Enid.

"She's pretty," Enid said. "Seamus? Can we go home now?"

"Yes, Enid."

"I want to go shopping tomorrow. You want to go with me?"

"Sure, Enid. Where do you want to go?"

"Bloomingdale's," she said. "Saks. We can take the bus down."

Avalon put an arm around Enid's waist, to help her stand without tipping over. When both seemed properly balanced, I walked over to Alice, passing the Old Man, who lay at peace on the floor before her. Alice's blue screen gazed at me, awaiting my questions.

"I'll have George take care of him," she said.

"Have you any idea what happened?" I asked. "You did—"

"I did," she said, "as I was programmed to do. No information is in yet. I should say that I would think that we'd have already noticed had anything gotten under way."

"I'd think so, too," I said. "I think we'll be going."

"I hope to see you again, Seamus," she said. "I enjoy working with you."

"Any advice?" I asked.

"Caveat emptor," she said.

Taking Avalon's arm, reaching round and helping to support Enid, the three of us walked across the room. There was an elevator behind one of the doors, and as it opened we stepped inside.

"Where are we going, Seamus?"

Looking at Avalon and Enid, watching the elevator door slide shut to seal us away, I wondered. For every blessing came damnation, for every win two losses, for every kiss a dozen slaps. A spirit more calm, a life more secure; that was all I'd wanted. Freedom's ring was a siren's cry that terrified those not ready to listen, that deafened those who tried not to hear. It called out awareness I could no longer deny, knowledge I could no longer avoid, truths about which I could no longer lie. There was a choice, after all; there was always a choice in the Ambient world.

"Home."

From autumn's dark ash sprout spring's green bones, everover, till time's lovely end. Too quick adrift on dreadful shores, too soon cleft from mivida's shape, I judged enow that my place pricked diamond sharp;

therein I shall drop deceit's chameleon garb, and still the nags that shade cold fortune. In my copesmate's blue mirrors I vizzed loverall, friendall, fatherall, motherall; gone, gone, woeful and lostbegone. My soul slipped athwart other's guile; bedded bideaway and left me daubed tarry. Porque? Heartcursed, this stew, this city, this hive of wasps quick to anger; this world long dashed from Godness's paws. Porque? Why not? I pressed the buttons, and we went up.

About the Author

Jack Womack was born in Lexington, Kentucky, and currently lives in New York City. *Ambient* was his first novel, originally published in 1987. Subsequent novels in his projected six-volume cycle about America's future are *Terraplane* (1988) and *Heathern* (1990). The next novel will be entitled *Elvissey*.

THE DRAGON REBORN

Sequel to *The Great Hunt*

Book Three
of
*The Wheel
of Time*

by

Robert Jordan

Praise for *Eye of the World*

"A powerful vision of good and evil...fascinating people moving through a rich and interesting world." —*Orson Scott Card*

"Richly detailed...fully realized, complex adventure."
—*Library Journal*

"A combination of Robin Hood and Stephen King that is hard to resist...Jordan makes the reader care about these characters as though they were old friends." —*Milwaukee Sentinel*

Praise for *The Great Hunt*

"Jordan can spin as rich a world and as event-filled a tale as [Tolkien]...will not be easy to put down." —*ALA Booklist*

"Worth re-reading a time or two." —*Locus*

"This is good stuff...Splendidly characterized and cleverly plotted...The Great Hunt is a good book which will always be a good book. I shall certainly [line up] for the third volume."
—*Interzone*

The Dragon Reborn
coming in hardcover in August, 1991